Philip ~~Gwynne Jones~~ was ~~~~ ~~~~ ~~~~ ~~6,~~
and lived and worked throughout Europe before settling in
Scotland in the 1990s. He first came to Italy in 1994, when he
spent some time working for the European Space Agency in
Frascati Philip now works as a teacher, writer and translator,
and lives in Venice.

PRAISE FOR PHILIP GWYNNE JONES

'ful novel, recounted by a witty and engaging narrator . . .
etian as a painting by Bellini (or a glass of Bellini). Oh,
s also an unputdownable thriller' – Gregory Dowling,
of *Ascension*, on *The Venetian Game*

'me book for people with sophisticated tastes: Venice,
renaissance art, good food and wine . . . I enjoyed all
nd more' – *The Crime Warp*

'Venetian setting is vividly described and Gwynne Jones's
, fluent writing makes for easy reading' – Jessica Mann,
ary Review

'A vilized, knowledgeable, charming antidote to the darker
reaches of the genre, full of entertaining descriptions of the
cit . . . Lovely. Makes you want to book a flight to Venice
straight away' – N J Cooper, Bookoxygen.com

Also by Philip Gwynne Jones

The Venetian Game

Vengeance in Venice

Philip Gwynne Jones

Constable • London

CONSTABLE

First published in Great Britain in 2018 by Constable

A CIP catalogue record for this book is available from the British Library.

ISBN: 978-1-47212-400-5

Typeset in Adobe Garamond by Hewer Text UK Ltd, Edinburgh
Printed and bound in Great Britain by Clays Ltd, St Ives plc

Papers used by Constable are from well-managed forests and other responsible sources.

Constable
An imprint of
Little, Brown Book Group
Carmelite House
50 Victoria Embankment
London EC4Y 0DZ

An Hachette UK Company
www.hachette.co.uk

www.littlebrown.co.uk

For Caroline, with my love

Vernissage [ver-n*uh*-sahzh; *French* ver-nee-sazh]

1. Also called *varnishing day*. The day before the opening of an art exhibition traditionally reserved for the artist to varnish the paintings.

2. A reception at a gallery for an artist whose show is about to open to the public.

Chapter 1

Gramsci hopped down from his window seat, padded across my desk and sat down on the keyboard. He prodded me in the chest and gave a little *meep* of satisfaction. Look at me. What a brilliant cat I am.

I stared at him, and then at the screen, which was now filling up with a succession of letter Ts. I pushed him off, and rested my finger on the backspace key until I'd erased what he'd done.

'Look, I know it's not the best thing I've ever written, okay?' I scrolled to the top of the document and reread my afternoon's work. He jumped on to the back of the chair in order to be able to look over my shoulder. I reached the end of the page and turned to look at him. 'To be honest, I think you probably understand as much of this as I do.'

I checked my watch. Time was getting on. I'd got up far too late, and wasted most of the day. I was nursing a mild hangover, building up a backlog of work, and this particular translation really did have to be finished that day.

Years that ended in an odd number were always good ones for business. Almost every vacant space in the city was being used as a venue for the great art Biennale, and every exhibitor wanted English translation work. Translating from Spanish, Italian and French alone would be enough to make me comfortable for months to come.

Gramsci hopped down from the back of my chair and came to sit in front of the fan. He did this on a regular basis. I had no idea why, as he didn't like it. He gave it two seconds, as he always did and then walked across the keyboard again. I sighed and looked at what he'd done. He sat down next to the monitor and stared at me.

I nodded. 'You know, I think you might actually be on to something here.' I read through the rest of my translation. 'I mean, it actually makes as much sense as everything else. I think you're getting better at this.' I scratched him behind his ears which he tolerated for a few seconds before snapping at me. He was becoming sentimental in middle age.

I reread the document but found it difficult to keep my eyes from slipping off the words. My words. Or at least, my translation of Josè Rafael Villanueva's. They sort of made sense in that they at least formed themselves into recognisable sentences and paragraphs but the meaning – and I was pretty sure there was a meaning to be found in there somewhere – refused to be grasped. And I'd written the bloody thing. What chance would other people have?

I sighed. How many of these things had I done in the past month? I was, of course, grateful for the mountain of work and yet I was starting to feel as if the more translations I worked on, the more I was losing my ability to speak my own language.

I printed it off, before realising that I hadn't erased Gramsci's key strokes. My finger hovered over the backspace key for a second, and then I stopped. I'd keep it as it was. Just to see if anybody noticed.

There had once been a time when I had loved the Venice Biennale, the great contemporary art exhibition that had run since the end of the nineteenth century (with a few short breaks for various unpleasant reasons). Every two years the great and not-so-great, good and not-so-good of the art world would make their way to the thirty national pavilions in the Giardini and the great exhibition spaces in the cavernous halls of the Arsenale. Almost every empty palazzo was pressed into service as a national pavilion for those who hadn't got in at the beginning and been granted a space in the gardens. Long-disused churches were opened up for the purpose of displaying art. Many of those that were still in use took advantage of the money flowing in to the city to host artists' works, subject, of course, to the work being of a suitably respectful nature. Between May and November, the city practically ate, slept and breathed contemporary art.

And I had loved it all. Ten years ago, when I had arrived in the city for the first time, I had spent the entire holiday moving from pavilion to palazzo to church in a Stendhal-like daze. It wasn't all brilliant, of course. Over the years, I'd developed a rule of thumb that about ninety per cent was rubbish. But that still left a substantial body of work that was, at least, pretty good, and it was the possibility, however small, of every unvisited space hiding something genuinely fantastic that kept me moving onwards.

Then it became part of my job, and everything changed. Every day I would feel myself drowning in an ocean of almost unintelligible verbiage. Every year I seemed to write more and visit less. Everything was starting to feel stale and second-hand, and when I did visit the Giardini or Arsenale I felt myself in need of an emergency visit to the nearest church to look at a Titian or a Tintoretto. Even a Palma il Giovane would some-times come as a blessed relief. I thought it was the fault of all the translation work. But I had to admit it was also possible that I was just becoming properly middle-aged.

The doorbell rang. Federica, of course. I buzzed her up. A hug and a kiss.

'So, did you have a nice time with Dario last night?'

'How did you know I was with Dario?'

She waved her hand in the direction of the kitchen. 'An empty pizza box and a bottle of beer. Nowadays you only get a pizza after a night out with Dario. Secondly,' and here she winced ever-so-slightly, 'Blue Oyster Cult on the hi-fi. Again, you only play Blue Oyster Cult after a night out with Dario.'

'That's only because you won't let me. But otherwise very good, *dottoressa*. Anything else?'

'Well, yes. You rang me at about a quarter to one to tell me how much you loved me.'

'Ah.'

'Ah.'

There was an awkward silence. I scratched my head. 'Yes. Yes, now you mention it, I do kind of remember that.'

'Oh good. I was hoping you hadn't forgotten.'

'Did you have an early start today?'

'Yes. As I told you last night.'

'Ah. Sorry, I'm afraid that bit's dropped off the end as well. Were you back at the Frari?'

'Yes.'

'On top of scaffolding? Very high up?'

'Yes.'

'The sort of thing you need a proper night's sleep before?'

'Yes.'

I nodded. 'Sorry.' I gave her what I hoped was my best disarming smile. 'But it was kind of a cool thing to do, wasn't it?'

She shook her head. 'No. Really not cool at all.' Then she gave up trying to look serious and smiled and touched my cheek. 'But it was nice.' She looked over at the desk. Gramsci, evidently worried about papers flying away in the breeze from the fan, had made himself a Useful Cat by sitting on top of them. 'How's it going?'

'Busy. Busy busy busy. This stuff is hard work.'

'I know. But still, it's only for a few months. And the money's good.'

'Oh yes. I mean, I'm almost having to turn work away. But I don't really enjoy it.'

She sniffed. 'Come on, it's got to be better than – what was the last thing you did – a frying-pan catalogue?'

'Frying pans are fine. I know what they're for. I even bought a few of them. In fact, the money I made on the translation I then immediately spent on buying the bloody things. But all this,' I waved my hand in the direction of Gramsci and his pile of papers, 'all this arty-farty stuff is doing my head in.'

'Think of the money, *tesoro*. You'll be able to take a month or two off after this. Maybe we can even go on holiday? And don't say arty-farty, it makes you sound like a philistine. You're not a philistine.'

'I just don't understand it. I've taken an unintelligible Spanish document and turned it into an unintelligible English one. Here, take a look at this.' I pushed Gramsci off the stack, and grabbed Mr Villanueva's abstract.

She took it from me and read for a few minutes. 'Oh right, it's about Chavez and the revolution.'

'It's the Venezuelan Pavilion. It's always about Chavez and the revolution. But does it actually make any sense to you?'

She read on. '". . . thus Josè Rafael Villanueva's installation refers back to classical Marxist theory of historical inevitability, whilst at the same time creating a new paradigm for a post-capitalist society. Dialectical materialism is dead. Long live bningydega.' She wrinkled her forehead. 'What's bningydega?'

I smiled. 'Gramsci did that. I think I'm going to leave it in.'

'You're not!'

'Come on, he's – what do you say – "made an intervention". I think it's rather good.'

She tried to look serious, failed again and laughed. 'Okay. It's funny. But you can't leave it in. This is your job. And who's that guy you know, the Venezuelan consul?'

'Enrico.'

'Enrico. He's sort of a friend isn't he? He could get into trouble if you let this go out.'

I sighed. 'I know. You're right.' I sat down and pushed Gramsci away. Then I changed the word 'bningydega' to 'dialectical materialism' and printed the whole piece off once more. 'I'll send him a copy tonight and he can get some laminates made up for tomorrow if he wants.'

I powered down the computer. 'And that, I think, is everything for today.'

'Great. So what are we doing?'

'I thought we might go downstairs to the Brazilians' for a Negroni. And then I'll cook dinner.'

'Lovely. What are we having?'

'Well it was going to be fish but, er, I didn't make it to the market in time. I've got some aubergines and some peppers. A few tomatoes. Best Pasta Dish in the World Ever?' I wandered through to the kitchen, and turned the oven on. 'If I put the peppers in on the lowest setting they should be properly roasted by the time we get back. I don't think there's a risk of the house burning down. Unless it's a multiple Negroni night, and I think we're both too old for that now.'

She smiled. 'Speak for yourself.' Then she pulled me towards her and kissed me. 'And I love you too, you know?'

Eduardo slid Federica's drink across the bar, and then made to do the same with mine. Then he paused, and tilted his head to one side, looking me up and down. Then he turned to Federica.

'He's looking well, you know.'

She smiled. 'He scrubs up well enough.'

'You can see the difference. He looks like a new man.'

'Well he's cooking properly again. That must help.'

'Not just that. He hardly has breakfast here any more. And those multi-Negroni nights . . . well, I don't know if we'll ever see them again. To be honest, takings are down. I might have to sell up.'

'You can't do that. You're the nearest thing he has to a father confessor.'

I waved at them both. 'I'm still here you know? And incidentally I have my cat to confess my numerous sins to.'

Ed passed my drink over to me. 'So, still working hard for the Biennale, Nat?'

'Yep. And likely to be for the next few months. The work for the national pavilions is done but there's always a bit of work for small exhibitions and independent shows. They don't pay that much, but they're worth doing.'

'And any free invites? Openings, meeting the celebrities – that sort of thing?'

'Tomorrow morning. British pavilion at the Giardini. A lot of the big hitters are going to be there. Journalists, critics, the British ambassador's coming up from Rome. The Biennale curator will probably drop by as well, what's his name?' I turned to Federica.

'Scarpa. Vincenzo Scarpa.'

Ed shook his head. 'I don't know him.'

'Neither do I,' I said.

Federica sipped at her drink. 'Very intelligent man. Ferociously intelligent, one might say. He's also the rudest man in Italy.'

'Wow.' Eduardo and I answered as one.

'Have you met him?' I asked.

'Once. At an opening nearly five years ago. He graced me with about thirty seconds of his precious time.'

'You didn't like him?'

'There are two sorts of people in this world. Those who hate Vincenzo Scarpa and those who haven't met him. Oh, and I suppose there's his mother. Possibly.'

'Blimey. You're kind of putting me off the whole idea of tomorrow.'

She shrugged. 'I wouldn't worry about it. He'll need to get around most of the main pavilions. He'll swan in for two minutes to be nasty to the artist, and then he'll head off again. He probably won't even speak to you.'

'But I'm the honorary consul.'

'Nathan, the rudest man in Italy works to a very tight schedule. If he has the chance of being rude to you or rude to the ambassador, who do you think he's going to choose?'

My face fell. 'I wish you were coming. I feel a bit scared now.'

'No time, *tesoro*. Why didn't you ask Dario?'

'I did.' She opened her mouth to speak but I interrupted. 'I asked him *after* you told me you were busy, okay? But if he's coming in to Venice in the morning he'd like to bring Valentina and Emily as well. Make a day of it.'

'And you couldn't get them a pass?'

'The problem is little Emily. There's a very strict no kids policy. No ifs, no buts.'

'Why's that?' said Eduardo.

'I don't know. Probably something terribly naughty. At least, that's what I'm hoping.'

Federica gave me a hard stare. I reached for my Negroni, and drained it. I checked my watch. 'The peppers should be roasted by now. Let's go and eat. I probably won't see you tomorrow, Ed.'

His face fell. 'But you do still love me, Nathan?'

'You know I do, Ed.'

He grinned. 'Have a good time, yeah?'

'I'm sure I will. The best part of the Biennale is always the *vernissage*.'

Chapter 2

It would have been nice to arrive by water taxi. In all my years in Venice I had never used one. There was something so grand, so sophisticated about the image of them, but they cost an arm and a leg, and occasionally another limb would need to be thrown in as a tip as well. It would, as usual, have to be a *vaporetto*. I made my way up to Rialto and realised I'd mistimed things.

The queue stretched out of the *pontile* and down as far the *fondamenta*. It was still early May but the weather was starting to get hot now and I really didn't want to have to stand for the whole journey, away from any source of ventilation. What to do? I could get a coffee and wait for the next boat to pass and hope to be first in the line for the following one. I checked my watch. No time.

The part of the *pontile* reserved for those disembarking was enticingly empty. There was also a No Entry sign. You were not, under any circumstances, supposed to wait in that area. Except, of course, unless you really wanted to. Everybody did it, from time to time. *In Through the Out Door*, as Led Zeppelin would have said. I strode up as if it were the most natural thing in the world, parked myself on a metal trunk that the *marinai* used for storage, took out my newspaper and pretended to read in order to shield myself from any accusing stares. It would, almost certainly, be all right.

It wasn't. An elderly lady with a shopping trolley started haranguing me as soon as I sat down. '*Signore! Signore!*'

I pretended not to have heard, and buried my head in the football results. '*Signore!* The queue starts outside. You mustn't wait there.'

'I'm sorry,' I said, 'I'm going to work. It's important.'

'I'm going to the shops. It's important for me too. I need to sit down.'

Someone else joined in. 'I'm going to work too. Get to the back of the line.'

I made one final, despairing effort. 'Look. There's room for us all here.' I patted the space next to me. 'Sit down here, *signora*.' I'd picked the wrong day, obviously. The entire front row was now shouting at me. Italians are very good at those strange conversations where people pretend to be shouting at each other and having a proper fight for five minutes before the situation resolves itself and the problem just goes away. I began to realise it wasn't going to be one of those occasions. When an ominously big and beardy fishmonger started remonstrating as well I decided to try and beat a dignified retreat. I folded my paper away and walked back to the *fondamenta*. Ironic cheers followed me along my way.

I was last on to the *vaporetto*, the *marinaio* practically having to push the last few stragglers on, like commuters on the Tokyo underground being stuffed on to trains. I shared half my personal space with the rucksack of the backpacker next to me, who ignored the *marinaio*'s plea to take it off and put it on the deck; something he might have been prepared to do had there been an inch of space there. Most people, hopefully, would be getting off at the San Zaccaria stop for Piazza San Marco. That was only twenty minutes away. But it was going to be a long twenty minutes.

Sometimes Venice could be a hard city to live in. Sometimes, I thought, you really had to want to live here.

The crush did indeed thin out a little, but I was still sweating uncomfortably by the time we reached the Arsenale stop, the last one before Giardini. I decided to get off anyway. It wasn't a long walk, and it might help me to cool down a little. Many of the great and perhaps not quite so good had parked their maxi-yachts along the *riva* here, granting them a magnificent view over the *bacino* of San Marco and, coincidentally, blocking off said view for the local residents.

After ten minutes' walk I was at the entrance to the Giardini, that great, green space that was one of Napoleon's better legacies to Venice. I walked past the statues of Wagner and Verdi, both of whom had had their noses removed in an act of vandalism a couple of years previously. There was no sign of the two of them ever being repaired. The two titans of nineteenth-century opera would probably always stare noselessly out at passers-by.

Venice is short of public gardens and so it had always seemed a shame to me that so much of its biggest park remained closed off for so much of the time. Indeed, the public wouldn't be allowed in for three days yet, as the art world's press mixed with artists, curators, collectors and oligarchs during the preview. Crowds were forming at the entrance. There was still a pecking order, even amongst the chosen few.

I had made up a little time so I stopped for a *caffè macchiato* at Paradiso, and took it outside. From here I could see the whole of the *bacino*, the island of Giudecca, the church of the Salute and the entrance to the Grand Canal. I hadn't been up this way since, when? The last Biennale? I'd forgotten just how majestic that view was. Oh yes, you really had to want to live in Venice. And this was why people really wanted to live here.

I walked past the ever-growing line and waved my pass to the guard. She took a brief look at it, and punched the number into her handset. Then she looked confused, looked at me again, and re-entered the number. Her device bleeped and flashed a red light in a way that didn't seem terribly encouraging. She drew a deep breath. 'This thing hasn't been working all morning,' and waved me through.

My feet crunched on the gravel as I walked. The sky was clear, the sun was shining and, away from the suffocating crush of the *vaporetto*, it was just – just – warm enough. It was pretty much the perfect time of year to be in Venice. And it was certainly the perfect time to be at the Biennale; before actually seeing anything, when everything was unknown and everything was potentially brilliant. I smiled to myself. Months of translation work had left me feeling more than a bit cynical about the whole jamboree but – despite oligarchs, maxi-yachts and unintelligible abstracts – there was still a bit of magic about it. Some of the pavilions – the clean, minimal-ist lines of Scandinavia and Denmark, the jaggy modernism of Alvar Aalto's Finnish building – seemed to reflect national stereotypes. Others were quirkier. The Hungarian pavilion was, somehow, the most Hungarian-looking building ever designed. The unfortunate Uruguayans were exiled to what had been a small warehouse around the back of the gardens. I stopped to give a quick wave to Enrico, engaged in conversation with a group of journalists outside the Venezuelan pavilion, a 1950s work by Carlo Scarpa.

'Nathan, Nathan, wait up!' I recognised the voice. I turned to see my Romanian friend Gheorghe jogging up the gravel path behind me, dressed, ever so slightly incongruously, in full evening dress. He smiled. 'What brings you here?'

'Meeting and greeting, Gheorghe. Opening day for the Brits. And, well, everyone I suppose. How about you? Come to cheer on the Romanians?'

'Maybe later, Nathan. First day of work.' He smiled.

'Work? I thought you were still carrying dogs across bridges?'

'I am, but I don't do so much leg work these days. That whole operation is kind of franchised out. Leaves me a bit more time for other projects.'

'That's brilliant. I'm glad it's going well. So what are you doing?'

'I'm a dancing Frenchman.'

'You what?'

'A dancing Frenchman. That's their installation this year. Half a dozen of us at a time, we're just dressed up like this, in evening dress. And when somebody enters the pavilion we do a little dance around them. There's some words to go with it as well. It's fun. Come along later.'

'I will. But, erm, why you? I mean, with you not being French and all.'

'They couldn't get enough, Nathan. An Insufficiency of Frenchmen, they're calling it. They wanted people who could dance a bit and do a French accent.'

'So they called you?'

'Bit of luck really. I was helping a young woman's poodle over the Rialto Bridge. That's a nice route to have, you can have a proper chat with people. Anyway, it turned out she's working for the curator, told me to get in touch.' He smiled. 'It's good pay as well. And nearly six months' work.'

'I'm glad. Could be a whole new career for you?'

'You never know. It's a bit of a niche market, mind, but the skills are transferable.' I could never quite tell when Gheorghe was being serious.

'They might have called me. I speak French.'

'Are you much of a dancer, Nathan?'

'Not for the dancing. For the translation.'

We strolled together along the gravel paths in the early morning sun, up to the three great pavilions of Germany, France and Great Britain. All imposing, and all just a little bit pompous in comparison to some of the more modern, funkier ones we'd passed. We shook hands. '*Buon lavoro*, Gheorghe.'

'Thanks. You too.' He looked around. 'There's a few photographers around. Maybe we'll both be in the papers?'

'That'd be nice. See you later.' He walked off, giving a little twirl along the way as if already getting into character.

A group of young people in regulation Art World Black T-shirts were handing out catalogues and goody bags at the entrance to the British pavilion. I took one from a young woman, and glanced around.

'No prosecco?'

She smiled. 'No prosecco! They won't let us. Too dangerous, they say.'

'Dangerous?' I checked my watch. 'I know it's only half past ten but what could be dangerous about a few drinks and *cicheti*?'

She smiled again. 'You'll see.'

I felt a hand on my shoulder. 'Don't tell me. It's another complaint about the lack of drinks, isn't it?' I turned around. The speaker was a man of about my age, wearing a dark suit over a plain black T-shirt. He had a thin growth of stubble, and hair just ever-so-slightly too long. He attempted to look serious, failed, and then grinned. 'I'm Paul Considine. And it's my fault that there's no prosecco.'

'You mean . . . ?'

'This is my pavilion. Hang on, that sounds a bit pretentious doesn't it? Anyway, I'm the artist.' We shook hands.

'I'm Nathan Sutherland.'

'Ah, Mr Ambassador!'

'Nothing so grand. Merely the honorary consul.'

'That still sounds quite grand. Pleased to meet you. I hope you enjoy it. So tell me, do you live here all the time?' I opened my mouth to reply, but he turned his head to look over my shoulder. 'Oh hell, I'm sorry but my agent's waving at me. He's probably worried I've forgotten my speech or something. I'm going to have to run. We'll talk later, okay?' He gave my arm a squeeze, and ambled off.

It felt a bit odd cruising a lap of the crowd without a glass in my hand, but I did my best. I spotted someone I vaguely recognised, an elegant grey-haired man in his late fifties in an expensive camel coat. The British ambassador. I walked over.

'Good morning. William Maxwell, I presume? I'm Nathan Sutherland.'

'Ah, our famous honorary consul. Pleased to meet you.' A deep, rich brown voice that could have been acquired at the same shop as the camel coat. 'I don't think we've spoken before, Nathan. How long have you been here?'

'Nearly six years now. Only two of them as consul.'

'That explains it. It would have been my predecessor who came up for the last Biennale. You're very lucky to live here. I'm very jealous.'

'Well, Rome must be lovely too.'

'Oh it is. But it's chaotic. It's so wonderful to get away from the traffic. I really must try and come up more often. Are you busy?'

'Not so much. The usual things. Lost passports, stolen property. Nothing terribly serious ever happens.'

He raised his eyebrows. 'Really?'

I knew what he meant, and gave a little smile. 'You heard about that then?'

'British consul rescued by man on motorcycle whilst attempting to stop a valuable work of art falling into the Grand Canal. Yes, it did rather make the news.'

'Sorry.'

He smiled and patted me on the back. 'So, do you know anyone else here?'

'No one at all. My partner met the curator once.'

Maxwell discreetly pointed his thumb over to the main doors – still closed – where a little man in horn-rimmed glasses was in animated conversation. He had the look of a slightly flabby Dmitri Shostakovich.

'That's him?' I said 'Vincenzo Scarpa? That's the demon curator?'

'Don't be fooled', said Maxwell. 'He punched someone in the face on live TV only a few months ago.' I whistled. He continued. 'The chap he's speaking to – the older one – is Gordon Blake-Hoyt. Affectionately known as GBH.'

'Oh him. I've heard of him. Works for *The Times*, or someone like that. Hates anything modern, doesn't he?'

'That's him. The two of them seem to be getting on rather well, don't they?'

Indeed they were. Scarpa's hand was resting on GBH's shoulder, and the two of them were laughing. They paused for a moment, as a third man joined them. Paul Considine. Then they started sniggering again, as if at some private joke that he was not privy to. Considine was trying to smile, but looked awkward and embarrassed. It was evident he was trying to join in with the conversation, but the others seemed studiedly bored by his company and paid him little attention. Eventually he gave up and wandered off, shaking his head.

'And who's that?' asked Maxwell.

'Now that's our artist. Paul Considine. We've just met, but I'm afraid I don't know very much about him.'

'Me neither. Only what I've read here.' He brandished a copy of the press release. 'These things never really add much, do they? At least this one's written in English. I do wonder about some of them.'

I gave a watery smile. 'Indeed.'

'I get asked to quite of lot of these sorts of things. I expect you do too. Never quite sure what to make of them. Still, the best part of the Biennale is— '

'—the *vernissage.*' We both laughed.

'Ah, it seems as if something's happening.'

A photographer was moving through the crowd, gently manoeuvring people into position outside the entrance. I found myself in the second row next to Shostakovich's chubbier double. I smiled at him as if to say, 'Isn't this terribly exciting and a bit embarrassing at the same time' but he didn't even meet my gaze. Without a word, he grabbed the shoulder of the man in front of him, pulled him back, and took his place in the front row next to Gordon Blake-Hoyt. My new companion turned to me and silently mouthed the word 'wanker' as he briefly flashed the *corna* behind Scarpa's head. I grinned and gave a little nod, and then the photographer was telling us all to hold still and smile. A few snaps, and then a guy with slicked-back hair and wearing a pin-striped suit walked out of the front row and turned to greet us.

'Ladies and gentlemen, *signore e signori*. Ambassador,' he nodded respectfully. 'Honoured guests. Thank you for your patience. I'm not going to say too much. We'll be going in in just a few minutes' time – some of you have seen it already, for the rest of you I'm sure you'll think it's been worth the wait. But in the meantime I'd just like to introduce my dear friend Paul Considine.'

There was a ripple of applause but nothing seemed to be happening. I looked to my left. Considine was staring into space, oblivious to everything. The woman to his left took his arm, and whispered in his ear. He shook his head, as if to clear it, stepped forward and turned to face us.

His friend smiled at him. 'Just a few words, Paul.'

Considine cleared his throat and half raised his hand. 'Erm, not much to say really.' He spoke quietly and I strained to hear exactly what he was saying. 'It's just brilliant to be here. Thanks to the British Council. Thanks to Lewis – Mr Fitzgerald – my agent here. For all the work he's done. And for being a great friend. It's fair to say I couldn't . . . No, fair to say, I wouldn't be here without him.'

His voice was cracking. He took a few deep breaths and continued.

'It's been difficult at times. It's difficult for me to be an artist at times. Sometimes we forget, that when we create something . . . when we put something out for people to look at, we give them the power to hurt us. So in a way, that's what this whole piece is about. It's called "Seven by Seven by Seven". It's all in the title.'

He stopped again. The air was thick with embarrassment. In front of me, Blake-Hoyt and Scarpa were whispering to each other. I stared at Lewis, trying to catch his eye. For God's sake, just step in and say something, please. But then Considine seemed to rally a little and gave a half-smile. 'Anyway, thanks to all of you. I hope – well, I just hope you like it. It means a great deal to be here. And I'm very proud, and very happy. Thank you again.' He gave a little bow and waved to the group of black-clad acolytes. 'I think we can open up then?'

Two of them walked forward and pushed open the great double doors.

Scarpa shook hands with Blake-Hoyt, patted him on the cheek and, without so much as a glance inside, headed off in the opposite direction.

The rest of the crowd streamed in. Before I entered, I turned back to look at Considine. He was standing by himself, staring into space and looking utterly, terribly alone.

Chapter 3

I immediately understood the reason for the 'no children' rule.

Glass. Glass everywhere. Great vertical sheets of broken glass, glass spikes, broken mirrors, powdered glass underfoot. Only a thin line of tape on the floor served as a barrier to the spectator.

I struggled to remember how the pavilion had looked on my last visit, two years ago. It had been a more conventional gallery space then, divided up into white cubes. Now it had been completely remodelled into one gigantic, single room. Two glass staircases, on opposite sides, led to an upstairs gallery, three narrow glass-floored corridors overlooking the central area.

I made my way upstairs, a little unwillingly. I've never been good with heights, but that wasn't the problem. It was the effect of feeling oneself suspended in the air above a valley of jagged, broken glass. The safety barriers – glass themselves, and a little lower than I'd have liked – provided no real feeling of security. One wall was lined with seven glass scythes. Another with seven swords. Another with seven daggers. It was simultaneously one of the most beautiful and terrifying things I'd ever seen.

As I looked down, the mirrors cast back distorted, broken reflections of my face. I rested my hands on the (glass) railing, closed my eyes and took a couple of deep breaths. Then I felt someone's hand clap me on the back and I choked back a scream. I turned around, ready to let rip.

It was my companion from the photo shoot, the one who'd been forcibly removed from the front row by Vincenzo Scarpa. Middle-aged, floppy-haired and slightly ruddy of complexion. He looked as if he'd enjoy a drink.

'Sorry, that was a bit thoughtless of me. Did I startle you?' He spoke in English, with only the lightest trace of an Italian accent.

I exhaled, slowly. 'Yes. I think you can say that.'

He chuckled. 'Sorry again. What do you think?'

'I think it's brilliant. It's scary as hell, but it's brilliant. How about you?'

He cocked his head to one side and gave a little grimace. 'It's, well, it's okay. I mean, I like it. It's good. And people's reactions are fantastic.' He grinned at me. 'But I don't think it's all that original.'

'No?'

He shook his head, and lowered his voice. 'No. I saw work like this last year at an exhibition in Stavanger. I think what he's done here – well, it's on a bigger scale. But like I said, I don't think it's original.'

'You mean plagiarised?'

He waved his hands to shush me. He was speaking in a whisper by now. 'I don't know. I hope not. I'm not going to say anything. Certainly not in front of his agent. But there are others here who might.' He gestured with his head towards the opposite gallery, where Gordon Blake-Hoyt was scribbling in a notebook, and making a great show of shaking his head. 'That's just for effect, you know. Scarpa gave him a personal tour yesterday. He's filed his copy already. There's a filthy review in today's *Times*.'

'So what's he doing here again?'

'Just to be nasty. Just to spoil the big day. Gordon Blake-Hoyt is like that.'

'Bastard. The poor guy looks in a right state.'

'Yes, I know. He's kind of fragile anyway.'

'I didn't know that.'

'There are stories. Booze and drugs hell. In the past. I think his agent does his best to keep him on the straight and narrow. I think he certainly earns his keep that way. You're not in the art world yourself then?'

'Me? No, I'm the honorary consul here. My name's Nathan. Nathan Sutherland.'

'Pleased to meet you Nathan. I'm Francesco Nicolodi. I'm with *Planet Art* magazine.' We shook hands.

'Are you in town for long?'

'Only for a few days. I'm going to be busy. See as much as I can, try and identify the big hitters. Copy to file for next week.'

'Are you going to Scotland and Wales?'

He shrugged. 'I don't know. I should make an effort, I know. But if you've only got a few days it's difficult to drag yourself away from the Giardini and the Arsenale. Are you going yourself?'

'Oh yes. One of the perks of the job as hon con. You get to go to lots of parties. And the Welsh pavilion was really good last time. But do come to Scotland, they always put on a good spread.'

He threw his head back and laughed. '"Put on a good spread"? You're a terrible old philistine, Mr Sutherland.' He paused. 'What sort of spread?'

'Hendrick's gin. In the afternoon.'

'I'll be there.' He checked his watch. 'Right, I've got to head over to France now, and then over to Germany. Come along, they always look after you well on *vernissage* day.'

'Don't mind if I do.'

We went down the stairs. As we left, I could see the figure of Gordon Blake-Hoyt staring down at us, both hands gripping the railing. I got the feeling he was going to make sure he was the last one to leave. Just to make a statement.

Considine was sitting by himself, as his manager Lewis talked to the ambassador and various members of the press. He was trying, and failing, to light a cigarette.

'Just a moment, Francesco.' I walked over to Paul, and fished a lighter out of my pocket. 'Light?'

He nodded. 'Thanks.' His hands shook a little as he took it. His face was more lined than I had thought at first. His eyes were red. He'd been crying. He dragged on his cigarette. Then he looked apologetic, and proffered the packet.

I shook my head. 'I'm trying to give up.'

'But you carry a lighter?'

'In case I decide to stop trying.'

It got a smile out of him. I was pleased. 'Listen,' I said, 'for what it's worth, I think your work in there is fantastic. Absolutely bloody fantastic.'

He said nothing for a moment. Then 'Thanks. Thanks, man.'

'So who gives a damn what that rude old bastard thinks anyway. That's just his job. Being professionally nasty.'

He reached behind me, grabbed a crumpled sheet of paper and pushed it into my hands. 'Today's *Times*. Hot off the press.'

It was Blake-Hoyt's piece, or most of it, crudely torn from the newspaper. I cast my eyes over it, but didn't want to read the whole thing. I didn't need to. 'I'm sorry,' I said.

He grinned, but his shoulders were slumped and his eyes were sad. He looked beaten. 'You know, my friend, after all these years I've learned one thing about people like this. That there's no point trying to be nice to them. They just see that as weakness. And they serve no socially useful purpose at all. They're parasites. Cancer.'

'I'm sorry,' I repeated, uselessly.

"S'okay. Thanks.'

He continued to smile. Then he offered me the packet of cigarettes. 'There's only a couple left. Take them for Ron.'

'For Ron?'

'For later Ron.'

We both laughed. He closed his clear blue eyes for a second, and when he reopened them he was smiling. Properly, this time.

I clapped him on the shoulder, then turned and made my way towards the French pavilion, in pursuit of Francesco.

Chapter 4

I'd just clinked glasses with Nicolodi and the French ambassador when the screaming started. Except it wasn't quite like that. Just a crash and a thud. A few raised voices. And then the screaming. Proper screaming. From the British pavilion.

People seemed frozen for a moment, and then Francesco and I broke into a run. Outside the main doors a young woman was sobbing hysterically as her friend hugged her and tried to calm her down. A black-clad acolyte was being violently and copiously sick.

We made our way inside. Lewis and Maxwell were darting from right to left, heads jerking this way and that as they tried to find a way into the maze of glass. I couldn't understand what they were trying to do. Then Francesco grabbed my hand, and drew it upwards. 'Look!' Difficult to spot at first, but as I concentrated I could see that a section of the safety barrier in the upstairs gallery was missing. Then he drew my hand down . . .

A vertical sheet of glass. Broken. Jagged. Dripping with blood. Not, perhaps, as much as you might imagine. When I had time to think about it, it made perfect sense. The impact must have been so fast that very little blood had been spilled at the point of impact. The considerable amount that there was, was now pooling at the base of the plate. On one side of which lay the body of Gordon Blake-Hoyt. And on the other, his head.

I gagged and considered running outside to throw up. And then it hit me. I'd probably seen more dead bodies than anyone else here. 'Okay, Francesco.' I grabbed his arm. 'I want you to go outside and make sure everyone's all right. Get them some water, sit them down. Don't let them leave. The police will want to speak with them.' He looked at me with a mixture of horror and confusion, but then nodded and ran off.

Lewis and Maxwell were still trying to find a way through the jagged maze. I hadn't even spoken to Lewis, and so I walked as calmly as I could up to the ambassador, and placed my arm across his path.

'Leave it. Come on. Leave it. Both of you. Let's just go outside.'

'We can't just leave him there.' Lewis' voice was a mixture of rage and hysteria.

'Yes we can. That's exactly what we're going to do. He's dead. There's nothing we can do. And we're not going to risk hurting ourselves.'

'And who the bloody hell are you?'

'I'm the honorary bloody consul in Venice, and right now I'm trying to stop anyone else from getting hurt. So step the hell back.'

The three of us stared at each other for a moment, but then Maxwell nodded, and we retreated outside.

*   *   *

'Christ, Sutherland, this is a bloody disaster.'

'With respect, Ambassador, it's a bit more serious for him than it is for us. So what do we do now?'

'"We?" What do you mean "We?"'

I breathed deeply. 'Okay. It's like this. I might not get paid, but I do know what I'm doing. The police will be on their way. There'll be an ambulance within minutes.'

'An ambulance?'

'Yes.' For God's sake, how long had he been doing this job? 'An ambulance. They'll remove the body and then the police will, well, do what they have to do.'

'And then?'

'I've got contacts with the police and the emergency services. I'll deal with them. Do you want to deal with the relatives?'

He remained stony-faced. Oh shit, it was going to have to be me. The very worst part of the job.

'Okay, I'll deal with the relatives. The police will put out a statement. That's fine as far as it goes, but it will be as bland as bland can be. So you need to put out a press statement too. For the UK press. Something that will keep them happy, that will make them think we're on top of the job. You understand? I can't do that. This is going to be a big story; you need to deal with that side.'

He took a deep breath. 'Fine. Thank you, Sutherland.'

'Call me Nathan, please. You did earlier. "Sutherland" sounds like you're my boss.'

There was no sign of either Considine or Lewis. I really, really felt the need for a cigarette. I looked around the crowd but nobody had lit up. Then I remembered Considine's packet and reached into my jacket. Roll-ups. Roll-ups rolled by an artist. I should feel honoured. Then I realised that my hands were shaking, and that the shock was hitting me, and I sat down and closed my eyes as I smoked quietly.

The ambulance men arrived first. And then the police. There were a few of them I knew, and they gave me a nod. The entrance was taped up as the forensic team arrived, and I was given to believe that my work was done.

Maxwell, Francesco, Lewis and I looked at each other. Of Paul Considine there was no sign.

I pulled out my mobile phone, and dialled.

'Dario. It's an emergency . . .'

Chapter 5

I went to speak to Lewis once the police had finished with him.

'I was a bit sharp back there, I'm sorry.' I said

He shook his head. 'No problem.' He offered me his hand. 'We haven't been formally introduced. I'm Lewis Fitzgerald. Paul's agent.' We shook hands.

'Speaking of whom . . . ?' I looked around. Still no sign of him.

'He sent me a text. He went back to his hotel before it all happened.'

'Is he all right?'

'Not really.'

I ran my hands through my hair. 'Look. You probably know this yourself. But I may as well tell you anyway – there is absolutely zero chance of this place opening up again. It's just not going to happen.'

He gave a brief nod. 'I assumed as much. What happens next? Or what could happen next?'

'Don't know. I really don't know. I mean, I saw him leaning on the barrier – we probably all did – and it looks like it gave way.'

'That's not our fault.'

'Well, the responsibility would probably lie with the fabricators. But this will take years to sort out. You understand? It'll take years.'

'My God. Oh bloody hell. I think this will kill him.'

We stood in silence for a few moments. Then I reached into my jacket, and gave him my card. 'Call me if there's anything I can do.' He nodded, and pulled out his mobile phone as he wandered off.

There didn't seem to be much else that I could do. I exchanged a few words with one of the cops, and explained that anyone at the *Questura* would be welcome to get in touch if I could help in any way. He nodded politely, and shrugged as if he thought it unlikely.

I made my way back through the Giardini. I paused at the exit. People were still coming in. The little matter of a violent death was not going to stop the great money-making machine. It would be nice to stop for a beer at Paradiso. God knows, I could do with one. But then I saw a *vaporetto* approaching and broke into a run.

I made it on to the boat with only a few seconds to spare, and went down into the rear cabin. There was nowhere to sit, of course. And then I saw someone wave from the seats outside. Francesco Nicolodi was sitting there and scribbling away in a notebook. He gave another wave and patted the seat next to him, shaking his head as a couple of other passengers asked if it was free. I squeezed my way through the crush to the back of the boat.

'I didn't see you leave,' I said.

'I spoke to the police for a bit and that was it. I thought I'd go back to my hotel.'

'I thought you'd have been doing the rounds of the other pavilions.'

He looked genuinely shocked. 'After what just happened? I'm not such a heartless bastard, you know.' Again, I was struck by how perfect his English was. He grinned. 'Anyway, there's only going to be one story that people are talking about. I thought I'd try and file my copy before anyone else can.'

'I didn't realise journalists still used notebooks and pens,' I said. 'There's something rather reassuring about that.'

'Most of us don't. But I'm a terrible typist – strictly one finger.' He paused. 'Listen, maybe there's something I can do for you?'

'Oh yes?'

'I heard you speaking to the ambassador. About informing the relatives. Now I do know a lot of people that Gordon works— ' He giggled. 'Sorry, worked with. I could let them know, if that would help.'

'Was he married?'

'Never married. Don't think he had a partner. But as I said, I do know some of his colleagues. I could let them know, and then they can pass on the info to his family, if there is one.'

I paused. It was my responsibility. But it was the very worst part of the job. I didn't have to do it very often, but it never got any easier. 'Okay. Thanks. It would be better than coming from a stranger. But only if you're sure.'

'I'm sure. It's not a problem.'

I gave him my card. 'Just in case you need to get in touch. And maybe I'll see you at Scotland or Wales tomorrow?'

'Free gin? I'll be there! Could do with a drink right now to be honest.'

'I'd offer you one myself but I'm in a bit of a rush.'

'No worries. Tomorrow maybe.' The *vaporetto* was pulling into the Spirito Santo stop. 'I'm getting off here.'

'I'm getting off at Zattere.' A quick walk over the Accademia bridge and I'd be just five minutes from home. 'I'll come with you. Save fighting my way through on my own.'

We made our way through the cabin, our plaintive cries of *Permesso* and *Scendiamo* growing ever more desperate the closer we approached our destination. Eventually, bruised of elbow and trodden of toe, we made it on deck to be rewarded with the lightest of breezes as the boat pulled in to the pontoon.

Everyone braced themselves for the habitual jolt as the *vaporetto* bounced off the jetty, and then the *marinaio* was there, tying up the boat with one hand and sliding back the bars of the gate with the other. 'Spirito Santo, next stop Zattere, finish Piazzale Roma.' Mirror shades, single black glove, cropped hair and designer stubble. In any other country, in any other city, he'd be a bus conductor. Here, he seemed like a rock star. 'Go inside the cabin please. Take off your rucksack.'

Francesco patted me on the shoulder. 'Okay, see you tomorrow I hope. Scotland and Wales, yes?' I nodded. He smiled, and made to step off the boat.

I felt something bounce off my shoe. I looked down and nearly clashed heads with a young guy with a backpack. I gave him a wave. 'I'll get it, okay?' Bending down with a rucksack on a crowded boat was likely to cause mayhem.

It was a plain black leather wallet. 'Is this yours?' He shook his head. Francesco was almost away down the bridge to the *fondamenta*. 'Francesco,' I shouted, 'is this yours?' He turned at the sound of my voice and I held the wallet high in the air above the heads of the crowd. He looked confused for a moment, and then his hand went to his jacket, to check.

'Not mine!' he shouted back.

The *marinaio* slammed the gate shut and cast off. I tried to attract his attention. 'I'm sorry, but someone's dropped their wallet.' But as I spoke, the same tourist backed into us, his rucksack managing to hit us both in the face simultaneously.

'Take off the rucksack please. Go inside please. Go inside please.' He probably knew how to say this in a dozen languages. The tourist shuffled off his backpack causing us both to step back and press ourselves against the gate as he did so. I tried again. 'This wallet isn't mine . . .'

Again, I was interrupted. A Frenchman, this time. 'I'm sorry, but we have no tickets. Can we buy tickets from you?'

If the *marinaio* was at all stressed, he concealed it perfectly. 'Yes, you can, sir,' he answered, in French.

'Thank you. Are we going the right way to San Marco?'

This time, the frustration couldn't be suppressed. 'Sir, San Marco is in that direction.' He jabbed a finger in the direction from which we'd come, where the Basilica, Ducal Palace and *campanile* dominated the horizon.

'Oh.' The visitor furrowed his brow. 'How do we get to San Marco?'

'Sir, get off at Zattere, go back in that direction, line number 2.' He was gesturing more forcefully now.

'Zattere? Where is Zattere? How do we get to San Marco? *Saint Mark's Place?*'

'One moment please.' He was sweating now, as we pulled into Zattere and he tied up the boat. He does this every day, I thought. Every day, for eight hours, at almost every stop.

He must have the patience of a saint. And he still looks better than I do.

I made an attempt at proffering the wallet, but he met my gaze and just shook his head. No time. *Go inside please. Take off the rucksack. San Marco, sir, wait here, take the next boat in that direction. Go inside please. Inside please . . .*

I stood on the *fondamenta* and watched the boat depart. When they decided to go on strike, I could curse ACTV, the public transport company, as much as anyone. And then there were those occasions which made me wonder how anyone could do their job without being driven clinically insane. I shook my head. To hell with it. I'd need to see Vanni at the *Questura*, sooner rather than later. There was an ACTV office with a lost property department nearby. I'd drop the wallet off then. I stuck it in my pocket, and made my way down to Accademia.

I met Dario at Bacarando later that afternoon. I felt a bit disloyal to Eduardo and the other Brazilians, but it was close to Rialto and would make Dario's journey back to Piazzale Roma, and Mestre, that much quicker. He'd been working in Venice that afternoon, but I was aware that I was pushing things a bit by dragging him out for a beer for the second time in three days. He smiled, as he always did, but he looked tired.

'Long day.'

'Long day, long night. Emily didn't sleep well, so we didn't. And my boss was in a bad mood for some reason. How about you?'

'A British national at the Venice Biennale got his head chopped off by a sheet of plate glass.'

He nodded and took a sip of his beer. 'Okay. You win.'

'So it's going to be a busy few days. Repatriation of body to sort out.'

'You've done that before though, right?'

'A few times. It's never nice though.' Given the sheer number of people who visited, it was inevitable that some of them wouldn't find their way home again. In some ways it was surprising how rarely it happened. But when it did happen, it was an unpleasant business to deal with. Francesco, at least, had saved me a potentially agonising conversation with Blake-Hoyt's relatives.

'So what happens? Post-mortem?'

'Dunno. I mean, the guy's head's come off. Can't see a post-mortem really adding very much to that. They might do one anyway, I suppose, just in case they decide to prosecute.'

'You think they might? And who?'

'Ah, someone's going to be in big trouble over this. Don't know who though. The guys who actually built the installation, most likely. Can't see how it's the artist's fault. Shit for him though. Biggest day of his career and then this happens. The poor guy looks like a wreck anyway.'

Dario checked his watch.

'You've got to go, haven't you?'

'Sorry.'

'It's okay. Thanks for coming out. I needed a beer.'

'You seeing Federica tonight?'

'Not tonight. She's at her place on the Lido. Sometimes I go over, but I worry about what Gramsci will get up to. You know, raiding the fridge, inviting unsuitable cats around for parties. That sort of thing. I'll have an early night, tomorrow's going to be busy.'

'More Biennale stuff?'

'Scotland and Wales. And it's unlikely the body will be released tomorrow but it's best to be prepared. I'm supposed to be there when the casket is sealed.'

'Okay. Just don't straighten his tie.'

I snorted the remains of my beer. 'We really shouldn't be talking like this.'

He shrugged. 'Black humour. It helps. Sometimes it was the only thing that kept us going in the army. Right, I've gotta go.'

'No worries. Don't forget, we'll have you round for dinner sometime.'

'That'd be great. Just let us know when, we'll get a babysitter for Emily.'

'Don't be daft, bring her as well. She can just sleep when she gets tired.'

'You sure? What's your cat like with kids?'

'As good as he is with the rest of the human species. And inanimate objects. But seriously, I haven't seen her in ages. Is she talking?'

His face lit up and the tiredness seemed to drain out of his face. '*Mamma. Papà.* And – get this – one time she said *Ummagumma!*'

'You're kidding?'

'Nope. She was just burbling away and then out it came – *Ummagumma.* I tell you Nat, I actually cried.'

I wasn't a hundred per cent convinced that Emily, apropos of nothing, had suddenly come out with the title of a progressive rock album from 1969, but I didn't like to say so. Dario was a happy soul by nature, but I didn't remember him ever looking quite so happy as this.

'That's brilliant. I'm happy for you, you know that?'

He looked at the floor, slightly embarrassed. 'Thanks, Nat.'

'Ah come on, let's get another drink in. And something to eat.' Bacarando always made me feel hungry. The glass cabinet held some of the best *cicheti* and *polpette* in Venice, along with skewers of meat, seafood and roasted vegetables. You could even get something that was the closest the Italians were ever going to get to a pie.

He shook his head. 'I haven't got time. I really haven't got time.' Then he smiled again. 'Okay, I've got time. But just a small one. And a skewer of prawns.'

'I'll get these.' I smiled at the *cameriera*. 'Two small beers, a skewer of prawns, and a portion of sardines. Or are they anchovies?'

She shrugged. 'Small fish.'

'A portion of small fish then.' Small crispy fish, species unknown, to be eaten whole with a squeeze of lemon.

Bacarando kept background music at a low volume, but we could just about make out the opening chords of 'Satellite of Love' over the noise of the crowd. We drank in silence as we listened respectfully to Lou Reed's sepulchral tones.

I gave a little shiver as the song drew to a close. Spine-chilling. And that was Lou in a *good* mood. 'We should come here more often, you know?'

'We should. It's not what I'd call *progressive* but—'

'It's old music for old people.'

'Exactly.' Dario extracted the final prawn from his skewer

and popped it in his mouth. Then he gave his beer a swirl, and drained his glass. 'And now I really have got to be getting back.'

I gave him a hug. 'Okay, go and get your tram. I'll see you soon. Love to your lovely girls.'

He strode off in the direction of Rialto, making his way through the early evening crowds in Campo San Bartolomeo. I thought about stopping off for a drink at the Brazilians on the way back home, but thought better of it. It was tempting to go and grab a pizza, but two pizzas in three days risked dragging me back into my bad old ways. I went up to the flat instead.

'How about that then, Grams?' I swept him into my arms. 'I think I'm growing up.'

He mewled, and swiped at me, missing my nose by a couple of millimetres.

'You're not impressed, I can tell. You'd like old useless Nathan back.' He yowled, as if to indicate that – in his opinion – old useless Nathan had never really gone away.

There wasn't a lot in the fridge, but my new regime of going to the shops occasionally was paying off. I skinned and gently warmed some chopped fresh tomatoes and garlic in oil, threw in a few torn basil leaves and used it as a basic pasta sauce along with some diced mozzarella.

I plopped myself on the sofa, along with a large glass of wine, and took my mobile out. Federica would have heard about the day's events by now. Hell, everyone would have heard. I was about to call her when I became aware of something in my pocket digging into me.

Considine's cigarettes. There was, I remembered, one left.

It put me in something of a moral quandary. I didn't smoke

in the flat any more. On the other hand, there really was only one left and so . . .

I went through to the kitchen, failed to find an ashtray, and returned with a small coffee cup. I went through my jacket pockets until I located the lighter, and then withdrew the final, slightly crumpled coffin nail from the packet. I lit up, and took a drag. A Paul Considine cigarette. Thinking about it, 'Considine' sounded like a classy name for a brand. I probably wasn't doing it justice.

There was something else in my jacket pocket. I fished it out. The wallet. I'd completely forgotten about it. No worries, I'd drop it off at the ACTV office on my way to the *Questura* tomorrow. I opened it up and flicked through it in the hope that it would give me a heads-up as to who it belonged to. No *Carta d'identita*. No *tessera sanitaria*. Presumably, then, not an Italian citizen or resident. There was no bank card, no credit card, no driving licence. An utterly, and somewhat surprisingly, anonymous wallet. Nothing, it seemed, beyond the small amount of money. Somebody, perhaps, had got there before me and stolen those things of value or those things that could be sold on. Still, there were a few banknotes. Why leave those? I riffled through them. Forty-five euros in total. Then I felt something else between my fingers. A blister pack of tablets. Something called Priadel.

What the hell was Priadel? It occurred to me that the owner of the wallet could, right at this moment, be desperately looking for their essential medication. Perhaps I needed to check it out. I went into the office, logged on to the computer and googled. Priadel. 150 mg. Lithium carbonate based. Typically used in the treatment of bipolar disorder. I took a closer look at the results. Okay, it was something you needed to take every day but there didn't seem to be any potentially lethal effects if you missed a dose.

I went back to the living room, and replaced the blister pack in the wallet. There was something else in there that I'd missed, in between the banknotes. A small, crumpled piece of paper. I brought it closer to my face. A fragment of newspaper, torn from *The Times*, with Gordon Blake-Hoyt's photograph above the strapline. There was something written on it, scrawled in block capital letters across the text.

JUDITHA TRIUMPHANS

Chapter 6

Gramsci was slipping. He wasn't the first to wake me up. The phone was ringing, a Rome number.

'Ambassador Maxwell?'

'Good morning, Nathan. I hope you managed to sleep last night. God knows, I didn't.'

'Well, it was – something of a shock, I think you'd have to say.'

'That's an understatement. Anyway, I just wanted to check that everything's all right with you? We've put out an official statement. I think the Biennale people have done the same. Now I take it the relatives have been informed.'

'Yes.' Well, hopefully.

'Okay. Good. Well there's probably nothing else that can be done from our end. Are you okay running with the rest of it?'

'No problems, Mr Ambassador. It might take up to a week for repatriation, but there's nothing to be done about that.'

'Right. Good man. Oh, I see our friend the journalist was quick off the blocks.'

'I'm sorry, who?'

'Fellow you were talking to. I've got his name here somewhere – Nicolodi. Francesco Nicolodi. He's got a column in *The Times* this morning.'

I jumped out of bed. 'He's what?'

'In *The Times*. A sort of eulogy for the unfortunate Mr Blake-Hoyt, and some not very nice things about Mr Considine.'

I wedged the phone under my jaw, struggled into my trousers and half-hopped into the office to switch the computer on. 'I've not seen it. I'll take a look now.'

'Well he's very nice about us. "British diplomatic service responded admirably." So I think we can feel quite happy about the part we played. Anyway, thanks for all your work yesterday, Nathan. If anything really urgent comes up you can always contact the embassy, but it seems you have it all in hand.'

'I think I do.' The hell I do. 'Thanks again.' We hung up. I brought up *The Times* website. Arts section. Oh hell, paywall. I didn't know if the *edicola* in Campo Sant'Angelo would have a copy at this hour, so I ran back into the bedroom, and took my wallet from my jacket. This needed to be checked right now.

'The British Diplomatic Service proved itself a model of grace under pressure despite . . . scene of horror . . . appalling tragedy . . . one of the country's best-known critics . . .' At least, I thought, he'd managed to avoid the word 'bloodbath'. And, I had to admit it was quite flattering. Good old Francesco.

'Serious questions will now need to be asked of the British Council. Namely, why did they choose Mr Considine – a man known to have serious personal and emotional problems – for such a high-profile event? Secondly, were they aware of the nature of the installation and, if so, were all appropriate steps taken to minimise the risk to the public? Finally, there are question marks hanging over the very originality of the piece and, again, were the Council aware of this? Providing full and frank answers to all these questions is the least the Council can do, by way of respect to the many friends and colleagues of Gordon Blake-Hoyt.'

You shit.

I heard the apartment door open. It gave me a little start. Federica. She'd had a key for months now but I kept forgetting.

'*Ciao, cara.*'

'*Ciao, tesoro.* Are you okay?'

'I was. Not so sure now.'

'What's wrong? You're in all the papers, you know.' She plonked a stack of them down on the table. 'There's a nice photo of you in *La Repubblica.*'

I leafed through the pile. *Il Gazzetino, La Nuova, La Stampa, Il Corriere della sera, La Repubblica.* We were on the front pages of every one. *La Repubblica* had printed the group photograph outside the main doors together with, perhaps inappropriately, a head shot of the unfortunate Mr Blake-Hoyt.

I tapped the monitor screen. 'Look at this. Just look at it.'

She pulled her glasses from her bag, and scanned the article. Then folded her glasses away again. 'Mmm. Not nice.'

'No. And I think it's my fault. I agreed with this guy that he'd contact Blake-Hoyt's colleagues. I didn't think he was going to use that as an in for his article.'

She patted my cheek. 'You worry too much, Nathan. He just made the most of an opportunity. Mr Blake-Hoyt was unlikely to be filing any more copy, so he just made sure he was the first to jump in. That's all.'

'It's shit though. The poor artist. He seems a bit fragile. I'm worried about what this will do to him. And this journalist – this Francesco Nicolodi – have you heard of him?'

She shook her head. 'Not him, not Mr Blake-Hoyt. And for that matter I don't really know all that much about Paul Considine. Only what's on the Biennale website.'

'He didn't seem like a bad guy. Francesco, I mean. He seemed nice. Genuine.'

She smiled, and gave me a hug. 'That's your problem, *tesoro*. You're just too nice.'

'I don't think so.' I drew myself up to my full height and put my hands on my hips. 'For example, it's,' I checked my watch, 'gone nine o'clock and I haven't fed Gramsci yet.'

'My goodness.'

Gramsci mewled upon hearing his name. I stared down at him. He glared up at me.

'Okay, I think my point has been made. He knows who the boss is.'

We went through to the kitchen, and I fetched down his box of food. I measured out one hundred grammes of multi-coloured biscuits and then set to picking out the yellow ones.

'What on earth are you doing?'

'Oh, I bought him a new brand of biscuits the other day. It turns out he doesn't like the cheesy ones.'

I made us a coffee. Before I washed the cups I unobtrusively tipped the cigarette ash from mine into the bin. Not quite unobtrusively enough. I caught her gaze. 'Not classy?'

'Do you really need me to answer that? Anyway, I thought you'd given up smoking in the house?'

'I have. This doesn't count. It was—'

'Just the one,' she completed.

'—just the one, and it wasn't mine. It belonged to the artist. I suppose it was a present.'

'You begged a packet of cigarettes?'

'Not the whole lot, there were only two left.'

'You begged a packet of cigarettes from an utterly distraught man who'd just seen the greatest day of his career end in chaos?'

'I think you're making it sound a bit worse than it actually is.'

She gave me one of her disappointed little looks. 'Well you're a catch, Nathan, aren't you? What a lucky girl I am.' She sniffed again. 'And get some windows open. What if you had a surgery today?'

'Okay, okay. I'm a terrible person. I know that. Anyway, and more importantly,' I produced the clipping with a flourish, 'there's something I need you to take a look at.'

She took it from me, and turned it over in her hands. 'Where did you get this?'

'Well, as well as begging cigarettes from a broken-hearted man yesterday, I picked up someone's wallet. On the *vaporetto*. I forgot to take it to lost property. No idea who it belongs to, there's no ID of any kind inside. I'm wondering if it's Considine's. He showed me a clipping from *The Times* just before everything kicked off.'

'*Juditha Triumphans*. After Vivaldi's opera?'

'Strictly speaking, it's an oratorio.' She glared at me. 'Sorry. It's just that it's rare for me to know something you don't so I always think I need to make the most of those very occasional opportunities.'

'Okay. Good recovery. Carry on.'

'*Juditha triumphans devicta Holofernis barbarie.* "Judith triumphant over the barbarians of Holofernes." Vivaldi wrote it in tribute to the Venetian triumph in the siege of Corfu.'

'And, of course, Caravaggio, Gentileschi et al. Judith of Bethulia beheads the Assyrian leader Holofernes in his tent.'

'Yep.' I remembered Caravaggio's work, Judith working with bloody, surgical precision as Holofernes awakes in the middle of the act, as the ancient servant on the right of the picture holds out a cloth to collect his head. Or the even greater violence of Artemisia Gentileschi's version, as Judith and her maid hold the struggling barbarian down as Judith sets about her work.

'So you're thinking "strange thing to find in a wallet"?'

'Yes. And why is it written underneath a picture of Gordon Blake-Hoyt?'

'You're not suggesting there's a link with his death?'

'Well, he was beheaded.'

'An accident. But even if someone had pushed him there'd have been no way of guaranteeing he'd have fallen in just the precise way to be decapitated. He could just have been mashed on the glass.' I winced. 'More likely that Mr Considine saw what happened and scribbled it down. Maybe he felt it was poetic justice.'

'I don't remember him being there at the time. Ah, you could be right though. It kind of makes sense.'

'No one's going to kill someone because of a bad review. And even if they did, there are easier ways of doing it. More to the point, why do it anyway? He'd know that would be the end of his installation.'

'You're right. Creepy thing to do though. Anyway,' I grabbed her and gave her a big hug and a kiss, 'we can have the whole afternoon together. Pavilions to be opened, art to be seen and drinks to be drunk.'

She broke into a smile which, as it always did, lit up the room. 'So who do we have first?'

'First one's the Welsh pavilion. The name is,' I checked my diary, 'Gwenant Pryce. At Santa Maria Ausiliatrice. Then on to Scotland. Guy called Adam Grant. They're just off Strada Nova. Not at all in the same direction, which is a bit of a pain, but it can't be helped.'

'Do you know anything about them?'

'Nothing at all. The Welsh were very good last time. Can't remember much about the Scots. That might have been the gin though.' I had vague memories of blagging my way into the Irish pavilion that same day, and what might have been New Zealand, but I couldn't swear to it.

'What about Northern Ireland?'

I shook my head. 'They don't seem to be here this time. Or if they are then no one's told me. Shame. I don't think I disgraced myself last time. What time do you finish work?'

'I should be able to get away at two.'

'Okay, I'll see you at . . . hang on.' The phone was ringing. The consulate phone, not the business line.

'British Consulate, Venice.'

'Who am I speaking to?' No please, no pleasantries.

'My name is Nathan Sutherland.'

'Are you the consul?'

'The honorary consul, yes.'

'Mr Sutherland, my name is William Blake-Hoyt.'

Chapter 7

It was barely seven-thirty back in the UK. William Blake-Hoyt, it seemed, had got up early for the express purpose of maximising the time available to shout at me. I held the phone a few centimetres from my ear so as to minimise the pain, whilst Gramsci stared at me as if in silent agreement with Mr Blake-Hoyt's every word.

And I had to admit he had a point. It should have been my responsibility to inform him. Instead of which, I'd dodged it and passed it on to someone who was more or less a complete stranger. It was a cowardly thing to have done.

His mood didn't improve when I told him that I wasn't in a position to tell him when his brother's remains would be repatriated. This was the truth. As his brother had died in unusual circumstances, to say the least, there could be a significant delay before we'd get permission.

I let him shout at me for a few minutes more, before I managed to placate him by saying I would immediately check with the police and call him back within the hour. It didn't stop him from telling me that I should already have done this. And again, I was forced to concede that he had a point.

I put the phone down, and rubbed my ears. Federica cocked her head to one side. 'That didn't sound good.'

'Not good at all. Tough morning in prospect.'

'Okay, I'll let you get on with it. I'm sure you can sort it all out. And then we'll have a nice afternoon together and you can forget all about headless art critics.' She kissed me. 'See you later.'

I rubbed my ears again, and then dialled the *Questura*.

'Vanni? It's Nathan here.'

'*Ciao,* Nathan, *come stai?*'

'*Abbastanza bene*. Actually no, that's not true. I'm not very well at all. You can guess why I'm ringing?'

'Mr Blake-Hoyt and his mortal remains?'

'The very same. I've just been on the phone to his brother. I feel like I've been in a fight.'

'My word. Well, I'm very sorry, Nathan, but I'm not going to be able to help you.'

My heart sank. 'No?'

'No. Investigations still continuing, and there's not much chance of the examining magistrate completing her report until tomorrow at the earliest. There are still a few "unaccountables", shall we say.'

'Oh hell.'

'Anyway, I'm glad you've called. There are a couple of things I'd like to speak to you about. Off the record of course, but as you were present at the – incident, I'd be interested to know your thoughts. Can we meet for a coffee? Maybe at F30, about eleven o'clock?'

'Eleven is good.'

'Excellent. Let's call it an extra breakfast. See you there.'

'Okay, Vanni, *a dopo.*'

I hung up, and placed the phone down on the desk. I stood up, put my hands on my hips, and stared at it. Gramsci stared up at me. Phones on tables were a red rag to him. He prodded it with his paw. Then again, and again, moving it closer to the edge of the table each time. I let it drop into the palm of my hand. Then I sighed, and prepared myself for round number two with Mr William Blake-Hoyt.

I hadn't seen Vanni for a few months. He looked tanned and relaxed, his moustache possibly even more luxuriant than usual. He smiled, and we shook hands.

'Let's get a table outside. It's always nice to look over the canal to the *Questura.* It reminds me how good it is not to be at work. What do you think, maybe just some *bruschette?*'

I nodded.

'*Spritz al bitter?*'

'You know, Vanni, I think maybe I'll just have a prosecco.'

He grabbed my arm, and peered very closely into my eyes. 'Are you okay, Nathan?'

'Well it's just that other people may be lining up to shout at me this afternoon. I thought it would be good to keep a reasonably clear head. And my doctor tells me that prosecco isn't like proper drinking.'

We moved outside and grabbed a table. The sun glittered on the canal as we gazed across to the unlovely space of Piazzale Roma, dominated by a multi-storey car park. To the right, the Ponte della Libertà led away in the direction of the mainland.

Our drinks arrived and we clinked glasses. 'So, what's this all about then?' I took a sip of my prosecco and Vanni swirled his spritz and speared his olive. I was already beginning to wish I'd ordered one as well.

'Nothing very much. We've just been going through statements again. Basically, everyone was outside, milling around. There was a crash from inside, people rushed in – the ambassador, Mr Fitzgerald, all those young people – and then you and *signor* Nicolodi arrived shortly after. Does that sound about right?'

I nodded. 'Exactly that. By the time we arrived, there was just the ambassador and Fitzgerald left inside.'

'And you shouted at them to get out?'

'It was the only thing they could do. They were trying to make their way through a maze of broken glass. And it was obvious the guy was dead.'

'Very sensible. Thank you for that. You probably saved the ambulance service a bit more work. Now have another think – do you remember if you saw anyone else in there?'

'*Boh*, I couldn't swear to it. I really couldn't. With all that was going on, you know, and the space is full of glass, broken mirrors and the like. Reflections everywhere. It was just too confusing.'

'I understand. Ah, here's our food.' We ate in silence for a few moments.

'So what do you think happened?' I asked.

'Oh, I can't tell you that.' We both laughed, and clinked glasses again. 'It's almost certainly the fault of the company in charge of the installation. One section of the barrier hadn't been fixed properly. The securing bolts are fastened with hex keys. A couple of them had been missed. So as soon as someone leaned on it with any weight—' He spread his hands. 'Boom. Crash. Thud.'

I shivered. 'Bloody hell. Just imagine how he must have felt. When he realised he was falling.'

'Not a pleasant thought, is it? At least he wouldn't have thought it for long.'

'So what happens now? The state prosecutor opens a case against the company involved and then we can ship Mr Blake-Hoyt off home?'

'Well probably. There is just one little thing, however.' He reached into his jacket and pulled out his mobile phone. 'Take a look at this. We found this in the outside pocket of his jacket.' He turned the phone to me to show me a photograph. A postcard, showing an image by Artemisia Gentileschi. *Juditha triumphans devicta Holofernis barbarie.*

'Oh hell,' I said.

I had some explaining to do. When I'd finished, Vanni took out a packet of MS and lit up.

'I don't suppose I could . . . ?'

'Yes, you can.' He passed the packet over to me. 'You know, Nathan, have you ever thought about just buying cigarettes? Like normal people do.'

I shook my head. 'Borrowed ones don't count. So, what do we do now? More precisely, what do you do now?'

'I think we have to call in Mr Considine for a chat.'

'Just a chat?'

He nodded. 'Just a chat. He hasn't given us a statement yet, so that's why we'll suggest he comes in.' He paused. 'Tell me, Nathan, what did you think of him?'

I raised my eyebrows. 'Do you want me to say I think he's capable of murder?'

Vanni looked pained and waved his hands. 'No no. But be honest, what's he like? It's easier for you to get to know English people. When we have to do it, the language always gets in the way.'

I nodded. 'I think he's a nice guy, but we only spoke for a few minutes. He seems quite vulnerable; no doubt about that. He was on the verge of tears during his introduction. On the other hand, he'd just seen a filthy review rubbishing the greatest day of his career. So, no wonder he was in a bit of a state. I don't think he's the sort of artist who'd just laugh off a bad review by getting cheerfully drunk.'

'Meaning?'

'Someone – a journalist – told me he's had his demons. Drink, I guess. But as to whether he's capable of violence, I'd say no. Anyway, it makes no sense, it's a stupid way of plotting to kill someone.'

Vanni nodded. 'Indeed.' He checked his watch. 'Okay, Nathan, I've got to go. The drinks are on me this time.' He sighed. 'You know, they say the canteen in our *Questura* is the finest in the Veneto. All the other cops are jealous. It's still nice to get away.' I smiled. 'Oh, just one more thing. I need that wallet.'

'Sure.' I slid it across the table to him. 'Is it evidence?'

'It might be. But it could belong to anyone. And, of course, your prints will be all over it by now.'

'Oh dear. Have I contaminated evidence? I really was just going to take it along to lost property.'

He smiled, and got to his feet. 'Don't worry, Nathan. I'll make sure you get a light sentence.'

Chapter 8

There was already a small crowd of journalists outside Santa Maria Ausiliatrice when I arrived with Federica. I recognised a few from the previous day. There was also another little group of black-clad acolytes. I felt sorry for them. Art World Black looked fine in May, and would come into its own in November but would feel unbearable in the heat of August. I made a brief speech and then we lined up for a few quick photographs.

A young man came over to me. 'Mr Sutherland. I'm Owen Pritchard, from the Arts Council of Wales. Can I introduce you to the artist?' He took us over to a woman in, perhaps, her early sixties. She was pretty, red hair with a single white stripe forming a striking contrast to her black shirt and jeans. She smiled. 'Mr Sutherland? I'm Gwenant Pryce. Thanks for the speech. I hope this isn't all too boring for you? Not too much work?'

'No, not at all. This is one of the nicest perks of the job to be honest. And don't worry about the speech.' I looked from left to right, and gave a stage whisper. 'I used the same one as last time, to be honest.'

'I noticed,' said Owen.

I must have looked shocked because he burst out laughing. 'Joking,' he said.

'Tell you what, come along to Scotland this afternoon and you'll get to hear it again.'

Gwenant smiled again, 'Am I getting a trace of an accent?'

I laughed. 'I wouldn't have thought so. But I spent five years at the university in Aberystwyth. Maybe a bit of it rubbed off.'

'*Siarad yr iaith?*'

'*Nac ydw.*'

'Don't worry. Me neither. Why Aber?'

'Oh, I felt I needed to get away. And there was the weather, of course.'

'The weather?'

'I was misinformed.'

We all laughed. 'Take a look around,' she said. 'Any questions, just ask me afterwards. It'd be nice to talk. Abstracts and press releases are all very fine, but it's not a substitute for an actual conversation.'

'Thanks.'

Federica squeezed my arm. 'What was all that?'

'She asked me if I spoke Welsh. I had to admit I didn't.'

'Welsh? That's a different language?'

'Older than yours. Older than mine. I should have made more effort with it, really.'

'And if you had, where would you be now?'

'Somewhere wet, I imagine.'

A mournful atmosphere hung around Santa Maria Ausiliatrice. It had had an unhappy history. It had originally been the residence of Franciscan nuns, all of whom – save one – had died in the great plague of 1630. It later served as a hospital and hostel for the poor until – inevitably – Napoleon suppressed it in 1807. There wasn't much of the interior that remained, save an eighteenth-century altar with an engraving of the Last Supper. It only added to the feeling of melancholy.

The space had been repainted since my last visit, when the brickwork had quickly been covered in a thin layer of whitewash. Now, a thick layer of an intense, deep blue had been applied. Klein blue, I wondered?

There was no internal source of light in the room as far as I could see. Instead, sunlight streamed in through narrow window slits just below the ceiling, and reflected off a large mirror positioned at one end of the room directly on to Pryce's canvas, which hung opposite the altar.

We took a closer look. A beach. A seated figure, in rich red velvet robes, hands grasping the arms of a throne. The robes were painted in oil, and were ornately detailed.

Federica whistled.

'Good?' I said.

'Damn good. Just look at that brushwork. The face though . . . ?'

I nodded. There was no face to speak of. Just a pale, pink, featureless blob. 'I don't get it,' I said. 'Why go to all that trouble to paint something like this,' I sketched out the form of the seated figure with my hand, 'and then leave it like this. Like it's unfinished.'

She shrugged. 'Let's ask her afterwards.'

We moved on. The second room was painted in a deep, rich purple. Again, the only source of illumination was reflected sunlight, bouncing off a mirror and directly on to the only canvas in the room. The image appeared to be identical.

'I don't understand,' said Federica. 'Why reflect the sunlight directly on to the painting? That can't be good for it.'

'I suppose it'll only be for a short period every day. As the sun moves, so will the reflection.'

She shook her head. 'No.' I opened my mouth to speak, but she put her finger to my lips. 'Just listen.' All I could hear was chatter and footsteps from the streets outside, but then I became aware of something else. A low, electrical humming. Federica smiled, walked back to the mirror and stuck her head behind it. 'I thought so.'

'Thought what?'

'The mirror. It's being moved automatically to follow the position of the sun. So the light is always shining directly on to the canvas.'

'I thought you said that'd be bad for it.'

'It is. Makes it interesting though, doesn't it? Come on!'

We walked through to the next room, painted in a sickly, bilious green. Again, there was one solitary canvas, but I gave it only a cursory glance. I grinned at Federica. 'I think I've got it,' I said.

'Oh good. Got what?'

'What it's all about. Come on. Next room.'

The next one was a burning, bright orange. The following one, the purest of whites. The one after that, a funereal violet. 'I'll just bet you the next one is black,' I said.

'Oh, I believe you. But just how do you know this?'

I brandished the abstract. 'Just look at the title. *Behind the Masque.* There's two things going on here. The first is all those obscured faces – as if by a mask, right?'

'Sure. And the second?'

I took her by the elbow, and we walked through into what I knew would be the final room. Black, pitch-black, except for a single canvas illuminated by a reflected ray of sunlight. I let go of Fede's arm, and moved to the middle of the room. I spread my arms wide, and turned in a circle. *'And darkness and decay and the Red Death held illimitable dominion over all,'* I intoned, in the most sepulchral tones I could summon.

She put her hands on her hips and her head to one side. 'Oh, *tesoro*, I do worry that one day I'll go to bed with you and wake up with Vincent Price.'

I worried that we were making too much noise. 'I'm right though, aren't I?' I whispered.

'*The Masque of the Red Death*. Edgar Allan Poe. Well spotted. I still don't understand the lighting though.'

'Still, it's great stuff, isn't it?'

'Oh, it's very good. She can paint, no doubt about that. I don't think it's the sort of thing that wins awards but it's good. Why are we whispering?'

'I don't know. It just seems appropriate.' I heard footsteps behind us, and I couldn't help giving a little start. Federica sniggered, and the atmosphere was broken.

We emerged into the sunlight. Gwenant Pryce smiled at us.

'They're beautiful,' said Federica.

I nodded. 'Wonderful.'

'Thank you.'

'Could I just ask you – the seated figure? Who is that?'

She smiled. 'Well now. Who do you think it might be?'

'Your husband?'

She looked genuinely shocked for a moment, and then laughed. 'Oh my goodness me, no. No, we split up years ago, I wouldn't waste any more paint on him.'

'Oh right. Sorry. I thought I was being ever so clever. Could I ask who it is?'

She smiled again, but her eyes looked sad and tired this time. 'That, *cariad*, is for me to know and you to find out.'

Chapter 9

It was, perhaps, a forty-five-minute walk to the Scottish Pavilion just off Strada Nova, a part of town that I normally tried to avoid. In the summer months it became blocked with the hordes of visitors making their way from the railway station down to Rialto. Whatever time of day you found yourself there was the wrong time of day. The sun inevitably seemed to be at its highest point, there was no shade to be found and there was always one more bridge than you might expect.

A shame in some ways, as there were some proper shops to be found mixed in amongst the tat. Some nice *cichetterie,* some decent bars and quite a few not-so-decent ones. A Wild West theme bar that I had never been into and almost certainly never would. And, everywhere, abandoned buildings had been pressed into service as temporary galleries for the purposes of the Biennale.

The street, in that first week of May, was less hellish than it would become at the height of the season. It was, nonetheless, a relief to turn off and make our way down a narrow *calle* towards the Palazzo Fontana. Part Renaissance-style, part Baroque, the façade had a curious asymmetry to it that made it look downright odd when viewed from the Grand Canal, as if they'd run out of money before they could finish off the left-hand side.

I recognised a famous Edinburgh arts entrepreneur from my time in the city, deep in conversation with a group of critics in the courtyard. I smiled at him and he nodded as if to say that he wasn't sure if he knew me at all, but thought it as well to be polite.

I took Federica by the arm, and steered her inside. A bar had been set up in front of the water gate, the light on the canal casting constantly shifting reflections on the ceiling.

'Is it time for a gin then?'

She checked her watch. 'It's not even four. Are you serious?'

'Oh absolutely.'

'And why gin anyway? Shouldn't it be whisky?'

'It probably should. But there's something about drinking whisky during the hours of daylight that seems a bit hardcore. Gin is different. That's almost like not drinking at all.'

She shook her head. 'I don't think I'll ever understand your culture.'

I walked to the bar and caught the eye of an inevitably attract-ive and black-clad young woman. My smiley request of 'two gins please' froze on my lips. There was only prosecco to be seen.

'No gin?'

She chuckled. 'Not this time. Not after the last one. It was a nice idea, and the sponsors loved it but—' She shook her head. 'Just prosecco this time.'

'Hell. Well in that case, two *prosecchi* would be lovely.'

Federica and I clinked glasses. She could see the disappoint-ment on my face. 'It's probably for the best, you know.'

'Oh I know.'

'And we don't really need to start drinking neat spirits in the afternoon, do we? Not yet, anyway.'

'I know. It's just that I remember having such a nice time two years ago.'

'Bachelor days, *tesoro*. Bachelor days.'

'Anyway, there was something you were saying earlier. Something about waking up with Vincent Price.'

'Go on,' her voice was full of doubt, unsure where exactly this was leading, yet at the same time sure that it couldn't be anywhere good.

'I mean, would it be so bad? I sometimes think a little pencil moustache might suit me.'

'You can have one after I'm dead, *caro*.'

I grinned and squeezed her arm. And then, in the middle of the crowd, I saw Francesco Nicolodi. 'Just one moment, there's someone I really need to speak to.' He was, I could see, *sans* drink. I grabbed another glass from the bar, gave the attractive black-clad girl what I hoped was my most winning smile and made my way over to him.

'Francesco!'

'Nathan. A pleasure to see you.'

I gently pushed the glass into his hand. 'Let's just step outside for a moment, eh? I could do with a cigarette.'

'Of course.' He laughed. 'You promised me some Scottish gin, Nathan. I'm disappointed.'

'Prosecco it must be, I'm afraid.' I firmly steered him to the courtyard and reached in my pocket for a non-existent packet. 'Damn, I'm all out.'

'No problems.' He produced a packet of Marlboro, and offered me one.

'Thank you. Oh, and thanks again for sorting everything out with Mr Blake-Hoyt. Did you pass my details on to his family?'

'Yes. Yes, well sort of. His colleagues at *The Times* said they'd pass the information on. He doesn't have a partner. I think there's a brother or something.'

'A brother or something. Good, good.' I smiled. 'Well, I expect he'll be in touch in the next few days or so.'

'I expect so.' We stood in silence and listened to the Edinburgh arts entrepreneur hold court. Nicolodi checked his watch. 'Four o'clock.' He dropped his cigarette, and ground it out with his shoe. 'Sorry, Nathan, can you just hold that for a minute. I need to make a call.' He pressed his glass into my hand, then took his phone out and walked away from me. I caught just the one word before he was out of earshot. '*Salut.*' Romanian. He was gone for, at most, thirty seconds. He smiled as he walked back to me, and took his glass.

'That was quick.'

He shrugged. 'My insurance broker. Just a reminder for him.' He drained his glass and looked keen to be away. 'Well, thanks for that, Nathan. Lovely to see you again.'

'The article,' I said.

'I'm sorry?'

'You should be.'

'I don't understand.'

'Yes you do.' He looked left and right as if hoping to find someone else he could go and talk to, but the entrepreneur had led his entourage inside. There was just us now. 'The article.' I repeated. 'In *The Times*. I've seen it.'

'Oh, that.' He flustered. 'I sorry, but I haven't even seen it myself. I had to file it extremely quickly, as you can imagine.

They asked me if I could contribute a few words. By way of tribute, that sort of thing.'

'You didn't care about contacting the relatives, did you? That was just a pretext so you could get your foot in the door. "By the way, I'm a journalist myself and saw the whole thing, I don't suppose you'd be interested in an article?" '

He flushed red. 'Now just hold on one minute, Nathan, you're not being fair.'

'Not fair? You were as nice as pie to Considine yesterday, and then you completely rubbished him in your article. You made him out to be mentally unwell, and practically accused him of plagiarism just to top it off.'

'That's not what I meant to say at all. Look, as I said, I haven't even seen the article yet. You know what editors are like. It's probably just been subbed poorly.'

'I don't think so. You exploited me under the guise of an act of friendship. Then you exploited a dead man, and a guy who'd just seen the greatest day of his career end in disaster. Are you proud of that?'

He raised his right hand, palm open, and for a moment I wondered if he was about to slap me. Then he took a deep breath, and patted me on the chest. 'Okay, Nathan. Okay. Just what, precisely, are you going to do about it?'

'I'm going to read every article you write over the next few weeks very carefully indeed. And if I find anything – anything at all – that I don't like, I'm going to tell every journalist I know exactly what you've done.'

'It's nothing illegal. Anyway, it wouldn't look so good for you, would it?' He seemed cockier now, convinced he had me. 'Might be seen as if you weren't doing your job properly, mightn't it. Might seem as if you were shirking?'

I shrugged. 'Maybe. What's the worst that could happen though. I lose my unpaid job?' I smiled back at him. 'So, this is what you're going to do. There's a lovely Welsh lady out at Santa Maria Ausiliatrice. You're going to write her a wonderful review. And I haven't even got so far as seeing the art here yet. I don't really care. I'm sure it's very good. And you're going to give them a very good review as well.'

He glared at me for a few seconds and then laughed. Then he turned, and slowly walked out. As he reached the exit, he turned to face me again and shook his head. Giving me the best hard-man stare that a middle-aged arts journalist could muster.

'Oh, Francesco,' I said, 'I'm not angry. I'm just disappointed.' I gave him a little wave of the hand, as if to indicate the way out, and then he was gone.

I smiled to myself, and made my way back to the bar.

Chapter 10

'You look pleased with yourself,' said Federica.

'Oh, I am, I am. So pleased I think I've earned another drink.'

'Shouldn't we have a look at the art first?'

'Hmmm. That is kind of why we're here. Okay then.'

We made our way upstairs to the *piano nobile*. The last time I'd been here, I remembered the space being full of light, of the sun reflecting off the water of the Grand Canal and on to the ceiling. Adam Grant, however, had done something quite different. The windows were shrouded in diaphanous white material which let in only a dim light. I took a closer look. White silk, but dusty and torn. A shroud? I looked to the ceiling. I remembered frescoes by a minor painter of the eighteenth century, and some *stucco* in need of restoration. This time, they were covered by the same dusty white silk material. I looked closer. No, not shrouds. Dresses. Wedding dresses and veils. And then, as my eyes adjusted to the dim light, I noticed more of them hanging from the ceiling, casting pale shadows upon the floor. All of them dusty and cobwebbed. The material seemed to intensify the heat, and the atmosphere felt thick, muggy and unhealthy. More

than that, there was something funereal about it. Something
sickly.

I turned to Federica but, before I could speak, she saw the
expression on my face and smiled. 'Your sort of thing?'

I grinned. 'Oh yes!'

She patted my cheek. 'I thought so. You really do like all
this Gothic stuff don't you?'

'Oh, but this is great. This is great. Just look at it. It's like
Miss Havisham's version of heaven. Or of hell, maybe.'

'Even better than that.' She passed me a leaflet. 'Just look at
the title. *Lohengrin*.'

I laughed. 'Fantastic. So Adam Grant's a Wagner fan.'

'Elsa of Brabant asks one too many questions of the perfect,
gentle knight Lohengrin . . . and so he's forced to abandon her
on their wedding day.'

'Exactly. I wonder where Mr Grant is. I feel the need to
buy him a drink.' I was about to expound some more, but was
interrupted by a clap on my shoulder.

'Mr Sutherland! How are you?' It was Lewis Fitzgerald.

'I'm very well, thanks. Or at least, much better than yesterday. This is *dottoressa* Federica Ravagnan.'

She made to shake hands and then gave a little start as
Fitzgerald took her hand and kissed it. '*Piacere, dottoressa*.' I'd
never trusted people who do that. I mean, why? Look at me,
I'm being introduced to a total stranger, wouldn't it be great to
pretend I'm in a nineteenth-century novel?

'How's Mr Considine?' I asked.

Fitzgerald sucked his teeth. 'Not so great, if I'm being
honest. I was hoping he'd be here. He knows the artist. I think
he's trying to sleep things off.' I remembered what Nicolodi

had written about Considine's 'personal and emotional problems'.

'It must be terrible for him.'

'Yes. I was wondering if you'd heard anything about the possibility of the pavilion reopening.'

'Not a thing, but I wouldn't know any sooner than anyone else. It won't be seen as any of my business.'

'It's just that you said you knew some people in the police. Not wishing to stereotype of course, but,' he chuckled, 'given that we're in Italy, I wondered if you could have a couple of well-chosen little words.'

'Mr Fitzgerald.' Federica put the lightest, most delicate of touches on the word 'Mr'. 'Nathan's very good at his job, but even he isn't going to be able to get the pavilion reopened. No matter how well he chooses his little words. And given that we are – as you reminded us – in Italy, the investigation into this is probably going to take years.' She gave him her most dazzling smile, one I had learned was reserved only for those she seriously disliked.

Fitzgerald opened his mouth to speak, then thought better of it. There was an awkward silence, broken by the arrival of the artist, resplendent in tartan trews and wedding dress. 'You're the consul, right? Mr Sutherland? We're just having a quick group photo downstairs if you'd like to—' He broke off upon noticing Fitzgerald. The two men stared at each other for a couple of seconds. 'Lewis. I didn't realise you were on the guest list?'

'I'm afraid I was terribly cheeky. I used my colleague's. Mr Considine's.'

'Paul? How is he?'

'Not so good.'

'I heard what happened, of course. I'm very sorry for him.'

'Thank you. I did rather think I might have been invited myself though.'

'You probably were, Lewis. The invitation must be in the post. Like one of your cheques.' He turned, and made his way downstairs.

Lewis smiled. 'Oh dear, I don't seem to be collecting many friends today, do I? Okay, you'd better rush off for your photo shoot, Nathan. Lovely to meet you, *signora* Ravagnan.' No *dottoressa*, this time. 'And do please call me if I can be of any help.'

'Spritz?'

'Spritz. Oh yes. Most definitely.'

We made our way back down Strada Nova to La Tappa Obbligatoria. I could have done without the endless music channel playing on the television, but there was no denying they did some of the best spritzes in this part of town. I helped myself to some chunks of fried bread sprinkled with salt and oregano from the counter.

'Is it just me,' I asked, 'or is there an unusually high percentage of utter bastards in the art world?'

Fede chewed on her olive, and put her head to one side as if giving the question some proper thought. Then she delicately removed the stone from her mouth, and plopped it into her glass. 'I don't think so. Maybe at this level, perhaps. But at this level it stops being about the art and becomes about the business.'

'I mean, I've met two pretty unpleasant people in the last twenty-four hours. There might even have been four if *signor*

Scarpa had deemed me worthy of attention and Mr Blake-Hoyt hadn't—'

'—been cut off in his prime?'

'Yes. The artists seem nice though. I have to give them that.' I checked my phone. 'It's gone six. I guess nothing's going to happen with the body tonight. Tomorrow might be busy though. So what are we going to do now?'

Her eyes sparkled. 'Well, I've got a few invites. Friends of friends of friends, you know. Fancy being my plus one?'

'Marvellous, *dottoressa*. I'd be honoured. What have we got?'

She rummaged in her handbag. 'Let me see. Ukraine are in Campo Santo Stefano. Angola at Palazzo Cini. You'll like that, you'll be able to look at art by dead people as well. And then there are a few private openings on the Zattere at which, I'm afraid, there will be music by and for young people. Can you manage that?'

'I'll try not to grumble too much. When are we going to fit in food?'

She checked her watch. 'Okay, let's grab some *polpette* at alla Vedova. Then get the boat down to Sant'Angelo. Knock off the Ukrainians, then a bite to eat at Da Fiore. Then off to the Angolans, and down to the Zattere. There'll probably be a few drinks available down there.'

I crunched on my fried bread. 'You know, some people might think we're only interested in the *vernissage*.' She grinned. I reached for another piece of bread, but she stretched her hand out and stopped me.

'You'll spoil your appetite.'

'I know. I mean, these things are nice but they're not *that* great. And yet I can't stop eating them. Why do you think that is?'

She swirled her drink. 'Probably something to do with the spritz. You know, you'd almost think they put something addictive in there.' She drained her glass. 'Right, let's go.'

I put a fiver down on the counter and gave a nod to the *barista*. We made our way over the road to alla Vedova, and ordered a plate of the best meatballs in town.

'There was one other thing I thought we should try and do,' said Fede, 'but I don't know if we'll have time tonight.'

'Where's that?'

'The podule.'

'The what?'

'The mobility lift on the Calatrava Bridge. The *ovovia*. I always think "podule" sounds nicer.'

'Is that even a word?'

She shrugged. 'It is now. Pod plus module. Podule. Anyway, you know how it's not been used for years?'

I nodded. The Ponte della Costituzione, or the Calatrava Bridge as everyone referred to it, in homage to the eponymous *archistar*, had – in its short life – never been without controversy. I'd always thought it looked beautiful, but it was an opinion I tended to keep to myself unless I was very sure about the sort of company I was in. The trouble is, as elegant as it looked, it failed at the basic purpose of being a bridge; namely facilitating the passage of people from one side of the canal to the other in a reasonably straightforward manner. The varying tread length of each step made the act of crossing akin to a contact sport unless you kept your eyes fixed firmly on your feet at all times. The glass steps were striking but scared the merry hell out of you when wet. And, crucially, nobody had thought about disabled access. The problem was meant to be solved by sticking a little red ovoid cabin on the side which, the theory went, would transport people across, via a track fixed to the outside of the bridge. It had worked for perhaps two months, and now sat there unused, unloved and – crucially – unmoving.

But now, Federica explained, a use had been found for it. A local artist had, somehow, got permission to use it as an exhibition space. The smallest exhibition space there had ever been, or was ever likely to be, at the Venice Biennale.

'So what sort of work is it?' I asked.

'It's a video work. The artist took a film from the podule crossing from one side to the other when it was still in operation. And so the idea is that if you can't actually use it, you can still have the virtual experience.'

'I didn't realise it was still working.'

'It isn't. Only the elevator mechanism. No one knows if the rest of it is ever going to work again.'

'I'm surprised the *Comune* are allowing it to be used like this.'

She shrugged. 'I suppose it's a bit of money coming in. Who knows, if they use it for every Biennale they might cover the cost of the thing by the end of the century.'

'And people say the *Comune* aren't far-sighted. It's actually a pretty good idea. As an artwork, I mean.'

'It is, isn't it?' She patted my cheek. 'Look at you, getting interested in contemporary art. I never thought I'd see the day.'

'Hmph.' I tried, and failed, to put on my best grumpy face. Then we drained our glasses and strode off, arm in arm, towards the *vaporetto*.

Chapter 11

There was no need for me to actually be there the following morning, when Vanni called Considine in for a little chat. Nevertheless, I felt sorry for the guy, and thought I might be able to help. He was dressed as I remembered him and unshaven, with dark circles under his eyes. He gave me a weak smile.

'Good morning, Mr Sutherland.'

'Call me Nathan, okay? How are you, Paul.'

He shook his head. 'Not so good. Just so tired, you know. I haven't slept properly since . . . well, you know. I finally fell asleep just before dawn.' He yawned. 'Didn't have time to shower and shave. I feel like a right mess.'

'Nobody's going to care. Don't worry. It's just a statement, that's all.'

I'd got him a lawyer. Fitzgerald and I waited outside for them, studiously avoiding each other's gaze. Fitzgerald broke first.

'So what's likely to happen?'

I shrugged. 'Difficult to say. But remember, he's not under arrest. He's not actually done anything wrong. All they're doing is talking to him.'

Fitzgerald gave a hollow laugh. 'That's what bothers me.' I looked at him, but didn't say a word. 'He's not good at this. You can tell that, can't you?'

'Look, there's a lawyer in there with him. There's an interpreter as well, so he'll know exactly what's going on.'

'You know them?'

I nodded. 'Fabrizio – he's the lawyer – is the go-to guy for this sort of thing. He's fine. Professional. The interpreter, Anna, I know quite well. Given we kind of do the same job.'

'Can I ask why you're not doing it?'

It was my turn to laugh. 'It wouldn't really be right. I mean, there's no law against it. But it would seem a bit weird. As if every British citizen in trouble is also a business opportunity.'

'And it's not?'

I stiffened. 'No. Not at all.'

We sat in silence for a few more minutes, and then he spoke again. 'What do you think is going to happen, Mr Sutherland? Really.'

I sighed. 'If I was a gambling man, I'd say nothing is going to happen. I think it's a tragic accident. I think the people who put the space together are going to get their arses seriously kicked. And by that I mean prison. But I don't think any of that is likely to apply to Mr Considine.'

Fitzgerald nodded, but his face remained impassive.

I paused, and then continued. 'There is just one thing . . .'

He looked quizzical, but said nothing.

'*Juditha Triumphans*.'

'You what?'

'*Juditha Triumphans*. It's an oratorio by Vivaldi.'

'I know what it is. I know what it is.' He waved his hand at me dismissively. 'What's it got to do with Paul?'

'Well, a scrap of paper was found in what I assume is his wallet with the words scrawled across it.'

'And . . . ?'

'The scrap of paper had been torn from *The Times*. It was part of Gordon Blake-Hoyt's review.'

'I don't understand. How did the police get hold of his wallet?' He was firing questions at me now.

'It was found on the *vaporetto*. I handed it in.'

'Well, there we go. Could have been anybody who dropped it. Anybody.'

I held up my hands, palms towards him in a placatory gesture. 'I know, I know. It's just that they might think it a bit . . . a bit . . .'

'A bit what?'

'A bit strange. That's all.' It sounded weak, even to my ears.

He shook his head. 'You want to watch what you say. You could get into trouble. Saying things like that.'

'Look, you asked me what I thought and—'

'He's a British citizen in trouble. Your job is to help him. Not your business to be casting aspersions behind his back.'

I was about to raise my voice when the door opened, and Paul Considine came out, accompanied by a couple of cops, his lawyer and his translator. Fabrizio smiled, patted me on the shoulder and walked straight out.

I gave Anna a smile. 'Coffee?'

She nodded. 'On the corner?'

'Great. Just give me five minutes.'

Fitzgerald gave Considine a quick hug and tried to steer him towards the door, but he grabbed my arm. His eyes were red. 'Will you help me, Mr Sutherland?' was all he said.

'I'm sorry?'

'Will you help me, Nathan? Please?'

'Look, Paul. You're not under arrest. All they wanted was to speak to you. Probably that's all it's going to be.'

He shook his head. 'I'm just so tired, you know? Hard to think straight, hard to answer all those questions.'

I took a deep breath. 'I'll do what I can, Paul. I can get you another lawyer, although I suggest we keep Fabrizio. If you want to talk to a priest or anyone I can do that, I can call people in the UK for you, I can—'

'Not do very much really,' Fitzgerald interrupted.

'I'm sorry?'

'Stop apologising. Please.' He turned to Paul. 'He can't do anything. He's just the pen-pusher. The admin person.' He smiled at me. 'No offence meant.' He grabbed Paul by the elbow and steered him out through the door. 'Thanks for coming in today, Mr Sutherland, we do appreciate it.'

I stood in silence, wrapped in my own thoughts for about a minute. Arrogant little bastard. How dare he? Then I shook my head. Not my problem any more. Let Lewis bloody Fitzgerald sort it all out. Sometimes I wondered just why I did this bloody job.

I walked out on to the *fondamenta*. I reached inside my jacket for my sunglasses, and realised I'd left them at home. Summer was coming now. It wasn't yet the time of the pitiless midsummer heat that made the exposed, shadowless spaces almost unbearable, but my jacket, I could feel, would be sticking unpleasantly to me by the time I got home.

The bar on the corner of Piazzale Roma would never have been my choice for a leisurely drink – there was nowhere to sit down for one thing – but the staff were nice enough and they never ripped you off. Anna was standing just outside so that she could smoke with her coffee.

I gave her a peck on the cheek. 'Same again?'

'That'd be nice.' I waved at the barman. '*Un caffè, un caffè corretto.*'

Anna raised an eyebrow. '*Corretto?*'

I nodded. The barman caught my eye. '*Con grappa?*'

'*Sì.*' I turned back to Anna. 'I'm pissed off.'

'Oh dear. What's happened now?'

'Considine's agent. Or manager, or whatever the hell he is. Arrogant little prick.' I took a deep breath. 'Anyway, that's not the problem. How was he? Considine, I mean.'

The barman slid two coffees across the bar. Anna took a sachet of brown sugar, tore it and stirred it in. 'Do you think these are getting smaller?'

'I think so. Must be a health thing.'

'Doesn't work though, does it? Because now one just isn't enough. So now I have to use two. Which means I'm using even more than before.' She laughed, her voice rough with cigarettes.

I took a sip of my coffee, and felt the caffeine and sugar mix hit me at the same time as the grappa hit the back of my throat. Best coffee of the day. 'As I was saying. What do you think of him?'

She looked sad. 'Poor man. He looks like he hasn't slept in days. He kept apologising a lot. Said he was so sorry about what had happened to Mr Blake-Hoyt.'

'So what else did he say?'

'Not much. Yes, it was his wallet. He'd had it when he left home on the day of the opening. Then realised he didn't have it when he got back to the hotel. He must have dropped it on the *vaporetto* because he remembered validating his ticket. No, that wasn't his writing on the piece of newspaper. Yes, he had seen the article in *The Times* before the accident because his agent had shown it to him. No, he didn't like Mr Blake-Hoyt but neither did he wish him out of the world.'

'His agent showed him the article?'

'Yes.'

'Just before his big event. Bastard. Why do a thing like that?'

Anna shrugged. She paused for a moment, and then continued. 'So all in all he didn't say much. The trouble is, he looks tired and he looks scared.'

'Hardly surprising, I'd have thought.'

'I know.' She fished her cigarettes out of her bag, lit one up, and replaced them before I had the chance to ask her for one. 'But sometimes . . . well, you know how things work . . . sometimes these things are misinterpreted.'

'Did they mention the drugs?'

'Drugs?'

'Priadel. For bipolar disorder.'

'Oh, those sorts of drugs. Yes, they did. He does take – Priadel, did you say? – because of his illness. He said he was diagnosed five years ago.'

'Right.' I took another sip of coffee. 'He asked me to help him. Really help him, I mean.'

'And?' She raised an eyebrow.

'And I don't think I can. There's nothing I can do. Not really.'

'Then don't worry about it. You're doing plenty already.'

'I know. It's just . . .'

She laughed. 'Oh Nathan, you are sweet at times. You'd make a terrible Italian, you know.'

I grinned. 'I would, wouldn't I?'

'If you ask me, they're probably not going to speak to him again. Somebody's going to be in big trouble but not him.' She looked at her watch. 'I've got to go. Love to Jean.'

'Jean?' I said. She looked confused. 'We've broken up.'

Her hands flew to her face. 'Oh my God. I did know. I'd forgotten.'

I smiled. 'It's okay. We're both fine. I'm with someone else now. Federica Ravagnan, I don't know if you know her? She works in art restoration.'

She shook her head. 'Well, you must both come round for dinner some time. You promise?'

'Of course. Or you must come round to ours.' We'd had conversations like this for the last five years. We knew we never would. She kissed me on the cheek, and left.

I should, I knew, be heading back home. There was still, then, no prospect of the body being released. There would be a long and shouty conversation to be had with Mr Blake-Hoyt's brother. Therefore, I needed a good excuse not to do so. I checked my watch. It was, perhaps, a twenty-minute walk to the Frari. I'd see if Fede was in the mood for a long lunch.

I don't know why, but I always seemed to get lost when walking to the Frari. It was annoying. I knew exactly where it was – indeed, you could hardly miss it - and yet the city seemed to move itself around as an act of petty spite whenever I was going there. It took me longer than expected and my jacket was clinging to me by the time I arrived.

It was a relief to get out of the early summer heat. The sheer solidity of the Frari meant that, like most churches, it seemed to take months to heat up properly and months to cool down again. The church was modestly busy with tourists, as it usually was, but it never attracted the numbers that crushed into St Mark's Basilica, and the vast scale of the interior meant that it never seemed to feel excessively crowded.

As ever, my gaze was drawn through the rood screen, down through the nave and to the great, golden glow of Titian's altarpiece, *The Assumption of the Virgin*. The painting's enormous dimensions were dwarfed by the surrounding space, and yet it was almost impossible not to have your eye drawn towards it. The apostles gaze and gesture in awe, as (a perhaps unsurprisingly surprised) Mary is carried up to the heavens on a cloud supported by a swirling group of cherubim. Yet for all its movement, it was that great blaze of yellow-gold from the heavens that never failed to knock the socks off me. I found it hard to believe that it wasn't illuminated, and wondered whether, if I passed by at night, I would see the windows glowing as if the interior was still lit by the golden, glorious light of Titian's art.

I could feel myself starting to cool down now, and made my way to my second favourite space in the church. Allegorical figures and a winged lion lay on marble steps leading up to a pyramidal structure in the centre of which stood a half-open door, outside of which a robed, cowled figure stood bearing an urn. It should have felt incongruous in its surroundings, but it was far too perfect for that.

The tomb of Antonio Canova. Or, at least, of part of him. Most of his remains now lay in his birthplace of Possagno. But like so many visitors before and after him, his heart would always be in Venice.

I stared at the enticingly open door. I'd never, ever been able to make out where it led to. A half-open door leading into a pyramid, with a cowled figure outside bearing an urn containing Canova's heart. I'd always wanted to take a look beyond the door. I wondered if Fede could arrange it for me?

Ah yes, Federica. I'd only just thought of her and remembered the reason I came, when she tapped me on the shoulder, making me start.

'You seem miles away, *tesoro*.'

'I was. Or at least, I was somewhere within the pyramid.'

She smiled. 'I've told you, there's not much to see. It's just an optical illusion. It doesn't actually lead anywhere. Nothing to get excited about.'

'Oh, don't spoil it.'

She gave me a hug. 'You watch too many Dario Argento films, *caro*,' and kissed me.

'Hmm, you'd better watch that. You'll get us both thrown out. Lack of respect, that sort of thing.'

'I suppose so.' She stepped back. 'There we go, we must be a good metre apart. I think that's sufficiently respectful. You look hot.'

'I'm cooling down now. But summer's on its way.'

'You could always take your jacket off?'

'I don't like taking my jacket off. It feels like I'm not dressed properly. See also shorts and sandals.'

She sighed. 'Let me guess, the honorary consul's job in Bergen was already taken? Now, to what do I owe the honour of this visit?'

'Oh, it's been a bit of a tough morning. If I go home I'll have to do some work and entertain the cat. I wondered if you fancied lunch?'

She shook her head. 'Sorry, no time today. The rood screen isn't going to clean itself. Come round tonight though. Mother's coming round for dinner.'

'Oh right. Good,' I said, with as much enthusiasm as I could muster.

She narrowed her eyes. 'Don't be like that.'

'Like what?'

'You know. And she does like you. Really.'

'Really?'

'Well, she quite likes you. That's progress. And I'll cook.'

'You'll cook?'

'She likes me to cook. It makes her feel like she's passed her skills on.'

'Oh good,' I said.

'You're doing it again, Nathan.'

'I'm sorry. What time?'

'Seven-thirty. I'll see you then.'

I made to kiss her, but she gently pushed me back and shook my hand instead. 'Sufficiently respectable, *caro.*'

I smiled.

Chapter 12

We'd never worked out what we were going to do about living together.

I enjoyed going over to the Lido. There was something relaxing and wonderfully romantic about travelling there at the end of the day; either sitting inside the cabin of the *vaporetto* as the rain and wind battered the outside; or sitting outside on the rear seats as the sun sank in the sky over the lagoon, the green dome of the votive temple for the fallen of World War I glowing like a beacon. Then arriving at Santa Maria Elisabetta, and looking back at the panorama of the city itself. I even liked the smell of petrol, and being in the presence of cars again. And to top it all, Fede's apartment was nicer than mine.

The problem was – in contrast to the Street of the Assassins – the Lido really wasn't much good as an office for the Consulate. In the event of having been robbed, or losing important documents (likely as not including *vaporetto* tickets) it wouldn't do to have to take a long boat ride out to the Lido. Whereas my apartment was about as central as it got.

The other problem was Gramsci. It would be unfair to say that Federica actively disliked him, and, indeed, Gramsci positively tolerated her. The trouble was that she had seen what he had done to my furniture and was in no great hurry to provide him with an exciting new environment full of destructive possibilities. And so we muddled on as best we could.

I might have caught a bus on a cold and rainy day, but the early summer evening made for a pleasant stroll. I'd picked up some flowers for *signora* Colombo along the way, and carefully picked off the adhesive label as I walked along. Fede's mum no longer lived in Venice, and we didn't see her that often. I thought she was, perhaps, slowly warming to me. Nevertheless, I wondered if we would ever be on first-name terms (let alone ever use the second person familiar between ourselves) or if she would always remain *signora* Colombo to me.

I made my way up the stairs, let myself in and immediately realised I'd made a mistake. She was standing in the hall, talking to Federica in the kitchen, and her eyes rested momentarily on the keys in my hand. She said nothing, but gave me a knowing glance. So, you have your own keys then?

I didn't know if we'd ever be on kissing terms, or even handshaking terms, so I settled for giving her my best attempt at a winning smile and proffering my flowers. 'Lovely to see you again, *signora*. These are for you.'

She smiled. 'That's very kind, Mr Sutherland. I'm sorry, I'm only going to be here for a couple of days . . .'

'Oh, what a pity,' I interrupted, and inwardly cursed myself. Trying too hard, Nathan, trying much too hard.

The smile didn't leave her face for an instant. 'I'll only be here for a couple of days, but we can put them in water and Federica can enjoy them after I leave. Although I'm sure you buy her flowers all the time.'

'Oh, all the time. Yes.'

Federica flashed her eyes at me. 'You never buy me flowers,' they said.

I gave her a sad little glance, trying to express the words 'I know. But I will in future. I promise.'

She nodded, as if to say she'd heard all this before. Which, to be fair, she had. 'Why don't you both go through and sit down. I'll bring dinner through in a minute.'

Her mother went through into the dining room, but I hung back. 'Anything I can do to help, *cara*?'

Fede shook her head. 'Even I can't get this one wrong. Onion, garlic, olive oil. Tin of tomatoes. More chili than strictly necessary.'

'And the basil. Don't forget the basil.'

'I can tear up basil leaves, Nathan.'

'And the *soffrito* of course. It's all in the *soffrito*.'

She took my face in her hands and smiled. 'I know it is, *caro*. It might not be up to your standards but it will be fine.' She dropped her voice to a whisper. 'Now go and join *Mamma*.'

I stared at my shoes. 'I'm scared,' I whispered.

'Don't be silly. She likes you. Well, she quite likes you. Now go and sparkle.' She patted me on the cheek, turned me around and gently, but firmly, pushed me out of the door and into the dining room.

Signora Colombo and I sat on opposite sides of the table, and smiled politely at each other. We said nothing. I smiled and nodded at her. She did the same.

Silence.

Smiling was starting to hurt my face. 'So, do you have any plans for the next few days?' I ventured.

She shook her head. 'Nothing in particular.'

'You're not seeing anything at the Biennale? I might be able to get you a pass for the Giardini.'

'Thank you, but I probably won't have time. And I have to be honest, I don't have the patience for the art Biennale. I do like the film festival. And the architecture Biennale.'

'Ah, now that leaves me a bit cold to be honest. Sometimes I think you need to actually be an architect to appreciate that.'

'Perhaps. I was an architect, you know.'

'Yes, I know,' I lied. What to say, Nathan, what to say? 'So, did you ever build anything nice?' Or should I just start sobbing uncontrollably?

She came to my rescue. 'You're not cooking tonight?'

I shook my head. 'Not this time.'

'But Federica says you are a good cook.'

'I don't know. Maybe sometimes I am. But I know Federica wanted to cook tonight.'

She nodded. 'My husband was a good cook. A very good one. I never had the patience for it. To be honest, I was never terribly interested in food. And now I understand that must have been quite frustrating for him.'

A question was left hanging in the air. I could see she wanted me to ask it, but I couldn't think of the words.

She helped me out. 'He found someone else to cook for.'

'What a bastard, eh?' The words just slipped out and seemed to echo around the room as if I'd shouted them at the top of my voice in St Mark's Basilica.

There was a moment of terrible silence, and then she put her hand to her mouth and laughed a gentle, crystalline little laugh. 'My goodness. Yes, indeed. What a bastard!' She laughed again, and I joined in, trying to keep the hysterical note of relief out of my voice.

She called out, 'Federica, *cara*. Can you bring some prosecco for Nathan and me?'

Nathan! I'd done it! After almost a year, I'd done it! I thought it best to be sure, however. 'That's a splendid idea, *signora* Colombo.'

'Call me Marta, please.'

Federica brought some prosecco through, we all clinked glasses, and she rested her hand on my shoulder and gave it an ever-so-delicate squeeze.

Marta finished the last of her *spaghetti al pomodoro,* and smiled at me. 'I see you were in the newspapers, Nathan.'

I nodded. 'Yes. I could have done without it, to be honest. But there's no way this wasn't going to be front page news.'

'Horrible. That poor man.'

'It's tough. I'm doing all I can to get his body repatriated but the police won't release it until their investigation's concluded.'

'But it was an accident, of course?'

'Of course.' Well, almost certainly. 'But there are people the police are speaking to.'

'They were speaking to the artist today, *Mamma,'* said Federica.

'And how is he? It must be terrible for him too.'

'It is,' I said. 'Yes, I think it is. He asked me to help him. Trouble is, I don't think there's much I can do.'

'And you feel sorry for him?'

'I do. I think he's got problems. Or at least, a journalist told me he'd had problems in the past. Maybe drink, maybe drugs, But he does seem terribly vulnerable.'

Marta nodded. 'I understand. But sometimes vulnerable people can do terrible things too. Although journalists—' She exhaled a long, contemptuous 'pffffft'.

'I guess that's true.' I got to my feet, and reached for the plates. 'Let me get all this cleared away. And can I make anyone a coffee?' They both nodded. 'And there's a bottle of grappa here if anyone would like one.'

'No thanks, Nathan. You know how I feel about grappa.'

'I'm afraid I agree with my daughter, Nathan. My husband was always one for grappa at the end of every meal, but I never understood why.'

'Me neither, *Mamma*. And that stuff that Nathan buys is like drinking a cigarette.'

I returned from the kitchen, bearing one bottle and one glass. 'Well, that's the brilliance of it,' I said. I checked my watch, and smiled. 'Just time for a quick coffee, and then I'll need to head off for my *vaporetto.'*

There was a slightly awkward silence. 'My cat will be missing me.'

'He won't,' said Federica, under her breath.

'Well, he'll need feeding. And I've got quite a busy day tomorrow.'

'Oh, anything exciting?' said Marta.

'Well, exciting-ish. There are a few artists at the Arsenale that I helped out with translation work. I told them I'd come along and see them. Now, I couldn't make it on opening day because of all the – unpleasantness – at the Giardini, so I might try and go along tomorrow. Chance to have a look around the whole thing properly.' I heard the Moka starting to bubble away on the hob, and went out to the kitchen to pour three cups. 'That is if I can get away from the office. I've got a surgery in the morning, and I think Mr Blake-Hoyt's brother is going to call me every day until I can get the body repatriated.' I stirred sugar into my coffee and knocked it back in one gulp. I hadn't let it cool enough, and it burned the back of my throat. No matter. I got to my feet and reached for my jacket. 'Okay, and now I really must be going. Lovely to see you again, Marta.'

She smiled. 'Likewise, Nathan. I hope we see each other again before I go back.'

'Me too.'

Federica walked to the door with me. 'I'll give you a call tomorrow, *caro*, okay?' Then she gave me a hug and a peck on the cheek. 'Well done,' she whispered in my ear.

I caught an empty *vaporetto* back to a near-silent Venice and a near-empty flat. I tossed a few balls to an uninterested Gramsci. Of course, there was no point in playing when I was in the mood. Far better to wait until the early hours of the morning.

The strange affair of Paul Considine and the head of Gordon Blake-Hoyt aside, it had been a good day. I thought back to Paul's interview at the *Questura*. How had he seemed? Fragile, yes. Frightened, yes. He hadn't slept properly for days. And yet, the greatest moment of his career had ended in a violent death. How was he supposed to react? The only person who'd told me about deep-rooted psychological problems was Francesco Nicolodi, and I didn't see any reason to trust him any more.

I shook my head and scanned the racks of CDs. Some late night Hawkwind perhaps? No. I had a better idea.

V for Vivaldi. In between Verdi and von Bingen. *Juditha Triumphans*. I poured myself a glass of wine and lay back on the sofa as the horns blared out the martial overture and led into the great opening chorus.

Arma, caedes, vindictae, furores,

Angustiae, timores

Precedite nos.

The Red Priest at his most militaristic and thrilling. *Let weapons, carnage, vengeance, fury, famine and fear go before us.*

I think I fell asleep shortly before Judith left Bethulia.

Chapter 13

The woman on the other side of the desk was crying. She'd been trying to hold it back since she came in, but now the tears were flowing silently. She'd arrived with her husband only two days ago. They were regular visitors, she said, and came every year. They always stayed at the same place, the nicest hotel on the Zattere. And then last night, just before dinner, he'd just stumbled and fallen during their evening *passeggiata*. Or at least that's what she thought. He'd actually suffered a heart attack. He'd arrested twice in the water ambulance on the way to hospital, but – from what she could understand – he was at least stable now.

I'd been consul for less than six months when I had to deal with a young woman in floods of tears whose husband of two days had slipped and broken his leg on the *fondamenta* of the Giudecca. I'd had no idea, absolutely no idea, as to how one went about dealing with this sort of thing. I did, however, very quickly learn that – in these sorts of situations – you really did have to come up with something rather better than 'Still, it could be worse, could be raining.'

I was better at it now. I let her cry for a few minutes, and ever so gently prodded the box of paper handkerchiefs on my side of the desk over to hers. She ran her hands through her hair and took a few deep breaths; then dabbed at her eyes. Gramsci watched her from the edge of the desk. I stared at him. Don't even think about it. He stared back and raised a paw. With a swift, flowing motion I half rose from my seat, grabbed him and forced him on to my lap. I don't think she even noticed. Gramsci squirmed and wriggled as I held him down under the pretence of stroking him. I felt a little like Ernst Stavro Blofeld.

She blew her nose, and then smiled. She looked over at Gramsci, trying to escape from my iron grasp. 'He's funny,' she said.

I smiled back at her. 'Better now?'

She nodded, and flushed. 'I'm sorry.'

'Don't be. It's okay. It must have been very frightening.' She nodded. 'Right, well there are certainly a few things I can help you with. But first things first. Would a coffee be good?'

'Yes please.'

'Would a *caffè corretto* be even better?'

She gave a little laugh. 'At this time? Do you think I should?'

'You've had a horrible shock. Yes, I think you should.' I tipped Gramsci off my lap and went over to the coffee machine. I'd never liked capsule coffee makers but I'd come to realise that – if a client appeared in need of one – it looked more professional to have one in the office instead of going out to the kitchen to brew one up in a Moka. I'd gone to the trouble of preparing a tray with a couple of espresso cups on it. One of them was even clean. The other would do for me. I wondered if it would be just a little too smooth if I were to trigger the machine from my smartphone. All I'd need would be a machine that could be triggered by a smartphone. And, of course, a smartphone.

I made two cups and passed one to her, along with a small wooden box with some sugar sachets in. Some of which read, 'Magical Brazilian Café San Marco'. I sat back down, opened the bottom left drawer on the desk, and took out a bottle of grappa. I liked the way it made me feel like a 1940s detective. I topped us up. 'Take a little sugar as well, it all helps.'

'You're very kind.'

'I'm not, you know. After a few months in this job I realised that too many people were leaving the office in tears. That's never good. If nothing else, the bar I go to is downstairs. I started to worry that the staff would think I was a loan shark or something.' She smiled again. I took another look at the notes that I'd scribbled down. 'Okay, let's see what we can do here. Your husband's in the *Ospedale Civile*, but the good news is he's stable now?' She nodded. 'Well, that's good, isn't it? Now, have you got a name you can give me – a consultant or someone like that?'

She fumbled in her bag, and took out a diary. She riffled through it. 'Dr Vianello.'

I grinned. 'Have you got another name? It's just that Vianello round here is like being called Jones in Wales.'

'Sorry. Yes, his first name is—' She screwed up her eyes. 'Thomas. Tommaso, would that be?'

'That's right. I know him. Nice man. Doesn't speak much English.'

She welled up again. 'That's right. It makes things a bit difficult.' I nodded. She continued, 'I don't speak much Italian. Well, I speak a bit. It's just you never expect to have to talk about something like this, do you?'

She was right. It doesn't matter how good you are in a foreign language, you're always grateful for a doctor or a barber who can speak English.

'Okay, when are you next going to visit your husband?'

'This afternoon. Three o'clock?'

'Right. Would it help if I came along? I can interpret for you if need be?'

'Would you? That would be so kind.'

'No, it's fine. And then when he gets out, we'll need to look at getting you both home. But that can wait for now. Anything else, are there any people you'd like me to contact?'

'No, that's fine. I think I've called everyone.'

'Good, good. Well, I think we're almost done. But is there anyone you'd like to talk to? A priest for example?'

She flushed.

'Would that be nice?'

She nodded.

'Anglican, Catholic? Sorry, I have to ask this,' I smiled.

'Church of England. Is there one here?' She sounded surprised.

'There is. Not many people know about it, but there is. St George's, in Campo San Vio. Can I pass your details on?'

'Yes please. Thank you again.'

'No problems. No problems at all.' I showed her to the door. 'I'll see you later this afternoon then.'

'Thank you.' She paused. 'Can I give you a hug? Or is that not professional?'

I grinned. 'Maybe not. But hugs are important at a time like this, so I'll let it go if you will.'

I walked her down to the street, closed the door behind her and picked up the few items of mail that there were for me. Then I skipped back upstairs. This was always the best part of the job. If you're a victim of crime, then – sorry – there's not much that I can do. I can be a shoulder to cry on but there's little I can do beyond telling you to go to the police. Lost your passport? I can tell you how to get another one, but not much more than that. But if you're alone in town, and something has gone a bit wrong and you feel scared because you don't quite understand what's happening – well, that's fine. That I can help with. That's when I can make things a little bit less frightening and horrible than they seem. And that's why it's the best part of the job. I dropped the mail on the desk. Mainly circulars from supermarkets but there were a few envelopes as well. Bills, of course. Still, Biennale years were good years and they worried me less than they might have twelve months previously.

There was a rattle of keys in the lock and Federica came in. 'All finished, *caro*?'

I checked my watch. It was a minute past the hour. 'All finished, *cara*.'

'I saw an elderly lady leaving. She was smiling. You must have worked your charm.'

'Her husband's in hospital. I'm going round to see him this afternoon.'

'Oh, you are nice. Sometimes, anyway.' She sat herself down in the chair opposite me. 'Lunchtime?'

'Lunchtime. Let me just check email.' I scrolled through. 'Nothing. Not even from Groupon. Right, let's cook.'

'Spritz first?'

'Not today. I need to be on good form this afternoon.'

She grabbed my face. 'Okay, who are you, and what have you done with Nathan?'

'I'm being grown-up, *cara*. Doesn't it suit me?'

'I'm not sure. Try doing it in easy stages.'

'Okay, prosecco then.'

'That's better.'

I went through to the kitchen and poured out two glasses. Fede checked her watch. 'I don't have much time, I'm afraid.'

'That's okay.' I filled a pan and stuck it on to boil. 'Spaghetti with lemon, basil and parmesan. You can be out of here in thirty minutes. Twenty-five if you don't stop to tell me how brilliant I am. And am I cooking dinner tonight?

'I think tonight I need to stay in with *Mamma*.'

'Oh, and I thought we were getting on so well?'

'You are.' She gave me a hug. 'I'm very proud of you. But I think we should have a girls' night in. Why don't you go out with Dario?'

'He's busy tonight. Which means—'

'Sad bachelor night in?'

'That sort of thing.'

'Takeaway pizza, too much beer and watch a creaky old horror film?'

'I thought about that. But I think I'm actually going to do some proper work. Trying to help someone who isn't even a friend. I think I'm going to do that.'

Fede smiled.

Chapter 14

I had a good afternoon and an unsatisfying evening. I spent some time with the elderly couple at hospital, translating what Dr Vianello had to say. Which boiled down to, *You've been very lucky.* Then I went home to book them a couple of budget flights with easyJet. And then the flat started to feel a bit lonely.

'Will you help me, Nathan? Please?'

I had, really had, intended to set to work on trying to help Paul Considine. But the more I thought about it, the less it seemed I could do.

I'd tried to go over the facts as best I understood them. The trouble was, there weren't all that many. It was, I supposed, entirely possible that Gordon Blake-Hoyt would have a copy of Gentileschi's *Judith Slaying Holofernes* in his pocket. A quick check had revealed that the original was in the Uffizi. Very well, then, perhaps he'd just returned from Florence. Hell, perhaps it was just his favourite painting.

And the wallet? Considine admitted it was his. Had he just written down a sick little joke on *The Times* review, and then stuck it in his wallet? And then dropped it on the *vaporetto*? Or had his pocket picked. I shook my head. That made no sense. If somebody had stolen it, they'd have taken the bank notes and then chucked it away. For that matter, if he'd just dropped it it surely wouldn't have taken long for someone to notice it on the floor of a crowded boat. So had he been on it at the same time as Nicolodi and myself? It seemed unlikely but, on a boat crammed full of people, not impossible.

That just left *Juditha Triumphans*. Okay, perhaps he had written it, and was too ashamed and embarrassed to admit it to the police. It would make sense. Perhaps I was just guilty of thinking that a little mystery would be a distraction from the treadmill of translating abstracts? It could all just be a coincidence, couldn't it?

No. It really couldn't.

It would be useful to speak to Paul again, but then it struck me that I had no way of contacting him. Or his manager for that matter. I should have taken their numbers. Vanni, I knew, would put me in touch if I said it was urgent consular business but that would involve having to lie to him. Then there was Nicolodi. I at least knew where he was staying, but was unsure if he could be any help at all given that we'd been together at the time of the accident. Besides, we hadn't parted on the best of terms.

At which point, I'd given up. I spent the rest of the evening listening to *Juditha Triumphans* in the hope of inspiration, as Gramsci and I competed to out-sulk the other.

Still, today would be better. I stuck my head out of the window and craned upwards. A grey day, but I could feel a warm, gentle breeze on my face. The smell of coffee and brioche wafted up from the Brazilians. Today was going to be a good day. No headless art critics. No neurotic artists or shady journalists. I was just going to enjoy the Biennale.

I grabbed a quick breakfast downstairs, and then set out to walk to the Arsenale.

I could have taken the *vaporetto*, but – the cloudy skies apart – it was an almost-perfect early summer's morning and the streets wouldn't be too crowded yet. It was best to make the most of the opportunity. I walked down to Piazza San Marco. Years ago, I remembered walking through it in the half-light of a winter's early morning, my only companions being a couple of street sweepers. I had never seen it like that since. Even now, at barely nine o'clock, the square was starting to fill up with early morning visitors, and crap merchants jostling for position. Tables and chairs were already in position outside Quadri and Florian, ready to receive those who would pay almost anything for admittedly excellent coffee and croissants in order to enjoy the view of the world passing by in 'the most elegant drawing-room in Europe'. Unless one were to pass through in the very dead of night, it was never going to be quite as perfect as one might like. It would still, however, take a heart of stone to remain unmoved by it.

I made my way through the square, past the Doge's Palace, on to the Riva degli Schiavoni and over the Ponte della Paglia. I stopped for a moment to look at the view over to the Ponte dei Sospiri, the Bridge of Sighs. Ruskin, I thought, had been right. It had a pretty name, but there wasn't anything particularly special about it. And yet, whenever you passed through this part of town, there was just something about it that made you stop, if only for a few moments, and look. Which is why, in the height of the tourist season, the Ponte della Paglia would become impassable and traffic would grind to a halt.

I walked on, past the statue of Vittorio Emanuele and the church of the Pietà. Vivaldi's church. Or sort of. Legend claimed that he'd worked with the architect, or at least advised on the acoustics; either way, the Red Priest was long since cold in his grave by the time it was finished. The façade itself had remained unfinished until the twentieth century. It was currently undergoing restoration, the enormous advertising hoarding that covered it almost concealing the fact that there was a church there at all. I'd only ever been inside once, when I'd gone to a concert of modest quality and immodest price in order to gaze at Tiepolo's ceiling frescoes.

Vivaldi brought *Juditha Triumphans* to mind again. I turned the case over in my mind again. Except, I reminded myself, there really wasn't a case at all. Just a horrible accident which would be sorted out within a few days.

I'd taken my mind off walking by now, and arrived at the Naval Museum almost before I realised it. I shook my head, annoyed with myself. A walk through Venice seemed like a waste if you didn't concentrate on it. I still had time for another coffee, and walked down to a bar I knew just outside the Arsenale, where four of the least convincing lions in the history of sculpture stood guard over the main entrance.

Not yet ten-thirty. A little early, even for me, for a spritz. I ordered a *caffè macchiato* and a glass of water and sat down outside. Then I realised I had nothing to read. Not a newspaper, not a book and only an unintelligent phone. I took a quick look around the other customers. A family with a pushchair and a small boy with a scooter. Venetian, then. A silver-haired businessman reading *Il Sole 24 Ore*. Another local. A group of young people, all wearing Biennale passes on lanyards. A white rastafarian on the next table, with a dog on a string. Almost certainly a tourist, I told myself, were it not for the dog. A young man with a man bun. Why the man bun? They were everywhere now. Yes, it looked good on Toshiro Mifune in *Seven Samurai*, but since then . . . ? Ah Nathan, I thought, you're getting old. My coffee arrived and I went through my usual ritual. Take a sachet of brown sugar, tap it three times on the palm of the hand. Empty sugar into cup. Stir twenty times clockwise. Every time. And it was never quite right if I deviated from the ritual.

'Mr Sutherland?' The words shocked me out of my grumpy little interior monologue. 'Mr Sutherland?' The words came from my right. Paul Considine was sitting there. I had no idea how long he might have been there.

'Paul. How are you?' He shrugged. 'Can I get you a coffee?' He shook his head. 'No, I'm getting you a coffee', I said. I motioned him to drag his chair over. I waved at a waiter and held a finger up for another coffee.

'I'm heading off to the Arsenale after this,' I said, 'how about you?'

He nodded. 'Yes.' Then his expression changed, just a touch of slyness. 'Well, I'm supposed to.'

'What about Lewis? Mr Fitzgerald, I should say.'

'Vincenzo Scarpa agreed to give him a few moments of his time. Lewis thought it might be good if I was there as well.'

'And you don't want to?'

'What's the point? He doesn't like me, I don't like him. It's going to be like last week, it's just going to be an excuse for him to be nasty.' He looked upset for a moment, then shook his head as if trying to shake out the bad thoughts.

I tried to change the subject. 'I was being serious, you know. When I told you how much I loved your installation.'

His face cleared. 'Thanks.'

'Why glass, though? Have you always worked with it?'

He shook his head. 'No. Something happened to me, years ago now.' I was about to ask him what it was, but he shook his head. 'I started thinking more and more about glass as a material. As an idea. How there's an innate tension in it. How you could make an object that's fragile, beautiful and deadly at the same time. You could make a stained-glass window and then kill someone with the fragments. And then there's all the other weird stuff. You know how they told us in school about windows in old buildings? How they were thicker at the bottom, because glass flows like a liquid?'

'Except that— '

'Except that it's not true. Can you imagine how disappointed I was when I found out? But then I read that the speed of light through glass is slower than it is through the air. Which means every time you look through your window you're looking just a little bit into the past.' He reached over and grabbed my arm. He grinned. 'Glass is a time machine, man!' We both laughed.

The waiter arrived with Paul's coffee. He toyed with a sachet of sugar for a few seconds, rolling it between his fingers and worrying at it before dropping it back on the tray. He stirred his coffee nonetheless. He took a sip and grimaced. Then he smiled. 'I'm sorry, Mr Sutherland. I've always hated coffee.'

I smiled back. 'I can tell. Drink it anyway. It'll do you good.'

'Do I look that bad?'

'Actually, no, you don't.' He did look a lot better. Still a little tired, perhaps, but he was showered and shaved and wearing a light linen suit and white T-shirt instead of the regulation black.

'I've been sleeping better. That's helped. And I had a nice long telephone call from an old friend yesterday. It made me feel better about things.'

'Good.' I paused. 'Paul, this is a difficult question to ask. But you asked me if I'd help you so . . .'

He shrugged. 'Ask away.'

'You take a drug called Priadel?'

'I do, yes. They found I was bipolar about five years ago. Which explained a lot of things. Why so?'

'I'm just thinking about your little chat with the police the other day.'

'Oh Christ, was it that bad?'

I held up my hands. 'I think they thought you were just tired. But do you ever forget to take your drugs?'

'No. I never forget. Trust me, I just don't.'

'I take it the police didn't give them back?' He shook his head. 'But you have enough with you to get you through your time here?'

'Yeah. You have to be so careful with that sort of thing, you know? I take 400 mg, but a lot of European countries don't sell anything stronger than 300. So I always need to have few aside for emergencies. In case planes are delayed, that sort of thing.'

'Nothing stronger than 300mg?' He shook his head. I'd seen the blister pack. 150 mg. I opened my mouth to speak, and then paused.

'Something wrong?'

'No, nothing at all.' I didn't think it would help to tell him, and changed the subject. 'So this meeting with *signor* Scarpa? Would I be right in thinking that Lewis is hoping to get the pavilion reopened?'

He nodded. 'That's the idea. Be honest, Mr Sutherland—'

'Nathan.'

'Be honest, Nathan, do you think there's any chance at all?'

I shook my head. 'Not a chance in hell. And to be honest, I don't know how *signor* Scarpa would be able to help anyway. He might be a big shot in the art world but we're talking about a crime scene and a potential death trap. I'm sorry.'

His shoulders slumped for a moment. 'So I'd just be wasting my time even speaking to him?'

I didn't want to hurt him, but knew I had to be honest. 'It'd be a complete waste of time.'

I was expecting him to be upset, but his face broke into a broad smile. 'That's what I thought.' He finished his coffee. 'Yuck. Okay, Nathan, you remember I asked if you could help me?'

I nodded. 'Yes. I remember.'

'Can you do me a favour?'

'Of course.'

'A big favour?'

I laughed. 'Depends how big.'

'I need a hundred euros. Maybe a bit more, but a hundred euros would be enough. At least I think so.'

'You what?'

He threw up his hands. 'I'm sorry. I shouldn't have asked. I'm sorry.'

'No, it's okay. But listen, why do you want one hundred euros?'

He said nothing. 'Paul, there's a Post Office with a *bancomat* just back on the *fondamenta*. Shall I take you along there?'

He shook his head. 'I don't have a card.'

An Italian card, I assumed he meant. 'I know. That doesn't matter. Mastercard, Visa, a British bank card. They'll all work.'

'No. I don't have a bank card, Nathan.'

I looked him straight in the eye. The British representative at the Venice Biennale. A man who had been nominated for the Turner Prize. A man who didn't have a bank card. I opened my mouth to speak, trying to think of a suitably diplomatic way to phrase my next question, but he saved me the trouble. 'I went bankrupt, you know. Five years ago.'

'Oh right. I didn't know that. Sorry.'

'It's all right. It's kind of common knowledge. You know the old saying, "If money could talk—"'

'"—the only thing it would say would be goodbye". I know. I've been there myself. Go on.'

He shrugged. 'I had other problems at the time. Lewis helped me out. I mean, really helped me out. I don't think I'd be here without him. He helped me straighten my life out.'

'Did he now?' I raised an eyebrow. Lewis Fitzgerald, I thought, what a lovely man you must be. 'You're still entitled to a bank card, you know?'

He nodded. Then shook his head. 'I don't want one. Lewis looks after finances, pays for everything, sticks the rest in the bank. All I have to do is concentrate on making art. Does that seem weird?'

'Erm . . .'

He laughed. 'Yeah, okay, it probably is a bit weird. But it keeps me on the straight and narrow. And every day that passes makes things a little bit easier.'

We walked back to the *fondamenta* and along until we reached the Post Office. The ATM gave me the usual warning that my bank would apply a couple of euros charge, but I didn't care. I counted out one hundred euros in twenties, and made to pass them to Considine. 'Just one thing. You're not going to do anything stupid with this are you?'

'Stupid?'

'Booze. Drugs. Gambling. Terrible acts of self-harm.'

He laughed. 'As I said, I really, really don't do that stuff any more. It's all a bit boring really. I'd just like to take an old friend out to lunch. Someone I haven't seen for a while.'

I smiled, slowly. The suit, the clean white T-shirt. The good shave. It made sense now. 'Oh, I see. Is it – shall we say – an *event* meal?'

'I don't understand.' I gave him a meaningful nod. Then he laughed. 'Oh right. No, no it's not an *event* meal. Just an old friend.'

'An old friend. Lovely.' I passed over the money. Then a thought struck me. 'Do you have anywhere in mind?'

'I don't really know the city. Could you recommend anywhere?'

'Sure.' I reached for my wallet and took out a business card. 'Ai Mercanti. Just off Campo San Luca. My favourite place for event and non-event meals. Tell them Nathan sent you, they'll look after you well.'

He looked delighted. 'Thanks, man. I appreciate this.'

'No worries.'

'Just one thing. If you run into Lewis, don't tell him eh? It's just that – well the other person involved – they don't get on.'

'Ah. Okay.' *Oh Mr Fitzgerald, you do have an interesting relationship with your artist, don't you?* Then I turned back to the Bancomat, and took out my card again.

'Everything okay?' said Paul.

'Everything okay. It's just that you might need more than a hundred euros. Even if it's not an event meal.' The machine whirred away, and I withdrew the money. I pressed it into Paul's hand. 'Quickest way would be a boat to Rialto. But you've got plenty of time. Might be nice just to take a walk. If you arrive early, Marchini Time is a nice place for a coffee. Or a pot of tea if you really can't face any more. Just stay away from the cakes.'

'No good?'

'Too good.'

'Thanks, Nathan.' I smiled. He turned and walked back in the direction of San Marco. 'Thanks again,' he called out over his shoulder.

I made my way back towards the Arsenale, a hundred and fifty euros the poorer. I folded the receipts away inside my wallet. Like Gramsci, I was becoming sentimental in middle age.

Chapter 15

The Arsenale. The great engine of commerce and war that established the dominance and greatness of The Most Serene Republic. The navy still owned a large part of it, typically kept off-limits these days. It also housed the control room for the MOSE project, a series of aquatic barriers that could be raised and lowered in order to prevent the phenomenon of *acqua alta*. At least, that was the theory. One day, the more optimistic Venetians predicted, it might even work. In the meantime, it served as a great financial black hole that had sucked in a seemingly infinite stream of money and the career of at least one mayor. I'd had the opportunity to look around the control centre and had been terribly disappointed to see that it was, in fact, just a nondescript computer room. For the amount of money involved, I'd hoped for something a little more James Bond.

I made my way to the entrance and checked the map. The South American guys that I'd done the work for were, inevitably, at the far end of the second great gallery. A distance of perhaps a kilometre. A couple of small electric buggies were used to ferry people from one end to the other, but were supposed to be reserved for the elderly and infirm. Just being a bit tired, I assumed, wouldn't be enough. I wondered if I should affect a limp, and then decided against it. I wasn't such a terrible person. Not quite yet. I set out to walk.

The exhibition space consisted of two great galleries and whatever outbuildings and warehouses could be pressed into service. Many of those countries that had never managed to find a permanent home at the Giardini now had their pavilions here along with individual artists and collateral events. The Arsenale covered about a sixth of the square area of Venice and seemed to hold an inexhaustible supply of art. It was everywhere. One year I had actually tried to see everything and gave up once I realised the exercise of ticking off installations one by one was a genuinely Sisyphean task. As soon as you thought you were finished, another space would appear as if by magic. Eventually it became too much, a complete sensory overload. By the end of it all I no longer knew what I was looking at. On one occasion I found myself staring at the interior of a shed, trying to decide if it was an installation or not. Art or shed? I genuinely couldn't decide. At which point I decided it was probably time to go home.

At the height of the Republic's power, it was said that the Arsenale could turn out a ship a day. I had no idea if that was true or not but, walking through the vast interior space of the first gallery, I wondered if perhaps it might have been. Here, in this vast, cavernous hall, the Venetians – by sheer weight of manpower – had pre-dated the assembly lines of the Industrial Revolution by over five hundred years.

Art slid by me. Huge kinetic sculptures. Tiny, scratchy little drawings. Light installations. Sound installations. Video work. It was impossible to take it all in. How, I wondered, was the casual visitor with a one-day ticket expected to do more than scratch the surface of it all? I'd come back later and do it all properly, I promised myself. Well, probably. Possibly.

I paused at the mid-point, wondering if I should break for a drink, when I noticed two familiar figures up ahead of me. Lewis Fitzgerald and Vincenzo Scarpa, deep in conversation. Good. I'd been hoping I might run into them. I walked up and gave them a jaunty 'Good morning!'

Neither of them seemed pleased to see me. Scarpa looked me up and down, and then turned to Lewis with a quizzical expression on his face.

'This is Mr Sutherland, *dottore*. He was at the opening of the British pavilion.' Scarpa moved close to me and stared up at me. He really was a very little man. No wonder he always wanted to be in the front row for photographs. He moved closer still, staring through those thick Shostakovich glasses of his, until his nose was almost touching the tip of my mine. Then he stepped back and shook his head. 'I don't remember you. Are you an artist?'

'I'm the UK's honorary consul.'

'Ah right. Yes, I remember now. You work for the ambassador, right?'

'No. Not exactly. I mean, he's not my boss or anything.' There was silence for a few seconds, as they stared at me. 'So. What brings you both here this morning?' I said, trying to inject as much breeziness as possible into my voice.

The two of them looked at each other. Scarpa shrugged his shoulders. Evidently he didn't do breeziness. Lewis turned to me. 'I just wanted to ask the *dottore* if he felt there was any chance of being able to reopen the Pavilion.'

I was prepared for this. 'I'm sorry, Lewis, but I don't think so. I mean, there's been a violent death there. There's still a police investigation going on.'

Scarpa gave a little smile and inclined his head. 'Are you a policeman?'

'Well, no.'

'Oh, I'm sorry. For a moment there I thought you knew what you were talking about.' I opened my mouth to protest but he shushed me. 'Presumably once the investigation is complete and actions have been taken, we will be free to open the space up again.'

I shook my head. 'The *Comune* will never agree. They—'

This time it was Lewis who interrupted. 'The *dottore* has been in Italy a little bit longer than you, Nathan. It's possible that he knows what he's talking about.' He gave me the warmest of smiles, which I returned. Both of us, I suspected, were thinking what it would be like to punch the other. 'Anyway,' I said, turning back to Scarpa, 'I thought you hated it.'

'I do. It's trash.'

'Trash, eh? Really. You hear that, Lewis? Trash.'

'The *dottore* has strong opinions, Nathan. That's not uncommon in the art world. But we'd both like to see it reopened.'

'Well yes. Who knows, perhaps it'll even bring more visitors in? The British Pavilion of Death. They'll be queuing up, Lewis. They'll be queuing up.' Lewis gave me a look of utter contempt, and the two turned to leave. I made my way after them.

'Can we help you with anything else, Sutherland?' Lewis, I had worked out, used my first name when he wanted to sound patronising and my surname when he wanted to sound threatening. He didn't seem to have any other settings, except, perhaps when he used an honorific in order to be obsequious.

'Well, I'm going this way anyway. I'm meeting a couple of Argentinian artists that I did some work for. Passarella and Kempes. Do you know them, *signor* Scarpa?' He nodded. 'And what do you think of them?'

'Trash.'

'Trash. Funny, but I thought you'd say that. Wonderful thing to have an open mind, isn't it? Don't you agree. Lewis?'

'Look, Sutherland, is there a point to all this?'

'A point? No, no point at all. Just nice to have some people to walk around with. Anyway, I just thought you might like to know that it seems that Paul won't be joining us.'

'What?'

'He won't be joining us.'

Fitzgerald looked thrown. 'That's annoying. I told him I needed him to be here this morning. And that after he could take things easy for the rest of the day.'

'Ah, well maybe not as easy as all that. He's off to—' I paused.

'Off to where?' said Lewis.

'Milan.' Why Milan, for God's sake, where had that suddenly come from? 'Yes, he's going to Milan.'

'You what?'

'Off to Milan. He wanted to see the Brera gallery.'

'How's he going to get there?'

'Oh, I've been there once or twice. Every so often I need to go to the High Consulate. I gave him some directions and told him what train he'd need to get.' I paused. 'I also lent him a few bob. You know. For his train fare.'

Lewis stopped walking. 'You gave him money?'

'A hundred and fifty euros. Enough for his train fare and a good lunch.'

'A hundred and fifty euros.' He rubbed his face with both hands and swept his hair back. 'You idiot. You bloody idiot.'

'Something wrong?'

'You bloody fool, Sutherland. He's not going to go to Milan. He'll be out buying booze. Or something worse.'

'I don't think so. He seemed very keen on the idea of Milan.'

Lewis raised his hand, and reached towards me as if to grab me. Then he thought better of it, and swept his hand through his hair again. 'Paul's had problems, you know that? Big problems. It's taken all I've got to keep him on the straight and narrow and now – and now you tell me you've given him over one hundred euros with which to get off his face. You imbecile.'

'No need to be rude, Lewis. And he seemed fine. Relaxed. Happy.'

He screwed his eyes shut. 'He seems fine because he's taking his drugs. If he stops taking them . . .' I could see him counting to ten under his breath. Then he opened his eyes, breathed deeply and turned to Scarpa. 'I'm going to need to go back to the hotel. He'll turn up there eventually. God knows in what state, though. What's the quickest way back?' He reached down to pick up a small rucksack at his feet, and slung it over his shoulder.

Scarpa removed his glasses and gave them a quick polish on his jacket. There was, I thought, the faintest of smiles on his lips. 'There's an exit point after the next gallery. You can get a buggy back to the entrance from there.' Lewis gave him a quick nod, and dashed off. 'I wouldn't run,' said Scarpa. Lewis disappeared through some heavy black curtains at the end of the corridor. A few seconds later we heard a loud cry, followed by some impressively creative swearing. Scarpa shrugged. 'I did tell him. There's a light installation in there. Almost completely black. You need to give your eyes a few seconds.'

There was, indeed, a warning sign at the side of the curtained-off entrance. I recognised the name of the artist, an American guy who I'd always quite liked. I jabbed my thumb at the plaque and looked at Scarpa. 'Trash?' I asked.

He shook his head. 'No. This one I like.'

We stepped through the curtain.

The room was, as expected, completely dark. Yet, as we stood there, we could see the far wall almost glowing with a faint grey light. As our eyes adjusted, the wall appeared to glow brighter still, and then dim again. The effect was similar to a work by Mark Rothko suddenly appearing and disappearing before your eyes. Hypnotic, beautiful, restful; save for the steady stream of expletives from Lewis.

I could barely make out his form, but he seemed to be bent double. 'Ran into a bastard bastarding bench.'

I stretched my hand out towards him. 'You want to sit down for a moment?'

He swatted my hand away and got to his feet. 'Just let me find the bloody way out of here.' He stumbled behind me. 'Bloody, bloody curtain is bloody here somewhere.'

Then I felt it. A brief tearing of fabric, and a shot of pain through my shoulder. The shock was greater than the pain, but enough to raise an 'Ow' from me. I reached my hand behind my shoulder and patted around. My jacket was torn, and my fingers came away wet. Had I stepped back and cut myself on an exposed nail in the wall?

And then Lewis screamed. 'God! My God!'

'Get the lights on,' I shouted. 'Get the bloody lights on.'

Lewis continued screaming. I could see his form, bent double, his hands clutched together. 'Are you hurt, Lewis? Tell me.'

A ripping sound came from the back of the gallery, and light flooded in. Scarpa had simply torn the curtains from their railing. Gallery attendants came running from both directions.

'My God. I think it's gone through. It's gone through my hand.' He held a bloodied handkerchief against his left hand. He sank to his knees. 'It's gone through my hand. Oh Jesus, my hand.'

'Someone go and get a first-aid box. There must be one nearby. And call an ambulance, he's going to need hospital.'

I swayed a little on my feet, and then someone gently manoeuvred me over to a bench. 'Sit down, okay. You've cut yourself. We'll call an ambulance for you both.' My head swam, and I bent and stuck my head between my knees, trying to breathe evenly. And then I saw it. Lying on the floor, stained with blood at the tip, was a glass spike. No, not a spike. An arrow. A perfectly cast glass arrow. And there, only a few feet away, lay another; this one now snapped in two. Glass arrows.

Chapter 16

The water ambulance raced across the lagoon, carrying the two of us to the Ospedale Civile on Fondamenta Nove. I'd only ever been in one once before, when a friend, under the influence of strong drink, had bounced downstairs at a wedding reception at Paradiso. It was actually quite a fun way to travel, unless your life was hanging in the balance. Free to ignore all speed limits in the lagoon, ambulance drivers were at liberty to hoon around as much as they liked in the case of an emergency.

Lewis looked grey and sick the whole time. The paramedic kept trying to console him. 'It's a bad cut, but you'll be okay. All right? Just keep your hand up, and keep the pressure on the bandage, okay.' He nodded, but was blinking away tears. 'It's gone through my hand,' he kept repeating.

They met us at the pontoon with a pair of wheelchairs. I felt slightly light-headed, but more from the shock than the pain. I thought I could probably walk, but it seemed rude to refuse. Lewis slumped drunkenly into his, his head bowed and hand held shoulder-high. They rushed us through the halls of perhaps the most architecturally schizophrenic building in Venice. Through gleaming white corridors that smelled of antiseptic, through to a courtyard in which half a dozen bored-looking cats lazed in the midday sun, through the frescoed and statue-lined corridors of the original building – the Scuola Grande di San Marco – and through to *pronto soccorso*, where we were wheeled our separate ways.

It was, the doctor assured me, nothing serious. It would just need a couple of stitches. The arrow had ripped through my jacket and shirt, and neatly sliced my skin. It had, of course, ruined a perfectly good shirt and my best jacket. No, more than that, it had ruined my only jacket.

The doc helped me as I struggled back into my clothes, and gave me a friendly pat on the other shoulder. 'Just come back in a week to have the stitches taken out. There, you're free to go.'

'Is my friend ready?'

His brow furrowed. 'Not sure, one moment.' He stepped out of the room, and returned just a few seconds later. 'He'll be okay, but it needs a bit more time.'

'Is he badly hurt?'

'Not badly, it seems, but he's in shock.'

'Will he need to stay in?'

He shook his head. 'No. But he needs someone to take him home.'

'Okay. I don't think he knows anyone in the city. I'll wait for him in the bar. I could do with a drink.'

The doc grinned. 'Good luck with that.'

The bar in the Ospedale had once been one of the best little bars in Venice. Panelled in dark wood with red leather padded chairs, it was part-gentleman's club, part-classic 1950s coffee bar. I remembered my first visit, when I'd thought that – if it were only a bit closer to home – I'd have been tempted to become a regular. But then they stopped you smoking. And then they stopped you drinking. And nowadays, although you could still get a decent coffee and brioche, it wasn't really a bar at all any more.

The *barista* laughed and shook his head when I enquired, more in hope than expectation, about the possibility of a *caffè corretto*. I sighed, and ordered a *macchiatone* instead. I had no idea exactly how long I'd have to wait. I wished I had something to read. I took a look around the bar in the hope that someone might have abandoned their newspaper, but I was out of luck.

I sat down and sipped at my coffee. And then a little more. And then a little more. And then I was finished. How much time had passed? I checked my watch. Five minutes. Great. I ordered another coffee and slid it over to the other side of the table in order to discourage me from simply knocking it back.

It lasted, perhaps, ten minutes this time. I sighed, and reached into my pocket for some more change as I made my way back to the bar. Eighty cents. Not enough. I reached into my jacket pocket for my wallet and extracted it with some difficulty, my pocket being jammed full of receipts and flyers, as was typical at this time of year.

I asked for another *macchiatone*. Three coffees in quick succession was not the smartest of ideas, but at least these were diluted with a healthy dose of foaming milk. I looked in my wallet. Not a five-, ten- or even a twenty-euro note to be seen.

The *barista* slid my coffee across the bar. I proffered a fifty-euro note. He gave me a sad little look.

'You don't want to take this do you?'

He shook his head. 'Got anything smaller?'

'I've got eighty cents.'

He stuck his hand out. 'That'll do.'

'You sure?'

'Sure I'm sure. If I give you change of a fifty it'll clear the till out.'

'Thanks.'

'You shouldn't drink so much coffee.'

'I know. It's not my fault you stopped serving proper drinks.'

He nodded, sadly. 'I know. It was better in the old days. More of a party atmosphere, you know?'

'Erm, yes. This is kind of a hospital, though?'

He shrugged. 'Can you think of a better place for a party?'

I took my coffee back to the table. I pushed it as far away from me as I could. Then I placed the saucer on top of the cup. That, I thought, should help me eke things out for a bit longer.

I placed my wallet on the table and reached into my pocket to have a clear-out of all the crap that was blocking it up. Receipts, mainly. I always kept receipts. As far as I knew, it was still the law that you had to keep receipts until you were at least one hundred metres from the place that issued it. Living upstairs from a bar therefore meant that I had acquired quite a collection over the years. Federica and Dario kept telling me that this was all a load of rubbish, and that the law had changed years ago. I, however, was not prepared to take any chances.

Receipts, then. And flyers. You always accumulated flyers during the Biennale. It reminded me of my brief period in

Edinburgh, when Jean and I would compete to see who could acquire the most flyers for *Accidental Death of an Anarchist* in a single day.

I stacked the receipts in one pile, the flyers in another. I replaced my wallet in my jacket. Then I removed the saucer from on top of the cup, took a mouthful of coffee, and replaced it. I felt quite pleased with myself. Then my shoulder twinged as I leaned back in my chair, as if to remind me of what had happened less than two hours ago.

How much longer could Lewis be? I took another look around the bar. A woman reading the *Corriere* was sitting at a nearby table, gently pushing a baby buggy back and forth with one hand. A young man, dressed in jeans and T-shirt entered. For a moment, her face clouded. Then he smiled at her, and they hugged. She started getting her things together.

Leave the paper, I thought. You've got lots to talk about. You don't need the paper. Go on, please leave the paper.

She left the paper. Just as I was about to rise from my seat, the young man suddenly turned and picked it up, rolling it up and sticking it in his back pocket.

Oh well.

I went back to the pile of flyers and leafed through them. Perhaps there'd be something worth going to. It was often the case that – even if the art didn't sound all that exciting – there'd be the chance to have a look round a normally closed palazzo or church. Nothing much of interest, however, until . . .

A postcard. When had I picked up a postcard? I took a closer look.

A pale white figure against a dark background. Nude, save for a loincloth tied roughly around his middle, one end trailing down to his feet. His hands, bound, behind his back. His face, beautiful yet anguished, surrounded by flowing shoulder-length hair and ringed by a halo.

I recognised the image at once. Andrea Mantegna's master-piece, from the gothic palace of Ca' d'Oro. The martyrdom of Saint Sebastian.

Saint Sebastian. His body pierced by multiple arrows.

Chapter 17

I had no time to think on what I'd just seen, as my eye fell on the figure of Lewis Fitzgerald, making his way uncertainly along the corridor outside. His face was pale and I could see that his hand was bandaged up, but he looked well enough; if lost. I stuck the postcard into my pocket, and ran outside to catch him up.

'Lewis! Wait up!'

He turned, slowly. 'What do you want, Sutherland?'

'I thought I'd hang around and see if you could use some help.'

His face twisted into something that approximated a sick little smile. 'Stalking me now, are you?'

'Don't you have to actively follow someone to stalk them? I don't know, I'm no expert. As I said, I just thought you might want some help.'

'All I want to do is get on a bloody boat, get back to my bloody hotel and go back to bloody bed. And I don't want any help from you.' He turned to walk away.

'Okay. But if you want the *vaporetto* stop I wouldn't go in that—'

He cut me off. 'I said I don't want any help from you.'

I went back inside the bar again and sat down. If he continued in that direction he'd walk through a cloistered garden populated by stray cats, a dark, statue-lined entrance hall and then into Campo Santi Giovanni e Paolo. At which point I assumed he'd give up. I gave him five minutes before I headed outside once more. He arrived just two minutes later, looking angry and flustered. He stared at me with an air of desperation.

'Do you want a hand?' I said.

'Are you trying to be funny?' He held up his heavily bandaged left hand.

'Oh God. I'm sorry. No I wasn't, really. Look, do you want me to show you the way to the *vaporetto* stop?'

He looked angry for a moment, but then his shoulders dropped and he nodded. 'Yes. If you would. Thank you.' The moment of calm didn't last. 'I mean, what is this bloody place? You're walking along a corridor, and it looks like a proper hospital with doctors and nurses and everything and the next thing,' he threw his arms wide, 'you're in a cloister full of bloody cats.'

I smiled. 'Yes, it is confusing at first. Come on.' I led him back through the hospital and out on to the *fondamenta* and the dedicated *vaporetto* stop. We sat in awkward silence for a while on the pontoon.

I was the first to break. 'So, how's the hand then?'

He shook his head. 'They don't know. It's a clean wound, at least. There might be some nerve damage, but they won't know that for a while.'

'I'm sorry.' Silence again. 'I'm all right, by the way.'

'You what?'

'I'm all right. I was hurt too, remember?' I turned my shoulder to him. 'Couple of stitches. Ruined my best jacket.'

'Oh my goodness. I'm so sorry. Here's me having lost the use of a limb and I never thought to ask about your jacket.' He lowered his head and stared at his shoes.

I shrugged. 'Just trying to make conversation.' I paused. 'But there is something I need to speak to you about. Something more serious.'

He raised his head and looked at me, but said nothing. I reached into my jacket pocket. 'I found this. Just now, when I was waiting for you.' I held the postcard up for him to look at.

'Saint Sebastian,' he said.

I nodded. 'Martyred in a hail of arrows.' He said nothing. 'This isn't mine, you realise,' I continued. 'I'd never seen it before ten minutes ago.' I paused. 'Have you checked your pockets?'

'What?'

'I was just wondering – maybe you have one of these as well?'

'Don't be silly.'

'I'm not being silly. But it's a bit of a coincidence, isn't it? We both get hit by arrows. I find an image of Saint Sebastian in my pocket.'

He shook his head. 'I'll tell you what happened. We're attacked by someone, I don't know who. You go rummaging in your pocket. You find that postcard – something you probably picked up months ago and forgot about – and then your mind starts working overtime and making all sorts of connection which aren't there. It's understandable.'

I sighed. 'You're probably right,' I lied. 'So the question remains – who?'

We could see the next boat arriving now, and got to our feet. The 5.1 service, smaller than the *vaporetti* that served the Grand Canal, and lower in the water. I waited until he was about to step on board. 'You think it was Paul, don't you?'

He stiffened but said nothing. 'You do, don't you?' I repeated.

He went down to the cabin in silence, and stood there waiting for me. I sat down. He chose a seat on the opposite side. The engines whined – there was always an unpleasant, piercing quality to the engines on the smaller boats – and we pulled away from the pontoon. For the moment, we had the cabin to ourselves, but more people would almost certainly be boarding at Fondamenta Nove. If there was going to be a scene, it would be better to have it now.

I stared across the aisle at Lewis. 'I like Paul. He seems a bit vulnerable, a bit head-in-the-clouds at times but that's all. But as soon as I told you he'd gone off with some money you went berserk. So what is it you're not telling me?' He stared right back at me. 'Come on, I'm trying to help him here. You must admit, both of us seem to be attracting trouble at the moment.'

He nodded, and sighed, and for a brief moment I thought I'd managed to get through to him. 'Now you listen here, Sutherland. As far as I'm concerned the only trouble we've attracted is you. Paul Considine is a good man, a decent man. And I know what you're trying to imply, and if I hear you repeat anything like that again, ever, I will sue you hard enough to impoverish your grandchildren.' I opened my mouth to remonstrate, but he jabbed one of his good fingers at me, his face flushed, 'Shut up! I don't want to speak to you, I don't want to hear another word from you. Ever. Clear?'

I raised my hands, and nodded. We sat in silence for a few moments, and then, from across the lagoon, I heard the wail of a siren. A police boat or an ambulance. I half-got to my feet, the better to look out of the window. There it was, an ambulance heading out on call from the hospital. Heading at high speed in our direction.

I sat down again and looked over at Lewis. 'I'd sit over here if I were you,' I said.

He stared right through me.

'Lewis, I'm being serious. I wouldn't sit over there.'

He continued to glare at me.

'At least close the window.'

The wail of the siren rose in crescendo as the ambulance flashed past us at high speed. The wake hit us seconds later, rocking the boat violently and sending a wave crashing through the open window and soaking Lewis from head to toe.

The siren wail receded, and the momentary silence was broken by the *marinaio* crying 'Next stop Fondamenta Nove.' Lewis Fitzgerald sat and silently steamed in his little pool of water.

'I'm sorry,' I said. 'I did try.'

He made no move, but sat and glared at me with an expression of the purest hatred.

Chapter 18

Federica gave me lots of hugs. So did Eduardo. It was gratifying to find oneself the most huggable person in Venice, but I was nonetheless grateful that Dario wasn't there. A Dario hug would probably have reopened the wound.

We clinked glasses. Then Federica spoke. 'But seriously, *tesoro*, this isn't funny. You really could have been hurt.'

'Killed, even,' said Eduardo.

'I know. Seems kind of unreal though. Thinking back, I'm not sure I even remember any pain. It was all just so quick. Pissed off about this jacket though.'

'I'm sorry, *caro*, but I never really liked it.'

'No?'

'To be honest, Nathan, I never really thought it suited you,' added Eduardo.

'You're kidding? And how long have I been coming here?'

'Maybe five years?'

'You could have told me!'

'Didn't like to. You seemed attached to it.'

'Great. Great. Well to hell with the jacket. It could be worse. It's a hell of a lot worse for Lewis. He might have some permanent damage there.'

'He's a shit, though,' said Federica.

'Oh, he is. He's a complete shit. But I don't want him to be, you know, maimed or anything. It's not his fault.'

'Not his fault that his client is a psycho?' said Eduardo

'Considine? I don't think it was him. Really. I don't think he's the type. He just seems too, I don't know, gentle.'

Federica spat her olive stone into her spritz. 'Maybe. From what you were saying, you were nice to him. So why would he want to hurt you? But you'll admit, that thing with the postcard is strange. First Holofernes, now Sebastian. Something's going on.'

'You're right. Something's going on. I hope it isn't what I think it is.'

She smiled. One of her big, lighting-up-the-room smiles. 'Ooh, does this mean we've got a new mystery?'

I shrugged. '*Boh*. I don't know. It just all seems a bit funny, and . . .' And then it hit me. I drained my glass and set it down on the bar. 'Come on. I've got a brilliant idea.'

'You have?'

'Yes.' I wagged a finger in the air. 'I'm going to prove that Paul Considine could (a) not have killed Gordon Blake-Hoyt and (b) not have attacked Lewis and me this morning.'

She looked confused but, nevertheless, put her money down on the counter and we left the Brazilians, arm-in-arm. '*Caro*, I'm not sure what you think you're doing?'

'Trust me,' I said, as I steered her down into Campo Manin where visitors posed for photographs in front of the statue of the man who had briefly re-established the Most Serene Republic before the Austrians had crushed him. We took a quick right, and bypassed the tourists queuing – even at this hour – to go up the spiral staircase of the Palazzo Contarini.

'Nearly there, *cara*,' We turned into the Calle dei Fuseri and the entrance to Ai Mercanti was before us.

The restaurant was closed.

'Oh crap.'

Fede looked at me. 'What's wrong?'

'It's closed. It's bloody closed. I hadn't thought of that.'

'It's Monday, Nathan. They're always closed.'

I rested my forehead against the door and screwed my eyes shut. I opened them again. It was still closed. 'Of course they are. Why didn't I know that?'

She patted my cheek, and smiled. 'Because, *caro*, I always make the bookings.'

I put my head in my hands. 'I don't believe this. If I'd just thought of another restaurant – any restaurant that opens on Mondays – I could have proved everything,'

'It's okay, *tesoro*, don't worry,'

I shook my head. 'You're right. Okay. I've got another idea . . .'

'Two in one day?'

'Oh yes.'

'As brilliant as the first?'

'Even more so. We'll pick up some pizza from Rosa Rossa. There's some cheap red wine on top of the fridge. And then we're going to watch a film.'

'A film?'

'Oh yes. Only Vincent Price can help us now.'

Federica's pizza lay half-eaten as the credits rolled.

'You watch this sort of thing for fun?' she said.

'*Theatre of Blood*. It's a classic!'

'It's absolutely horrible.'

'Your people gave the world Lucio Fulci and *Zombie Flesh-Eaters*. You do not get to judge what is and what is not horrible.'

'Nathan, there was a man's head on a milk bottle.'

'Arthur Lowe's head. The pompous bank manager in an old British sitcom. You wouldn't know him. That's what makes it funny.'

'It wasn't funny. It was just horrible.'

'Well maybe just a bit. But you get the idea. Vincent Price plays a scorned Shakespearean actor who goes around killing his enemies according to the methods of despatch detailed in the plays.'

'Yes, I get that. And you think Considine is doing this?'

'No. Not Considine. Doesn't make sense. I can see he might have had a grudge against Blake-Hoyt but Lewis is his manager. And I was positively nice to him.'

'Mistaken identity?'

'Could be. Whoever it was, was firing arrows into a dark room. They can't have been able to see very much.'

'What about the postcards?'

'Easy to slip one into a pocket during the confusion. Maybe they just got the wrong person.'

'Meaning?'

'Scarpa.'

She nodded. 'I thought so.'

'Absolute unholy shit of a man. Enemies that can be counted in four figures. People probably queuing up to kill him.'

She nodded again. 'I think you're probably right, *caro*.'

'Probably?'

'It's just . . .' she paused.

'Go on.'

'It just seems a very complicated way of going about it.'

Chapter 19

Federica headed off to the Frari at about seven the next morning. I had no surgery and figured I could treat myself to a lie-in, at least until such time as Gramsci decided he needed entertaining.

It was not to be. I was woken up by the sound of the entry-phone buzzing incessantly. I struggled out of bed and scurried to the phone as quickly as I could.

'*Chi è?*' I could only think it was an unfortunate tourist, perhaps with something important stolen, who needed help at short notice. In which case I could just ask them to come back the following morning or, more likely, do what I could immediately and grumble away to myself later.

'Nathan. It's me. It's Lewis.'

'Lewis?' I couldn't think of anything else to say.

'We need to talk. Please.' He didn't sound angry this time. Desperate perhaps, but not angry.

'Uh, okay. Sure. Look, there's a café next door. Just go and grab a bite to eat and a coffee and come back in twenty minutes, okay?'

'Nathan, I think this is urgent.'

'Lewis, right now I am trouserless and my cat is about to start demanding food. Trust me, twenty minutes would be best. Make it fifteen if you think it's that important.' I hung up.

The entryphone rang again precisely fifteen minutes later, and I buzzed him up without even bothering to check who it was. He looked tired and dishevelled as we stood in my front room, both of us wondering how to break the ice. After a few seconds of awkward silence, he broke and held his hands out in a gesture of peace.

I paused, then nodded. 'Okay. Come on through.' I led him into the office. I had a fair idea what this was about but wasn't going to let him off the hook so easily. 'So, what is it? Stolen passport? *Vaporetto* ticket gone missing?' I glanced at his left hand. 'Emergency travel insurance?'

If I'd riled him, he didn't show it. 'It's about Paul,' he said.

'Oh yes?'

'He didn't come home last night. Back to the hotel that is. Which means that no one's seen him since . . . since . . .'

'Since I gave him one hundred and fifty euros to go and drink himself to death with?' I suggested.

He gave a hollow little laugh. 'Well, you said it. I don't suppose you've heard from him?'

I shook my head.

'There's more. That card you showed me yesterday.'

'Saint Sebastian?'

'Yes. When I got back to the hotel yesterday, I was changing out of my jacket and found – this.' The postcard he slid across the table was identical to mine. I picked it up, and turned it over. No message, no writing of any kind, no means of identification at all.

'So what are you thinking, Lewis?'

'I don't know what I'm thinking. I'm just worried that's all.'

I leaned forward and folded my fingers together. 'Do you think Paul had anything to do with what happened to us yesterday? And with what happened to Mr Blake-Hoyt?'

He sighed, and seemed to be weighing his words carefully. 'No. No, I don't. But I worry that people will think that. What's going to happen about yesterday?'

'Well unless you or I make a *denuncia*, nothing.'

'Nothing?'

'No. It's up to us to make a complaint. Now, I've only got a minor scratch. Shame about the jacket, but I can live with that. But you got properly hurt.'

He stared down at his hand, as if he'd forgotten it for a moment. 'It's not too bad. The painkillers help. So if I don't make a – *denuncia* – then the police won't investigate further?'

I shrugged. 'It depends. There were other people there and, technically, one of them could make one. Did you see how many visitors there were?'

He shook his head. 'I'm not sure. When the lights went on, I could see, I don't know, maybe another half-dozen. And Scarpa, of course.'

'Okay. Well, it's been nearly twenty-four hours. If anyone had been to the police, we'd normally have been contacted by now. And Scarpa has a vested interest in keeping this quiet. Closing down one pavilion in isolation is one thing. Closing off a section of the Arsenale would create all sorts of hassle for him. More than that, it might even seem as if he wasn't quite on top of things. So unless we go . . . it can all be swept under the carpet. An unfortunate accident.'

He nodded. 'That's great. Thank you. Really. As for your jacket—' He reached for his wallet.

I shook my head. 'I'm not that broke, Lewis. So what are we going to do about Paul? He didn't have much money, no – legal – means of getting any more, and so he must still be in Venice or nearby.'

'There are a few people in the UK that would wire him some money. If he asked. I can check with them.'

'Okay, you do that. Does he know anyone in Venice?'

'Not really. Okay, there are the people working at the pavilion but he doesn't really know them. The Welsh artist – the Pryce woman – he knows her.'

'Right. Do you want me to speak to her?'

'I'll do that. I'm going to be in that part of town today anyway.'

'Okay, not a problem. And Adam Grant? I got the impression they knew each other.'

'They do. I'll speak to him.'

I paused. 'I thought you two didn't get on?'

'We don't. But he likes Paul. He'll want to help.'

'Fine. Anything else we can do?'

'I can only think – *signor* Scarpa. Think about yesterday. I think the real target in that room was him.'

I'd thought that too, but saw no reason to tell Lewis. 'Why's that?'

'He's written stuff about Paul in the past. Bad reviews. I mean, really bad reviews.'

'Was the word "trash" involved?'

'Oh yes. And more. He has a quite a wonderful line in invective.'

I nodded. I remembered the opening. Scarpa and Blake-Hoyt, laughing and joking together and completely ignoring Considine. Laughing and joking in the full knowledge that GBH had just done his very best to destroy the biggest day of Paul's career.

'So I suppose we need to speak to him,' Lewis continued.

'And say what, exactly?'

'I don't know. Maybe find out if he's been passed one of these things as well.'

'Okay. And then what?'

'I don't know. I don't know. Just hope we find Paul and then take it from there. Do you have a better idea?'

I shook my head. 'Okay. But this is not going to be a lovely job.' There was silence. 'You want me to do it, don't you?'

He nodded. 'Would you?'

'Why me? You seemed to be getting on fine yesterday.'

'That was yesterday and that was business. Today I'm just a guy who's caused more trouble for him. I don't think he'll welcome my company.'

I sighed. I scribbled away on my notepad. 'Don't speak to nice Welsh lady. Speak to rudest man in Italy instead. Okay, I think I've got that. Not quite sure how I'll find him. I guess I'll speak with the Press Office at the Biennale.'

'Thanks. Really. So I'll call you this evening, okay? Just to see how we're getting on.' He slumped back in his chair, and looked relieved. 'Are we okay now?'

'Sure we are, Lewis.'

We shook hands.

Chapter 20

I sat on the back of the *vaporetto* and gazed out upon the Grand Canal, the water shimmering in the midday sun. I was setting out for an appointment with the rudest man in Italy and, for some reason, felt ridiculously happy. Perhaps it was just the weather. Jackets rather than coats, and not yet the unbearable heat and oppressive cobalt-blue skies of the height of summer. I got off at Ferrovia, and made my way to the podule at the base of the Calatrava Bridge.

It wasn't strictly true to say that I had an appointment with *signor* Scarpa. More that an old friend of Federica's, working in the press office, had agreed to give me his schedule for the day. At one o'clock he was taking a tour of the Biennale's smallest installation. I had no real idea why, but suspected that it might just be that he saw any day without his photograph in the paper, or his name in the news, as a day wasted. For Vincenzo Scarpa, all publicity – whether punching someone on live TV or presiding over a bloody, fatal accident on the opening day of the world's greatest art fair – was good publicity.

I found him at the base of the bridge, surrounded by his security people, a couple of journalists and a small group of curious tourists. Security people – I hadn't noticed them yesterday. Did he always walk around with them, or was he just taking extra care? He posed with one hand raised in a wave and the other resting on the open door of the podule. A sardonic smile played about his lips. I wondered if he had any other way of smiling. I hung around at the back of the group until he stepped inside and then, just as the doors were about to close, threw myself forward and into the seat opposite him. He had no time to react as I punched the button to close the doors, and then the one to set the podule in motion. Briefly taken aback, his security people started to hammer on the door, but it was too late as the podule slowly raised itself out of their reach.

He stared at me in absolute fury and opened his mouth to speak but I didn't give him the chance. 'Nice to see you again, *signor* Scarpa.' I gestured at the video screens suspended above our heads. 'I must say I'm looking forward to this.'

'What the hell is the meaning of this, Mr . . . Mr . . . ?'

'Sutherland. Nathan Sutherland.'

'I'll have your job for this.'

'No you won't.' Well, probably not. 'Come on now.' I checked my watch. 'The journey takes about forty minutes I believe. That leaves us plenty of time to chat.'

He reached over me to stab at the emergency stop button, but I was too quick for him and covered it with my hand. 'No no. Let's watch the video first, eh? This is why you're here, after all.'

For a moment, I wondered if he was going to punch me. Then I wondered if I would punch him back. We sat there, glowering at each other, sizing each other up. It must have been like this, I thought, when Ali met Foreman for the first time. If, that is, Ali and Foreman had been a couple of out-of-shape white guys who smoked and drank too much.

I held up my hands in a placatory gesture. 'Come on, Vincenzo. Let's watch the damn film eh?'

A vein in his temple was throbbing alarmingly, yet he suddenly nodded and sat back in his seat. And for the next twenty minutes we sat and watched the video screens positioned above each other's heads, as they did their best to mimic the experience of being transported across the Calatrava Bridge. A view that few people had ever experienced. I wondered how the artist had managed to do it. The podule was supposed to be restricted to those with mobility problems, and access to it was granted remotely, via a video link with an operator. It had been reported that – of the few people that had ever successfully managed to use it – the vast majority had been heavily laden shoppers. Perhaps he'd simply turned up with a big trolley.

We didn't exchange a word until we virtually reached the other side of the bridge, and started our journey back. It was Scarpa who broke the silence. 'Well now, Mr Sutherland . . .'

'Well now, *signor* Scarpa.'

'So what are we doing here?'

'Oh, we're here to see the installation. And to take a ride in the podule. Have you been in here before?' He glowered. 'No. Silly question really. Me neither. Anyway, what do you think of it?'

'Trash.'

'Trash. Yes, I thought you might say that. Funny, but I—' I was interrupted by him slapping me across the face. There was no great power to it, and it stung more than hurt, yet there was such a precision to it, such a finicky expression of irritation that it shocked me out of my act for a moment.

He smiled. 'Now you listen to me for a moment, you little shit.' He looked at his watch. 'I think there's maybe twenty minutes until this trashy little ride finishes. Which means you have twenty minutes to persuade me not to call my three gorillas down there to be ready to haul your arse off and hurt you. Understand?'

'I understand.' I rubbed the side of my face.

He leaned back in his chair, crossed one leg over the other and spread his hands wide. 'Go ahead. Convince me.'

'Well, I was thinking of appealing to your better nature.'

'I haven't got one. You should know that. Try again.'

'Also that you are a high-profile public figure and it wouldn't look good to be seen beating up a humble little *apparatchik* like me.'

'Mr Sutherland, I once broke someone's nose on national television. The award for "Best TV Moment of 2010" still sits on my mantelpiece. You'll have to do better than that.'

'Okay, what if I were to say that I'm trying to save you from a violent death at the hands of an art-obsessed serial killer?'

He said nothing.

'So can I continue?' I asked.

He nodded.

I ran him through the theory. He rubbed his chin. 'So, the idea is that someone killed Mr Blake-Hoyt because of a bad review. But then they tried to kill you and Mr Fitzgerald. I don't understand?'

I ran my hands through my hair. It was starting to feel unpleasantly hot. 'I think they were trying to kill you, *signor*

Scarpa. I think someone is going around trying to kill some of the major critics in the art world.'

He shrugged. 'Is that it?'

'What do you mean, "Is that it?"'

He chuckled, and laid his hand on my knee. 'My dear fellow, I am so sorry.'

'What?'

'I am so sorry that your life is so dull that you have to invent a *stupidaggine* like this to entertain yourself.'

I screwed my eyes tight shut. '*Signor* Scarpa, you're trying to make me angry, aren't you?'

'Well of course I am. It's working isn't it?'

I took a deep breath, and reached into my jacket pocket. I took out the two cards. 'Can I just ask you – and I really am trying to be serious here – have you ever seen these before?'

'Gentileschi and Mantegna.' He shook his head. 'No. No. I have spent thirty years as a critic and writer. I have never heard of Gentileschi and Mantegna.' He laughed and shook his head again.

I snapped. I leaned over and jabbed my finger at him, trying my best to ensure my fingertip remained at least an inch from his chest. 'Now you listen to me. I don't know why I'm doing this but I'm trying to save your miserable, graceless little life.'

The two of us, now, were on our feet, slapping and jabbing at each other in what was, perhaps, the most rubbish fight ever. Out of the corner of my eye, I noticed people on the bridge had stopped to watch. Perhaps they thought it was part of the installation.

I held my hands up to try and ward off his slaps. 'Can we stop this? Look, can we please just stop this?' My words made no impression. Perhaps an appeal to his vanity would work? 'People are looking at us. People are pointing and laughing at us.'

He slumped back into his seat, and took out a handkerchief with which to wipe the sweat from his brow. Then he tugged at his collar. The heat was starting to become properly uncomfortable now. Nobody had ever thought that the podule would require air conditioning. I searched for a handle on the window, and then realised that nobody had thought it necessary to provide it with windows that would open either.

I struggled out of my jacket with difficulty, as it clung to me in the heat. 'Can I finish speaking? Or haven't you finished slapping me yet?' He said nothing so I ploughed ahead. 'Gordon Blake-Hoyt was beheaded. In his pocket was an image of Judith beheading Holofernes.'

'And so? How could someone plan for the unfortunate Mr Blake-Hoyt to lose his head? It's impossible. He might have been impaled, lost a limb, missed the glass altogether. How could this mysterious assassin possibly know the precise manner of his demise? Dear Mr Consul, this is a nonsense.' He chuckled again.

'Now listen.' I held up my hands, partly in a gesture of peace, partly so as to give them something to do instead of punching him. 'Of course he couldn't have known. I think it was just a kind of a calling card on his part, a statement of intent. Call it what you will. Whatever happened would have been close enough. And then Lewis and I had arrows fired at us. Glass arrows. We both found that an image of Saint Sebastian had been planted on us. You were in the room with us at the same time. I think those arrows were meant for you.'

He said nothing for a few seconds, and I thought he was just weighing his words for maximum insulting effect. Then he sighed, and tugged at his collar again. The sun was now shining directly into the cabin. I wished I'd brought my sunglasses with me. 'If this is true,' said Scarpa, 'why did I not receive one of those images?'

'I've got to be honest, I don't really know. But the three of us were close together – we had been for a while. And whoever did this was firing arrows into a dark room. They couldn't be sure who they'd hit. As long as someone had that card on them, maybe they thought that would be enough?'

He nodded. 'Okay. Again, if this is true, why would anyone wish to kill Mr Blake-Hoyt or myself?'

'Blake-Hoyt had a lot of enemies. He seemed to delight in being as nasty as he could to people.'

'Not a reason to kill someone, though.'

'Careers could be damaged. Ruined, even.' And just maybe, I thought, if you were unstable that would be reason enough in itself.

'And why me?'

I gave a little cough. 'With respect, *signor* Scarpa, you do carry a reputation as the rudest man in Italy.'

He smiled, for the first time, I thought, with genuine pleasure. 'Yes, I do, don't I?'

'Some might say,' I continued, 'the most hated man in Italy.'

He grimaced. 'Berlusconi usually beats me on that one.'

'I'm sorry,' I said.

He shook his head. 'It's okay. It just the way things are in this country. It's who you know. Anyway, even if I accept what you are saying, what should I do about it?'

I actually hadn't thought of that. 'Erm, well I suppose you have your three gorillas, as you said. And if you receive anything strange – you know, a postcard of a historic painting showing a grisly death – give me a call.'

'Oh good. Yes of course I will. If I feel my life is being threatened I will of course turn to the British consular service to defend me.'

I sighed. It had sounded more than a bit weak, even to my ears. Something else I hadn't really thought through. 'Just one more thing, *signor* Scarpa. Just why were you meeting with Lewis Fitzgerald yesterday?'

He laughed. 'Am I obliged to answer that, *Tenente Colombo?*'

I shook my head. 'I just wondered. If you hated Considine's stuff so much, why even consider the possibility of reopening?'

He seemed genuinely surprised. 'As I said, this is nothing to do with some trashy art. It's just business.'

'Just business?' He nodded. 'Is it ever about the art any more?'

'I'm not sure it ever was. Now my dear fellow, the cabin is about to descend. How fast do you think you can run?'

The podule started to move. I looked downwards, to where Scarpa's gorillas were taking position. I looked across to Scarpa, who was grinning. 'I don't suppose you could have a word?' He shook his head.

Another ten seconds and we'd be there. I lunged across the cabin and slammed the emergency button with the flat of my hand. The podule ground to a halt and the video screens flickered for a moment before powering down. Scarpa shook his head in mild irritation, and reached across me to press the 'operate' button.

Nothing happened.

He pressed it again. And again. And then again. The podule refused to move. The video screens remained dimmed. The 'mobility cabin' that had worked for just a few short weeks in its lifespan had died yet again.

'You idiot. You imbecile.'

'I'm sorry. You didn't leave me much choice. It was either that or get my head kicked in.'

'I'll make damn sure you do get your head, as you say, kicked in.' He was on his feet now, gesticulating wildly and raging at me. People on the bridge were again stopping to point and stare.

'I'd calm down if I were you. Let's just sit down and wait, eh?'

'I'm not going to calm down, you cretinous halfwit.'

I shrugged. 'Suit yourself. It's just the last time this happened I seem to remember it took about two hours to rescue the occupants.' I unbuttoned my collar and cuffs. 'And it's not going to get any cooler.'

'Fede?'

'*Ciao, tesoro.*'

'Are you free for a drink? Right now I mean.'

'It's a bit early isn't it? There's stuff that I could really do with finishing today.'

'Sorry. It's just I've had a bit of a trying day.'

'Where are you? Could you drop by the Frari?'

'I don't think they'd welcome me at the moment. I'm outside that bar next to the Scuola Grande.'

'Okay. I'll see you there in five minutes.'

I'd forgotten to ask her what she wanted to drink, and so ordered a prosecco – her usual not-really-drinking-when-at-work drink – to go with my spritz. I saw her making her way across the campo, and held my hands up as she bent to kiss me. '*Noli me tangere.*'

She jerked her head back. 'Not much chance of that. My God, you stink.'

'Yes, I'm aware this doesn't look good.' My clothes were drenched in sweat, my hair plastered down over my forehead and my face still flushed bright red. 'Just as well the weather's nice. I don't think they'd have been keen on giving me a table inside.'

'What on earth happened to you?'

'I've just spent the last two hours imprisoned in a small unventilated space with the angriest man in Italy.'

'Oh. And how is he?'

'Not any less angry. I did try to explain that I was trying to save his life, but he wasn't having it.' I filled her in on the rest of the day's events. 'They got us out after about two hours. I didn't think I'd be very welcome on the *vaporetto* so I decided to walk home. *Signor* Scarpa kept telling me he had something very important to go to later on, so I imagine he's gone back to his hotel to freshen up. Oh, and three very large friends of his seem quite keen to catch up with me later.'

'You are mad. No, more than that, you're insane. I do love you, but you're insane.'

'Anyway, I thought I deserved a drink.'

'Only a spritz? Don't tell me you think it's too early?'

'*Beh*, it's just that I don't like drinking Negronis anywhere other than Ed's. It feels like I'm cheating on him.'

'So tell me more about Fitzgerald. Why do you think he wants you to help him?'

'Because of Paul.'

'Because he really believes in him and wants to help?' She sounded dubious.

I shook my head. 'Because he's a meal ticket for him. Lewis seems to have, I don't know, something like Power of Attorney over his finances. Paul just gets pocket money.'

'That makes no sense. Why would he allow that?'

I shrugged. 'Maybe he really is that bad with money. Maybe he just wants to concentrate on his art.'

She shook her head. 'Sounds unlikely. Would anybody really be that unworldly?'

'Unlikely, but just about possible. Have you ever heard of Peter Maxwell Davies? British composer. Nice bloke by all accounts. He entrusted all his finances to his manager. Then one day, he goes to the bank, tries to get some money out and – empty. All gone.'

'Wow.'

'He'd been ripped off for about half a million quid. Think his manager went to prison for false accounting.'

'And you think that Lewis is doing the same?'

I shrugged. 'I don't know. But, like I said, Paul is his meal ticket. Hence persuading me not to make a *denuncia*. If we don't make a complaint the only problem that Paul has is the death of GBH. And that, likely as not, is going to be laid at the door of the construction team.'

Federica took a sip of her prosecco. 'Do you really think Considine is going around trying to murder his critics?'

'I don't, no. But somebody might be. What do you think?'

'No. If you were going to do that, why do it like this? It's silly and over-complicated. And it would just draw attention to yourself. Like in that horrible film you made me watch.'

I sat my glass down with a little more force than necessary. 'As I've said before, *Theatre of Blood* is a classic. But, I admit you're right. That sort of thing wouldn't work in real life.'

'Exactly. And when you were hurt it would have involved someone firing arrows into a dark room. Stupid way to try and kill someone.'

'Yes. And that got me thinking.'

'What?'

'There was a thick, heavy curtain covering the entrance to the room. We were in complete darkness. If somebody had moved aside the curtain to shoot at us, there'd have been a flash of light, and I'm certain there wasn't.' I took another drink of my spritz, savouring its crisp, bitter coolness. 'I think whoever did it was in the room with us the whole time.'

'Every gallery has CCTV. One of them might show something.'

'It might do. Of course, it was pitch-dark. I don't know if anything useful would show up. More to the point, I don't know how the hell to go about getting access to that sort of thing.'

She frowned. 'Okay. Leave it with me. I don't know anyone directly, but there might be friends of friends who could help. I'll be discreet.'

'Brilliant.' I drained my glass. 'Okay, I'm going to go home and attempt to become less disgusting. Will I see you later?"

She shook her head. 'I'd like to, *caro*, but I should spend some time with *Mamma.*'

'Bring her over. I don't mind cooking for three.'

She touched my cheek. 'That's kind. But she doesn't like cats. I mean, she really doesn't like them. You know what Gramsci would do.'

'Yes. He'd want to be best friends. No problems. Give her my best.'

'I will. It's only for a few more days. And it sounds like you'll be busy anyway. More sleuthing tomorrow?' I smiled. 'You're enjoying this, aren't you? Despite being attacked by a crazy guy with a glass arrow and threatened by the nastiest man in Italy, you're actually enjoying this.'

I smiled. 'It's an adventure, isn't it?'

Now it was her turn to smile. 'Yes. But just be careful, okay?'

'I will.' I got to my feet. 'I'll call you tomorrow.' She moved towards me and I held up my hands. 'I'm not nice to be near, remember?'

'Don't be silly.' She gave me hug, and a peck on the cheek and, if it was horrible, she did a good enough job of hiding it. 'Speak tomorrow. Love you!'

'I love you too.' And with that I made my way soggily across the campo, and towards home.

Chapter 21

Lewis never called me that evening. He didn't do so the following morning either. That didn't particularly bother me. I was in no hurry to speak to him and, besides, I had a surgery to attend to. But three hours later, with not so much as a lost *vaporetto* ticket on which to spend my time, I decided that perhaps it might be best to give him a call.

There was no answer. I left a message for him and fixed myself a sandwich as I thought.

The most likely solution was that Lewis had found Paul and then he'd booked them on the next flight back to the UK. Paul wasn't being held or charged, there was no reason why he shouldn't leave the country. In some ways the police would probably prefer it. The death of Gordon Blake-Hoyt would be laid at the door of the construction team, and – after a few years' wait – be laid to rest with a generally unsatisfactory verdict. Yes, they'd probably gone back to the UK. It had been a week since the opening, and artists and their entourages tended not to hang around once the initial blitz of parties, openings and deals had come to an end. At this very moment, Lewis was probably imagining my potentially violent meeting with Vincenzo Scarpa, and laughing. The more I thought about it, the more it seemed like he'd just set me up in the hope I'd get a good kicking. His idea of a little joke.

I took a bite of my sandwich, and leaned back in my seat. The sudden twinge from my shoulder served to remind me that, convenient as this solution might be, there were still far too many loose ends for it to be convincing. Someone had attacked us only two days ago, and Lewis, at least, had been badly hurt. It needed investigating.

Actually, it probably didn't. But I was going to anyway.

Lewis had told me that Paul knew both Gwenant Pryce and Adam Grant. Well enough to be able to tap them for money, if need be. There was a chance, albeit a small one, that they'd know what was going on.

I took a look at the webpages for both the Scottish and Welsh pavilions and sighed. There were no numbers to call. Of course. The exhibitions were only temporary, the staff likewise. Why have a fixed telephone line?

Scotland and Wales, then. And Lewis had volunteered to go and meet Adam Grant himself, a man who gave every impression of disliking him immensely. There was something about that which made Scotland the more interesting proposition. Hopefully, Grant would still be around. I took my jacket off the hook. I'd stitched up the back as best I could, in a manner that could be described as almost acceptable. Federica, I knew, would demand that I throw it away as soon as she saw it, but it would do for now. Besides, I was going to meet arty people. They'd probably think it a deliberate affectation.

'I'll see you later, Gramsci,' I cried. 'The game is afoot!'

* * *

A walk along Strada Nova in the middle of the day would be hot and hard work, so I took the boat up to San Marcuola instead. Then I walked past the casino where grumpy old Richard Wagner had breathed his last, and on to the main drag.

A young woman was in attendance downstairs, sitting behind a desk displaying catalogues, postcards and souvenir bags.

'Is Adam Grant in today?' I asked. She made no reply, hunched over her phone. 'Adam, the artist. Is he here today?' I repeated, just a little louder.

She looked up with a start, and tugged the headphones from her ears. 'I'm so sorry. I was miles away.'

I smiled. 'It's all right. I imagine it gets a bit dull at times?'

She nodded, then looked embarrassed. 'Well, sometimes. When nobody comes in. It's nice when people want to talk about the art, though. And it's good experience, just being here.'

'You're an art student?'

'Second year. Glasgow School of Art.' She paused. 'Do you live here?' I nodded. 'That must be lovely. I wish I did.'

'Maybe you will, one day. I hope so. God knows, we could do with more people.'

'So you must have seen lots of things. At the Biennale. What's the best thing you've seen?'

'Apart from the Scottish Pavilion, you mean?' She laughed, and nodded. 'Difficult to say. I've not had much free time this past week.' She looked disappointed. 'I'm told I should go and see the dancing Frenchmen. They sound like fun.'

Her eyes widened. 'Oh, I love that! My flatmate, Rhona, she's taking part in that. She's one of the dancers.'

'Rhona? That's not a very French name.'

'She's Scottish.'

'Oh yes, I'd heard. The insufficiency of Frenchmen. It must be hard work, though?'

'Well, they do it in shifts. Two hours on, two hours off. She says the morning session is best. Nobody really comes in at that time, but at least it's cool. It's so much hotter in the afternoon, and there're more people. You have to be so much more careful dancing around all the visitors.'

'I guess so. Still, I'm sure it's nothing that can't be sorted out by choreography.'

She smiled, again. I'd almost forgotten why I came when she added, 'I'm sorry, is there anything you'd like me to explain? About the art, or the artist. Would you like a catalogue? Or a bag?' Souvenir carrier bags from the last five Biennales were scrunched up in a suitcase on top of my wardrobe. But still, the offer of a free bag was never one to be taken lightly, so I rolled one up and tucked it in my pocket.

'I was wondering if the artist was in today?' I said.

'Oh yes. He's upstairs. You're in luck, it's his last day.'

'Thanks. You've been very helpful. Enjoy the rest of your time here.' I patted my pocket. 'Thanks for the bag.'

Again, she looked embarrassed. 'I'm sorry, but they're supposed to be 15 euros.'

'Oh. Oh right, sorry. Of course.' I fished out my wallet and paid up. It was another souvenir, I supposed.

'Would you like a catalogue as well?'

I shook my head. 'Maybe not. Thanks anyway.' And I made my way upstairs.

*   *   *

Adam Grant was wandering in a distracted manner through Elsa of Brabant's nightmare. He stopped as soon as he saw me. I couldn't read anything on his face, but that might, perhaps, have been the veil.

'Mr Honorary Consul.'

'Nathan, please. Can I call you Adam?'

He shrugged. 'If you like.'

'Can I just say, that's a fabulous dress. Do you do this every day? The wandering around, I mean.'

'Aye. It's part of the performance. While I'm here. I'm off home tomorrow.' He threw back the veil so we could talk more easily.

'Right. Is someone else going to double for you? A sort of stunt bride?'

He scratched his beard thoughtfully, and shook his head. 'No. I wouldn't trust anyone else to do it right. D'you like it?'

'Like it? I think it's brilliant.' He smiled. 'I mean, you might actually be genuinely, properly mad. But it's still brilliant.'

'I thank you. I think. So what can I do for you, Nathan?'

I drew a deep breath. 'It's kind of complicated. You know Paul Considine?'

'I used to. We kind of lost touch years ago. Why so?'

'He's gone missing. A couple of days ago.'

'You sure? Not just gone back to the UK?'

'Well maybe. But I can't get hold of his agent either.'

'Fitzgerald? Well that doesn't bother me. Shouldn't bother you either, Nathan.'

'I don't care about Lewis Fitzgerald. But I'm worried about Considine. And I think something strange is going on.'

'Okay. So tell me about it.' He stretched and gave a little grimace. 'Back's killing me. These heels. D'you mind if I sit down.' I shook my head, and he made his way over to the fireplace where he sat himself down in an antique and slightly wobbly chair. He motioned me to take the one opposite. 'Tell me about it,' he repeated.

'I will. But it's long and it's complicated. Could you start by telling me what Lewis wanted to talk about when you saw him the other day?'

'The other day? Nathan, apart from a few well-chosen words at the opening, I haven't spoken to him in over five years. And if he'd come here to speak to me on his own, I'd have punched his lights out.'

'You what?'

'I said I'd punch his lights out. You sound surprised.'

'Not at that. I mean, you really haven't seen him since opening day? He hasn't been back to speak to you?'

'No. Why would he have?'

'He thought you might be able to help. With Paul. You and Gwenant Pryce both.'

Adam laughed. 'Ah Lewis, Lewis. He never changes. I'm sorry, Nathan but I think he's been taking you on a very long ride.' Then he looked serious for a moment. 'He didn't ask you for money did he?'

'No.'

'Okay. That's something, anyway. Just another of his little games.'

I slumped back in my antique chair. 'Oh hell.'

'Ah, don't feel bad. This is just what he does. At least it's only your time he's wasted.'

I got to my feet. 'Seems like it. Thanks anyway, Adam, I appreciate your time.'

'No worries.' He rolled up the left sleeve of his dress to check his watch. 'Well, it's my last day. I can knock off early if I want. Come along with me. Let's go and pay a call on Gwen Pryce.'

'Why?'

'Oh, we can tell you all about Lewis Fitzgerald. You may as well hear the story from both of us. Besides, I don't know when I'll next see Gwen again. Come on.' He got to his feet.

I looked at Adam Grant, resplendent in bridal wear and tartan trews. 'Er, are you going like that?'

He seemed baffled. 'Yes of course. Part of the performance, isn't it.'

'Shall we get the boat, or just walk?'

'In these heels? Let's get the boat.'

We made our way back to the *vaporetto* stop. He gave a nod of his head as we walked past the casino. 'I read that you can visit Wagner's rooms, you know. I asked someone how you booked and they didn't seem to know what I meant.'

'Ah.' I thought I knew what was coming next. 'What did you say?'

'How do I book a visit to the casino?' He pronounced it in the English way.

I smiled. 'The trouble is you say casinOH if you mean the places with the blackjack tables and roulette wheels. Whereas you say casEENoh if it's a brothel you're after.'

'Oh. I thought they gave me a funny look.'

Chapter 22

Nobody batted an eyelid at Adam. You could walk around wearing anything in Venice at any time of year and people would assume you'd turned up late for Carnevale, early for the Biennale, were making a film or had just arrived from a country where people dressed like that normally. It was nevertheless surprisingly easy to get seats on the *vaporetto*.

Gwenant gave me a little wave. 'Mr Sutherland. How nice to see you again.'

'Call me Nathan, please.'

'And Adam. How are you, *cariad*?'

He pulled back his veil so he could kiss her properly. 'I'm well, hen. Heading back tomorrow.' He tugged at the veil. 'You know, I think I can take this off now. Can you give me a hand, Nathan? It's just pinned in at the back there.' I fumbled away as best I could until he was able to pull it free. 'Phew. Much better.'

Gwenant, I noticed, had been working away at a painting, illuminated by a heavy UV lamp.

'Something for your next exhibition?' I asked.

'Something for this one, Nathan. The work hasn't been developing as quickly as I'd have liked. I'm trying to speed the process up a bit. This is the last one.'

I shook my head. 'I'm sorry. I must seem terribly ignorant, but I don't understand.'

'You will, *cariad*, I'll show you in a minute. It's lovely to see you, anyway. What brings you both here?'

Adam gave a big, broad grin. 'Lewis Fitzgerald,' he rumbled, lingering over the words and rolling the R.

She laughed a tinkly little laugh. 'Oh my goodness. That awful man. I hope he's not been trying to take advantage of you, Nathan.'

'He seems to have sent our friend on a bit of a wild-goose chase,' said Adam.

'Oh dear. No money involved, I hope.' Adam shook his head. 'Well, there's a relief.'

'It seems his latest cash dispenser has disappeared. He thought the honorary consul might be the man to help him.'

I was starting to find the incessant to-and-froing irritating, and slightly unsettling. 'He also thought you might be able to help,' I said.

They both laughed. 'Well I can't think why he'd think that,' she said, ever so sweetly, as if she were tucking her favourite grandson up in bed and wishing him sweet dreams.

'I can't think why, either,' said Adam. 'I don't think we feature very highly on his list of favourite people, do you, Gwen?'

'I don't think we do, Adam.'

Then they stopped talking and both looked at me. I was starting to find it uncomfortably hot in there, a combination of the Venetian summer sun and the UV lamp. Why the lamp? In this heat? She must have noticed my glance. 'I said the work wasn't developing as I wanted, Nathan. I'm using these to speed the process up.' I shook my head again. 'The faces, I mean. They're covered in a very thin wash of watercolour. Watercolour fades in natural light.'

'But there's plenty of natural light in the space, especially with those mirrors set up.'

She shook her head. 'Not over the last week. Too much cloud. The UV lamps are to speed things up. I need to know things are going to work properly before I leave for home.'

I looked past her, into the opening that led to the first room of the exhibition. She nodded. 'Please, Nathan. Do go and have another look.'

Adam chuckled, as if he were privy to some private joke. 'Aye, go on, Nathan. Take a good look.'

I got slowly to my feet, and walked to the entrance. I turned to look back at them but they showed no sign of moving. Gwenant gave a gentle little motion of her hand, and mouthed the words 'Go on.'

I stepped through, into the dark, and measured my pace as I walked up to the first canvas, uncertain as to what to expect. Nothing seemed to have changed. There was the same figure in those great, rich Tintoretto-style robes; the same unidentifiable face that was little more than a pink blobby mask. I looked closer. Was it possible that there were some physical features there? A nose, a mouth, eyebrows? I shook my head. Gwen and Adam, for reasons best known to themselves, were trying to spook me, and I was seeing things that weren't there.

I moved on to the next room, and stared at the second portrait. Then I screwed my eyes shut, and shook my head trying to blot out what I had just seen. Then I opened them again. There was no doubt. This time the image was clearer, this time there was a definite face there.

I moved from room to room. From blue to purple to green. Clearer, ever clearer. Orange to white, and clearer still. I was running now, my heart pounding not with the effort but with fear. The violet room.

I stopped in front of the canvas and, again, I screwed my eyes shut. I rested my hands on my knees and breathed deeply. I had to be certain. I opened my eyes and looked once more.

The features were distorted and twisted, but clearly visible under the thin veneer of watercolour.

I knew who it was.

I ran through into the black room. The canvas had been removed, as I expected. Then I forced myself to catch my breath and gather my thoughts. I stepped back into the entrance hall, and stopped dead. Gwenant and Adam appeared not to have moved. They were both smiling. I stared at them for a moment, then grabbed the easel and dragged it round to face me.

It was the painting from the black room. The face was unmistakable. Bloodied, and scarred, and horribly torn, with eyes that seemed almost insane with pain. An image from one of Francis Bacon's nightmares. But recognisable nonetheless.

The face of Lewis Fitzgerald.

Chapter 23

Adam was the first to break the silence. 'I think we've spooked him, Ms Pryce.'

She laughed her bell-like little laugh again. 'I think we have, Mr Grant.'

I stared again at the horrible image on the canvas, then back at Adam and Gwenant. 'You've killed him. Oh my God, you've killed him.' I could barely stammer the words out.

Silence hung in the hot, suffocating air. I tried to gather my thoughts. Gwenant was slightly built and perhaps twenty years older than me. Adam was a big guy but still, in those heels, I could at least outrun him. I inched my way around the wall, making for the door. If he gave the slightest sign of taking his designer wedges off I'd be out of there.

Then, as one, they both burst out laughing. 'Killed him? Oh Nathan, you are a silly!'

Adam dabbed at his eyes. 'Aye. Oh, we'd make a right fine pair of murderers, eh Gwen?'

I felt my muscles relax. Just a little. I shook my head. 'I don't understand,' I said, trying to keep my voice as neutral as possible.

'No. You don't, do you? Sit down, Nathan, you're shaking. I'll make you a nice cup of tea.'

I opened my mouth, then closed it again. 'Don't forget the arsenic, Gwen,' said Adam. 'Joke!' he added, as I started, and I did my best to join in as they both laughed.

My hands shook a little as I took a biscuit from the packet that Gwen proffered. I laid it in the saucer and stirred my tea. 'Well now,' I said, 'it seems you've got stories to tell about Lewis Fitzgerald.'

'Only one story, my dear,' said Gwen.

'But it's the same one,' finished Adam.

'Which is?'

'He's a chiselling little spiv and a crook,' said Gwen as Adam nodded.

'Hmmm. Okay, that doesn't entirely surprise me. Tell me more.'

'It was back in the late eighties. I was quite young then, just starting out.'

'Oh, very young indeed, I would have said.'

'There's no need to be *faux* gallant, Mr Sutherland. Please let me continue.'

'Sorry.'

'He had a gallery in London. He can only have been a few years older than me, and he seemed quite glamorous. He was already building a reputation. And he offered to represent me. It was a good deal, I thought. There wasn't much of a scene in Cardiff at the time.'

'And then?'

'Oh, he got me work, I'll give him that. But then cheques started arriving late. Or not arriving at all. And then I discovered that amongst his many talents is a genius for creative accounting.'

Adam nodded. 'Same here, Mr Consul. I came out of Glasgow School of Art in the mid-nineties. Gwen and I didn't know each other then. So I signed up with Mr Fitzgerald. Five years later, I'd had exhibitions in London, Stockholm, Berlin, Paris – you name it – and somehow I had less money than when I was a student. Because that mendacious wee shite had been ripping me off. For years. And we could name a dozen more young artists who found themselves in the same situation.'

'I don't get it. Why didn't you take him to court?'

'You need money for that. And Fitzgerald's got a lot of it. Ours, to be precise. He could afford some pretty heavyweight representation. Super-injunctions and the like. Very little of it made the newspapers. And we both got some pretty scary letters. Not all of them from lawyers, if you know what I mean. Better to start over again. Forget about it.'

I turned to Gwen. 'Except you haven't forgotten about it, have you?'

'I had. For years. And then I learned that Paul had signed up with him. I knew him, years back, when he was still a student. We were – are – good friends. Paul's not like us, Mr Sutherland. He's away with the fairies. He's not capable, really not capable, of managing his own affairs.'

'And now, Lewis Fitzgerald is?'

Adam nodded. 'Aye. And Paul Considine has earned one hell of a lot more money than Gwen or I ever have.'

'Bloody hell.'

'So you see, Mr Sutherland,' continued Gwen, 'when I learnt that Paul and I would be in Venice at the same time, along with the famous Lewis Fitzgerald, well, I knew that my work would have to be a reaction to the circumstances.'

'But he was never going to see it. At least, not like this,' I gestured at the horrible image on the canvas.

'That doesn't matter. At some point, between now and November, somebody will see it. And they'll recognise it. And, hopefully, it will make them laugh.'

'Laugh? My God!'

'Oh, it made me laugh, *cariad*. All the time I was working on them.' She held my gaze, without blinking. 'Every single brush stroke. They made me laugh.'

I couldn't suppress a shudder. 'I thought you were just a lovely Welsh lady.'

'I am a lovely Welsh lady. This is just my little way of taking revenge on him.'

'You have to admit, Nathan,' said Adam, 'it's a more elegant way than just killing him.'

I nodded. 'Okay. But I don't understand where the wedding dresses come into it. Unless – unless they're a symbol of betrayal?'

Adam stroked his beard. 'Naw, I hadn't thought of that. I just like wedding dresses.'

'Oh.'

'So tell us, Mr Consul. Why exactly are you interested in Lewis Fitzgerald?'

'I'm not. That is, I wish I wasn't. But I think something strange is going on. And I'm starting to think that the death of Gordon Blake-Hoyt might not have been an accident.' I ran through the incident with the glass arrows and the two postcards.

'So you think someone is running around trying to murder people using methods depicted in historic paintings?'

'It sounds crazy, but yes. It seems to make sense.'

'It's a brilliant idea, I'll give you that. I wish I'd thought of it. Don't you, Gwen?'

'Oh yes, Adam.'

'So my question is,' I paused and dunked my biscuit in my tea, 'do you think Lewis Fitzgerald is capable of murder?'

There was silence for a moment, broken only by a sad little 'plop' as the edge of my biscuit dropped off into my tea. Adam shrugged. 'He's a bastard. Is he a murderous bastard? I don't know.'

'Besides,' added Gwen, 'you said yourself that he was injured by one of those glass arrows.'

'True. Straight through his hand. Must have hurt like hell. I could almost feel sorry for him. But only almost. So here's the more difficult question: do you think Paul Considine is capable of murder?' There was silence again, but neither of them showed any sign of breaking it. 'Is that a maybe?'

'It's a no, Mr Sutherland.'

'A mentally fragile man takes revenge on his greatest critic and someone who he thinks has ripped him off. It's a motive.'

'Mentally fragile. Why do you say that?'

'Because,' I struggled to think, 'because I know he's had his demons in the past. He seems to depend on Lewis. It makes him seem a bit vulnerable.'

She nodded. 'You're right. He is, or was. There were times when he seemed to be in his own little world. And I just wanted to mother him. And then there were times when he'd talk about his work, and it was like he became a different person. When all those words, when everything that was blocked up in him just came tumbling out and he'd fix you with those great blue eyes of his and . . .'

'And?'

'And then I wouldn't want to mother him any more.' There was silence for a moment. 'So maybe there's a motive, Mr Sutherland. But I don't believe it. I'll never believe it.' She sounded tired, and sad. 'I don't know. It's up to you to find out.'

'Just me?'

'We're both going home in the next couple of days, Mr Consul. So it looks like it has to be you. You've got to be the one who asks too many questions. You've got to be like Elsa of Brabant.'

'Oh. Can't I be like Lohengrin?'

Gwenant chuckled just a little too long for my liking, and Adam shushed her. 'No no. He's just a knight in shining armour. Elsa's the awkward one who asks the questions that everybody else is afraid to ask.'

'But it destroys her life!'

'Well yes. But hopefully that won't happen to you.'

I closed my eyes, and rubbed my face. 'More tea?' asked Gwen.

I shook my head, and got to my feet. 'No thanks. I'll be on my way. I've got dinner to cook. And difficult questions to think of. And when I've done that, I'll try and think who to ask them of.'

Chapter 24

Francesco Nicolodi.

He'd been with me on *vernissage* day at the Giardini, and seen pretty much exactly what I had. I couldn't be sure if he'd spoken to Considine himself, but it would seem unlikely if he hadn't. But just maybe he'd seen something else. And if he had, he'd almost certainly be saving it up for another exclusive. Where had he said he was staying? The Hotel Zichy. To be precise, the Hotel Ferdinand Zichy.

I should have thought it seemed a bit odd at the time. The Zichy was a low-budget hotel, not far from Spirito Santo. I'd occasionally had to deal with unhappy visitors there. Yes, it was cheap, but in Venice you got what you paid for. The Zichy was, I suppose, a few steps up from an actual flop-house, but had acquired a reputation for dubious hygiene and things going missing. More than one couple had arrived back after a day's sightseeing to find their room safe empty. After the third occurrence of this I'd complained to Vanni. He'd shrugged. Yes, there was probably something illegal about it all. No, they couldn't possibly prove it. It seemed, therefore, a very unlikely place for an international art critic to choose to stay.

There was no reason at all to go round there. Given the circumstances of our last meeting, I couldn't imagine Nicolodi would be pleased to see me. Nevertheless, it was just possible he might be able to help.

Work took me back to the Ospedale, where I did a final bit of interpreting and paperwork on behalf of the elderly couple. I carried their cases to the Alilaguna stop and waved them on to the next boat to Marco Polo airport. Then I took the next *vaporetto* round to the Giudecca canal. It was outside the rush hour by now, and there were seats free inside. I chose instead to sit outside, to feel the breeze and to look over to the island. I didn't have much occasion to come round here these days, and the view never became stale. I remembered the story of doomed, tragic Ezra Pound, and how he cried when he realised he would never see the Giudecca again.

The boat pulled into the Zattere stop where the family next to me alighted. No shopping trolleys, big cameras, and dad wearing shorts despite it being relatively early in the summer. In his left hand he held a Russian edition of a popular eating and drinking guide. If they turned left, I'd bet any money that they were heading to Nico's. They did indeed, and I watched them walk along the *fondamenta* to the *terrazza* that was already starting to fill up. Well deduced, Nathan, I thought. Fede would be proud of you.

I'd always loved this part of town. I came here less often that I should, but there had been a time when it seemed no problem was so insoluble that it couldn't be fixed by a spritz at Nico's. I turned and gazed across the canal to Palanca. Sergio and Lorenzo would be drinking and playing cards in the communist bar. We'd promised to keep in touch, but it had been over six months since we'd last met. The boat set off again, and, just two minutes later, we were at Spirito Santo. It was one of the stranger *vaporetto* stops in the city. The casual visitor might be forgiven for wondering why it was there at all. The reason was a depressingly simple one. There were no longer any grocery stores in the area, all having been turned into tourist shops. There was therefore a need to simplify the way of getting an ageing local population to the nearest supermarket at San Basilio. And so, under pressure from the few residents that remained in the area, the *Comune* had added an extra stop. Every year they threatened to take it away again. And every year, local pressure just about succeeded in keeping it open.

The pontoon was moored outside the long-abandoned church of the same name. Its doors hadn't opened in over a century, and probably never would again. Rumours persisted that some works of art still remained inside, leading to occasional break-ins, but the official line was that everything of value had long since been removed to the Accademia. Even Federica had never seen the interior. There was, she said, supposedly nothing of interest to see inside and the structure was in poor condition, leaving it useless even as a temporary space for the Biennale. The windows were boarded up now against the elements, as the plaster fought a losing battle against the effects of *aqua alta*. Tourists scarcely gave it a passing glance. It was, after all, just another dead church.

I turned left after the church and made my way down to the Hotel Zichy. The lobby was smart in the way that disappointing hotels always seem to have smart lobbies. Reception was unattended, whilst a bored-looking young man with a man bun polished glasses at the bar to my right.

I stood at the reception desk and waited. And waited some more. I smiled over at the young man. He smiled back at me and nodded. I waited a little more. And then I walked over to the bar.

'I'm here to meet a friend of mine,' I said.

'Sure.' I couldn't quite place his accent. Romania, Moldova? That way on. 'Just ask at reception.'

'Of course.' I nodded.

I went back to reception. And waited some more. I glanced over at the young barman, still polishing his way through glasses with Eastern European efficiency. I gave a little cough. 'Erm, there doesn't seem to be anyone here at the moment?'

He nodded. 'Not at this time of day. Only me.'

'Ah, right. Maybe you can help me?'

'Of course. Spritz? Beer? Wine?'

I shook my head. 'No no no. There's a friend of mine,' I lied, 'staying here. I wonder if you could just call his room.'

'Okay. You just need to ask at reception.'

'There's no one here.'

'Not at this time. Come back at six.'

This was going nowhere. I needed to reset the parameters of our relationship. I walked over to the bar. 'Okay. Can I have a beer please?'

'Moretti?'

'Nastro Azzurro, if you've got it.'

He nodded, fetched me a bottle from the fridge, cracked the top and passed it to me.

'Could I have a glass please?'

He slid one over to me.

'Maybe some crisps?'

He reached behind him for a small glass bowl, and then brought forth an industrial-size packet from which he transferred a few handfuls.

'Great. Thanks. Would you like one yourself?' He looked surprised. I looked around, exaggeratedly, and said in a stage whisper, 'Ah, go on, no one's around. I think you've probably earned one.' He gave an approximation of a smile, and then went back to the fridge for another Nastro Azzurro. He was about to drink from the bottle, but I shook my finger. 'Stick it in a glass. Bottles are just for *ultras*.' He grinned.

We clinked glasses. '*Noroc!*' I said.

He gave a little start. '*Vorbiti romana?*'

'*Numai putin. Lucrez ca traducator.*' I switched back to Italian. 'I have a friend who's Romanian. He taught me a bit. Maybe you know him. He has a business on the bridges. Carrying dogs, you know?'

He broke into a broad smile. 'Mr Gheorghe! Yes. He's a legend.' We clinked glasses again. I finished my beer. 'Same again? And have one for yourself.' He fetched another two bottles. I stretched my hand across the bar. 'Nathan.'

'Adrian.' We shook.

'Tell me Adrian, can we smoke here?'

He shook his head. 'Of course not. But everybody does.' He reached into his trouser pocket and pulled out a crumpled packet of something I'd never seen before. He extracted two cigarettes. 'Here. My treat this time.' I took a light from him and took a cautious drag.

My new friend kindly offered me a paper handkerchief with which to wipe away my tears. Eventually, I finished coughing and took a draught of my beer. 'Smooth,' I croaked.

He grinned. '*Carpati*. Cheapest cigarettes in Romania. My dad's favourite. He was in Revolution Square back in 1989. Always said he was more scared of the cigarettes than the *Securitate*.'

I took another, delicate little puff. 'He was a wise man, your father,' I said, dabbing at my eyes. We smoked and coughed in silence for a few minutes. 'So tell me, Adrian,' I said, 'what's it like working here?'

He shrugged. 'You've seen the reviews?'

'Yes.'

'They're kind of right. It's not so great. And sometimes stuff goes missing, you know. And one of us gets the blame.'

'But not you?'

'Not me. I'm too smart.'

'I'm glad to hear it. Listen, Adrian, I think you've got a guy called Francesco Nicolodi staying here at the moment.'

He looked blank for a moment, but then his face cleared. 'Southern Italian guy? Maybe drinks a bit too much? Here for the Biennale?'

'Two out of three at least. I can't swear to the second. Is he here?'

He shook his head. 'Not any more. Checked out this morning.'

'Ah shit. Do you have any idea where he went? Back down south or off to the UK?'

'No idea.'

'Hell. It might be important. You really have no idea at all?'

'Sorry.' Then he looked over his shoulder. I followed his gaze to the clock on the wall. One o'clock.

'I suppose,' I said, 'the rooms haven't been cleaned yet?' He nodded. 'So I guess that – hypothetically speaking – someone might be able to have a look around there.'

He shook his head. 'I'd lose my job.'

'Yeah, but it's a shit job.'

'True enough.' He beckoned me over to reception and took down a key. 'Just put in a good word for me with Mr Gheorghe, eh? It sounds more fun than this place.'

I grinned. 'I most certainly will.'

I wasn't quite sure what I expected to find. I wasn't even one hundred per cent sure what the hell I was doing there. Maybe it came down to just two things. Considine seemed like a nice guy, fragile, but a nice guy at heart. Francesco, I didn't like. More to the point, he'd made a fool of me. Deep down I was hoping to find something that proved it was his fault. Or, if not that, at least something that showed it wasn't Considine's doing.

And in the end, I found precisely nothing. The room was clean enough, although on the small side; a faded carpet lay on a parquet floor in need of sanding and revarnishing. There was the lingering smell of stale cigarette smoke. Residents here, I imagined, just preferred to ignore the rules. A small safe was fixed to the usual position in the wardrobe. No electronic code here, just a very basic key. One that would be very easy to copy. It helped to explain those visitors who'd come to me with stories of things going missing.

I opened drawers, checked the waste bin and even the bathroom cabinet. Nothing. But what had I expected? A match book? A map with circles drawn on it? A silly idea. I went back down to the lobby. Adrian was still at reception. I passed the key back to him.

'Did you find what you were looking for?'

'Not a thing. Sorry, I've wasted our time.'

He shook his head. 'No you haven't. We had a beer. That makes it a better afternoon than most here.'

'Thanks. Okay, I'll be off. I'll have a word with Gheorghe, as I promised.' I turned to leave, and then something caught the corner of my eye. An old-fashioned telephone cubicle. 'Wow. Does that thing still work?'

He laughed. 'Not since I've been here. Even here, all rooms have a telephone. It's a wifi point now. Just a shared PC.' It figured. Why spend money on wifi throughout the hotel when most people would probably have a smartphone? If you were running a hotel on the cheap, it was a good budget solution. A thought struck me.

'Could I just have a quick look?' He seemed surprised, but nodded anyway. I walked into the cubicle, and closed the door behind me. The authentic smell of the 1950s. No telephone now, just a budget-brand laptop secured to the wall with a cable. I tapped the keyboard a few times until the screen powered up, and opened the browser. I clicked the 'History' tab.

I almost laughed. It hadn't been configured to clear the history after exiting the browser. It was all there, at least for the past few days. I scrolled through. Mainly news sites in various different languages. And then Francesco's name. He'd googled himself. He'd actually googled himself. There was his *Times* article and his name seemed to be mentioned – alongside mine – in a couple of news reports. That was it. Except

– no – as I rechecked I could see a ten-minute gap between Francesco's search and that of, presumably, the next user who was looking at a Bangladeshi news site. And directly after Francesco's search for himself came the address of the Palazzo Papadopoli. One of the most exclusive hotels on the Grand Canal and about as far removed from the Hotel Zichy as one might imagine. He'd clicked on the 'Accommodation' tab. Naturally. The Papadopoli was not a place to have anything as vulgar as 'Rooms'. There was no room rate mentioned. If you had to ask, you almost certainly couldn't afford it.

So Francesco had gone from one of the cheapest places in town that still dignified itself by use of the word 'hotel', to one of the most exclusive. He could, I supposed, have been spending the money he got for his article. No. I had no idea how much money *The Times* paid for an unsolicited column, but I was pretty sure it wouldn't buy you a night in the Palazzo Papadopoli. Come to that, it probably wouldn't even buy you a spritz in the Palazzo Papadopoli. Interesting though. Something to think about.

I exited the cubicle and smiled at my new friend. I left five euros on the bar for him and gave him a nod. 'Have another beer on me,' I said.

Chapter 25

Gramsci was in a fractious mood. He was too dignified ever to have anything that could be considered 'a mad half-hour' and preferred to express himself in casual, petty acts of destruction. In this case, scrabbling away with his claws at the base of the sofa; directly next to his scratching post, as unmarked and pristine as the day I unwrapped it.

I ignored him. He scrabbled away a little more. He'd invented a new game recently, where he'd stretch full length, sink his claws into the sofa and pull himself upright. Federica was stretched out on the other sofa. Her mum was still away visiting an old friend in Chioggia, giving her another night off. 'He needs entertaining.'

'He'll get bored in a minute.'

She peered over the top of her glasses at me. 'He won't. Will he?'

'No.' I said. The scratching continued. I sighed. It had only been a few months since Fede had persuaded me to have the sofas re-covered. I reached for his ball. He reacted with excitement, jumped on the sofa and hunkered down behind the arm in a defensive position. I walked as far away from him as I could and tossed the ball in my hand a couple of times. 'Okay

Grams, the usual thing is it?' His claws scrabbled happily. 'I'm bowling, is it? You don't feel like having a go for once?'

'Why do you speak to him in English?' said Federica.

I gave myself as much of a run-up as I could manage in the confined space of the living room, delivered an overarm bowl, and watched Gramsci bat it straight back to me with his paw. 'Clever cat. Well done.' I turned to Fede. 'I don't know. I just always have.'

'But he's an Italian cat.'

'Yes, but English is his first language.'

'He's bilingual? You have a bilingual cat?'

'He might be.' I took another run-up. 'He's very clever, you know.' Gramsci took a wilder swipe this time, and the ball pinged off the coffee table as Fede – who was becoming used to this sort of thing – removed her wine glass just in time. She tossed the ball back to me.

I sat on the floor at the base of the sofa, and leaned my head against Federica's shoulder. She kissed the top of my head. 'I suppose he is quite clever. You've got him very well trained.'

'I have, haven't I? It took some time, but I got there in the end. I even managed to get him to fetch a ball once. 2013 I think it was.'

'I was talking to the cat, Nathan.' She took a sip of her wine and passed me the glass to put down on the table, which I did after grabbing a quick sip myself. 'So, have you got any work to do tonight?'

'Me or the cat?' She peered over the top of her glasses again and frowned. Sometimes I wondered if she genuinely needed them or if they were just a prop for expressing disapproval. 'Nothing important. Nothing that needs to be done right now. Mr Blake-Hoyt is obstinately remaining dead, which is going to annoy his brother, but there's not very much I can do about that. Oh, and there's investigating Francesco Nicolodi.'

'Do you think he's got anything to do with it?'

'I really don't know. But I can't think of anything else. I think Lewis and Paul might actually have left town. That whole business with Scarpa the other day, I think he was just hoping I'd get beaten up. Nicolodi's kind of like a last throw of the dice. And if that doesn't work, well I think I'll just have to give up. Did you find anything with the CCTV?'

'Sorry, *caro*. I did check it out, but the recordings are deleted every twenty-four hours. And as there was no incident reported, no *denuncia*, there was no reason why anybody should have thought to keep them.'

'Damn. That's a shame. Oh well, like I said, Nicolodi's kind of like the last chance now.'

She closed her laptop, and checked her watch. 'Still only half-past ten.'

'Is there anything good on RAI?' We looked at each other wordlessly for a couple of seconds, and then laughed.

'Okay,' she said. 'I'll have an early night. Are you coming to bed?'

I was about to say yes, and then the sound of claws against fabric came from the other sofa. Gramsci, clearly, had other plans.

'I'll be along in a minute.' I sighed.

I tossed some balls for a few minutes until he curled up on the sofa for a sleep. I wasn't entirely sure that this wasn't a cruel ploy, however, and didn't think I could risk going to bed yet. I sat down at my desk and logged on to my computer.

Francesco said he worked for *World of Art*, or something like that. No, that wasn't it. *Planet Art*.

I brought up their website but it was only a cobbled-together skeleton. There were various images of famous contemporary works on the home page, but it didn't look like a professional job. I clicked on the 'Articles' and 'Subscription' tabs but both just led me to a 'Page under construction' message. The 'About' tab had a generic blurb about 'Exploring the worlds of contemporary art' and listed a Francesco Nicolodi as founder and editor-in-chief. The English was shonky, as if run through Google translate.

That was it. I supposed it was possible they just hadn't got properly off the ground with their electronic version yet. I did a search on British art periodicals but could find no reference to *Planet Art*.

This got stranger and stranger. I ran through the facts again. Francesco Nicolodi arrives in Venice for the Biennale, claiming to be a journalist with an art magazine that seems not to exist. He checks into a fleapit of a hotel for a couple of days and then upgrades to one of the most exclusive residences in Venice.

I had no idea at all if he had anything to do with Gordon Blake-Hoyt's death. Almost certainly not; he'd been with me nearly all the time as far as I could remember. Nevertheless, I'd promised myself that I'd try and help Considine, and Francesco was pretty much the only lead left.

Something to check out in the morning. In the meantime, Gramsci seemed fast asleep. I could turn in for the night. I got to my feet as quietly as I could. Not quietly enough. The chair scraped across the floor, and I froze. Gramsci didn't stir.

I padded across the floor, until I reached the bedroom door. I'd done it.

A yowl came from behind me, followed by the scrabbling of claws against fabric. I sighed, again, and bent to pick some balls up off the floor.

Chapter 26

I held a surgery the following morning. Nobody turned up, but I received some flowers from the elderly couple as a token of thanks. They looked lovely, and a simple substitution of labels meant that I'd be able to give them to Federica later on. It was therefore early afternoon by the time I set out for the Palazzo Papadopoli. San Silvestro would be the nearest *vaporetto* stop but I didn't fancy standing on a crowded boat. It was a lovely day, so I decided to take the *traghetto* from Sant'Angelo to San Tomà and walk up from there.

I rarely used the *traghetti* these days. If you had a season ticket it was cheaper just to use the *vaporetti* to cross over the Grand Canal. Yet there were times that it was still the quickest way of crossing from one side to another, although there were fewer and more sporadic services every year. At one time, when the Rialto Bridge had been the only means of crossing the Grand Canal, there had been over thirty routes. Now we were down to just seven. Dario had once told me, with a warm glow in his voice, of how the *traghetti* would run all night when he was young. And now they all finished before sunset. I wondered if I'd still be in Venice when the final service closed for the last time.

I shook my head. The thought had brought a little cloud of gloom to hover over me. If anything could clear it away, a brief gondola ride across the canal could.

There were just a few of us in the queue at Sant'Angelo, waiting as the boat made its way from the San Tomà station on the opposite side. *Traghetti* were typically manned by ex-gondoliers who didn't quite want to give up their work just yet, and younger ones waiting for a place on a gondola station that would permit them the lucrative work of a regular gondolier.

I didn't recognise the old guy, his face lined with broken veins and weatherbeaten to a deep nut-brown after years of working outside. The other, however, was a young woman. The only female gondolier in Venice. We'd met a few times, always on this same route, but weren't quite on first-name terms. She recognised me and gave me a smile.

I smiled back, '*Come stai?*'

'I'm very well thanks. Can we use English?'

'Sure. Sorry, is my Italian that bad?'

'Not at all. But I need to practise.' Fair point. Gondoliers needed a high degree of fluency in at least one other language.

'How's it going? With getting a place on a station, I mean?' I asked as we pushed off.

'Not too bad. Maybe another year, maybe two. But I'll get there.'

'Good. I hope so.' I couldn't help but notice that she had the most extraordinary painted nails. 'I'll never know how you manage to keep your fingernails looking like that.'

She grinned. 'Practice.' She nodded at the old guy up front. 'You should check out Marco's. They're even more beautiful.'

'I'll make sure I do when I get off.'

The Venetian tradition was to stand on the *traghetto*, whilst tourists tended to sit. This was one of the occasions on which I was happy to look like a visitor. I'd only been in the city for a couple of weeks when the wake from a speeding ambulance nearly pitched me over the side. The gondoliers preferred to have you sit if you looked as if you might be somebody that would need rescuing.

The crossing took less than two minutes. But two minutes to look up and down the Grand Canal, under a clear blue sky. I'd been in Venice for over five years, and yet this service was the closest I'd ever been to being on an actual gondola.

We arrived at the San Tomà station, and I waved good-bye. Marco did, indeed, have beautiful nails. I set out for the Palazzo Papodopoli, the crossing, as expected, having blown away the dark clouds.

It was possible to reach the palazzo directly from the Grand Canal. Indeed, if you could afford to stay there, it would be bizarre to arrive any other way. George Clooney, of course, had been on the front page of almost every newspaper in the world when he arrived for his wedding via the front entrance the previous year. I was using the rather more modest rear entrance. Which, in a strange way, was technically the front entrance. I buzzed the intercom, and stepped back to give an ingratiating smile to the security camera. It must have been convincing enough, as the gate clanked open. My feet crunched on the reassuringly expensive-sounding gravel path as I walked to reception.

My invitation to Clooney's wedding had, unfortunately, gone missing in the post. This was, therefore, the first time I'd been inside. I was forced to concede that my pal George did indeed have extremely good taste. If you liked the baroque that was. If you liked rococo as well, hell, it was even better. I studied the ceiling. Cherubim and seraphim under a swirling pinky-blue sky. Almost certainly . . .

'Giambattista Tiepolo.' I gave a little start. The speaker was an attractive blond-haired woman in middle age, immaculately dressed in a black trouser suit.

'So I was thinking,' I said.

She smiled. 'Lots of people think that. I'm afraid not. It's just a copy from the late nineteenth century. However we have a suite on the *piano nobile* which has the real thing.'

'Is that where George stayed?'

'Of course.' Her expression changed ever so slightly, became quizzical. 'Can I help you in any way?' The subtext, of course, being 'I don't know you. You're not a guest here.'

'Perhaps. My name's Nathan Sutherland. I'm the British honorary consul in Venice.'

'Pleased to meet you, Mr Sutherland. Can I help you in any way?' she repeated.

'Well possibly. I met one of your guests the other day. A man called Francesco Nicolodi. He's a journalist. We were at the opening of the British pavilion.'

'Oh my goodness. Really? I read all about it of course. Dreadful.'

I nodded. 'Anyway, if it's possible, could you just call *signor* Nicolodi and tell him I'm down here. There's just a few things I'd like to talk over with him.'

She frowned. 'This isn't police business is it?'

'Oh no. Nothing like that. It's just . . .' I paused. What

kind of business, precisely, was it? Just trying to help out someone I hardly knew who might be on the verge of landing in serious trouble? 'Well, we were both witnesses to what happened. But it's nothing to do with the police, don't worry about that.'

She went to the reception desk, tapped away at a keyboard, and then picked up the phone and dialled. 'A Mr Sutherland is here for you, *signor* Nicolodi.' A brief pause, then 'Okay, I'll let him know.' She turned to me. 'He'll see you upstairs in the lounge in a few minutes.' Her phone bleeped, and she checked it. Then she looked across the reception hall to the water gate facing on to the Grand Canal. 'I'm sorry, we have guests arriving now. Please excuse me.' She made her way over to the water gate, where she was joined by five other members of the hotel staff. Two porters, a young woman bearing a tray with four glasses of prosecco, one man holding an empty silver platter and yet another holding a tray with a silver dome on it.

As I watched, a water taxi arrived. The two porters scurried outside and, seconds later, returned with the guests' baggage. A family of four disembarked, with the help of the driver. A couple in, perhaps, their seventies, presumably with their children. The manager greeted them as if they were the oldest and best of friends. Hot towels were proffered from underneath the silver dome, whilst glasses of prosecco were offered from the other side.

The manager caught me staring, and smiled politely. I gave her a little nod and made my way up the staircase. My buddy George really did have impeccable taste. And Francesco Nicolodi, it seemed, was definitely on his way up in the world.

*   *   *

'*Mister* Sutherland.'

  '*Signor* Nicolodi.'

We stood in silence for a few seconds, then Francesco spoke. 'Let's get a table, eh? It'll be a little more discreet. This is a such a nice place, I don't think they'd appreciate a scene.'

  'Oh, I was rather hoping to avoid a scene.' I said. We took a table by the window.

  'Quite a space, isn't it? And quite a view.' He grinned. It certainly was. Francesco Nicolodi, I thought, you lucky bastard. 'What's the building opposite?' he continued, point-ing at an elegant Renaissance-style palace that dwarfed the buildings on either side.

  'The Palazzo Grimani. It's Venice's Court of Appeal.'

  'Oh. I thought it was a museum.'

  'That's the Palazzo Grimani di Santa Maria Formosa. The one over there is the Palazzo Grimani di San Luca. There were rather a lot of Grimanis.'

  'Must be a nightmare to keep track of them all.'

  'It's a tightrope, Francesco. A regular tightrope.'

  'I'll bet.' He waved at the barman. 'We should get some drinks. They mix an excellent Bellini here, you know.'

  I shook my head. 'I've always found them a bit too sweet to be honest. Even when they're freshly made.'

  'What would you like, Mr Sutherland? Prosecco?'

  'A spritz, I think.'

  'With *Aperol?*'

  I shook my head. 'Still too sweet. *Al campari.*'

  'My goodness me. You really are a bitter man, aren't you?' I smiled. Our drinks arrived with a selection of luxury nibbles. Nothing so commonplace as mere crisps here. We clinked glasses. 'So why are you here, *Nathan*? I take it it's not just to check if I've written a good review for the nice Welsh lady?'

'No. But have you been there?'

'No. Don't need to. I'll google for a few images and the background info and do the rest from here. I'll make sure it's nice. Will that be good enough?'

'I guess so. Although I do wonder where I'll be able to read it.' He looked puzzled, and opened his mouth to speak, but I pressed on. 'Given that *Planet Art* magazine doesn't appear to exist.'

'What on earth do you mean?'

'I mean it doesn't exist. There's no such magazine. All there is is a website with hardly any content on it. What there is is written in lamentable English. And your English is perfect. No, that site looks like you've paid someone to knock it up in twenty minutes.' He was silent now, and sipped at his Bellini, as if giving himself time to think. I continued. 'You're not actually a journalist, are you, Francesco?'

'I—'

I waved my hand. 'No no no. You're not. You're not a journalist. You've had nothing published in Italy at all. Which makes me think you don't actually have a journalist's card. Which therefore makes me wonder how on earth you managed to get accredited for the Biennale?'

'*Planet Art* only has an online presence at the moment, and the website is, well, having some work done on it.'

'So somewhere in Italy, you have an office with dozens of journalists beavering away and a team of techies passing sleepless nights working on your website.'

'Something like that.'

I shrugged. 'As you wish. Nicolodi. Unusual surname you have, Francesco. I'm sure that's your real name, of course.'

He rolled his eyes and gave a theatrical little yawn. 'I could show you my documents.'

'Yes, yes. Of course you could.' I looked around at our opulent surroundings. 'Anyway, you must be doing well for yourself, Francesco. This is a bit of a step up from the Hotel Zichy.'

He gave the thinnest of smiles and drained his Bellini. He looked over his shoulder at the bar and looked faintly irritated when the barman was not there. A moment later, and the reason became clear, as he appeared, ghostlike, behind Francesco's shoulder. Francesco gave a little start, and then relaxed. 'The same again please. Mr Sutherland?'

I shook my head. 'Not for me thanks. I've got to cook dinner after this. Marvellous staff here, aren't they? Just look at him, he moves like a dancer. Mind you, the barman at the Zichy is a nice bloke too. I get the impression he's a bit easier to talk to, as well.'

'Are you following me, Sutherland?'

'Good heavens, no. You gave me your address yourself, remember? But I'm just a little bit interested in your sudden change in circumstances. You'll admit it's a bit of a leap from the Zichy to here.'

'*The Times* paid well for that article. So thanks for that.' The sun was shining directly through the windows now, and it was starting to become ever-so-slightly uncomfortable. Francesco's face was flushed and he tugged at, and then unbuttoned, his collar.

I laughed. 'Oh Francesco, I don't think so. A first-time commission from an unknown writer? It wouldn't even cover the cost of these drinks.'

His second Bellini arrived, which he grabbed from the barman before he could set it down. He placed his hands on the table, and closed his eyes. Counting to ten. Then he opened them again, and forced a smile on to his face. 'Sutherland, is there any reason I shouldn't just call our friend over there,' he jerked his thumb over his shoulder in the direction of the bar, 'and have you thrown out?'

'None at all.' Now it was my turn to play for time. I took a sip of my drink. 'You know, they do a top spritz here, Francesco. You really should try one before you leave. Anyway – and this may seem a little strange – I'm not actually here for a fight.'

He raised his eyebrows. 'No?'

'No. Just the opposite. I want your help.'

'Seriously?'

'Seriously.'

'What about?'

'Paul Considine. And Lewis Fitzgerald.' I explained as much as I felt necessary. 'I'm hoping they've just gone back to the UK and that Lewis just isn't answering my calls. Have you heard from either of them?'

Nicolodi shook his head. 'No. But then there's no reason why I should. I don't know either of them. But they won't have gone back to the UK.'

'How can you be so sure?'

He shrugged. 'Considine has another exhibition. He won't have gone home before that opens.'

'Another one? I don't understand.'

Nicolodi sighed. 'He had his personal exhibit at the British pavilion. You understand that, at least?' I opened my mouth to remonstrate, but he shushed me and continued. 'And he's part of the group show on Lazzaretto Vecchio, which opens tomorrow. You know where that is?' I nodded. The plague island. Abandoned for years now, but occasionally pressed into use on special occasions, such as the Biennale. It lay just off the coast of the Lido, not very far from Fede's apartment. 'You should come along. You seemed to like Mr Considine's work so much. You might enjoy it.'

'Perhaps I will.'

'So. Is there anything else I can help with?

'I was thinking about the day of the accident. You were with me at the time. Okay, you didn't see it happen, but there might have been something else you saw.'

'I gave my statement to the police at the time, remember?'

'I know. But just have a think. Anything else that comes to mind. And there's another thing, Francesco. GBH wrote a filthy review of Considine's work, and now he's dead. Vincenzo Scarpa did the same. There was an – an incident – at the Arsenale four days ago. I was in the same room as him. So was Lewis. We both got hurt, but I think Scarpa was the target. And that piece you wrote for *The Times* – where you practically accused Considine of plagiarism – that wasn't exactly complimentary, was it?'

'What are you saying, Sutherland? Is that a warning?'

'If you like.'

'I'll be very careful, I promise. I'll make sure to look out for Mr Considine running at me with a glass scythe.'

I shook my head. 'It's not Considine. I'm sure. He just doesn't seem the type.'

Francesco snorted out a laugh. 'What's so funny?' I asked.

'"Doesn't seem the type"? You're not in the art world, are you, Sutherland?'

'No. You know that.'

'"Doesn't seem the type." For Christ's sake. You might be a good consul, Sutherland, but you're a shit private detective.'

'What do you mean?' I could feel myself getting angry now.

'It's hardly a secret. In the art world. Don't let all that head-in-the-clouds nonsense fool you. He's got a nasty streak. You know he nearly went to prison ten years ago?'

My spritz stopped on the way to my mouth. 'You're kidding?'

He grinned. He'd got me on the back foot now and was enjoying it. 'Not a bit of it. I told you he'd had problems with drink. Know what he did? He got drunk one night and glassed someone with a broken bottle. Because he'd looked at him in a funny way.' I said nothing. 'Don't take my word for it. Look it up. It's all out there. Cuddly Paul Considine just happens to have a bit of a thing about broken glass, it seems.'

Ah, shit. I got to my feet. 'I'm sorry.' I dragged the words out. 'It seems I've wasted our time.'

He spread his arms wide, and looked around him. 'Not at all. Anyway, I can't think of a better place to waste time than this.'

'I'll pay for the drinks.'

'No you won't. My treat. As you said, they're a bit expensive here.'

'Thanks.' I turned and made for the stairs.

'Don't worry, Sutherland. I'm not angry. I'm just disappointed.'

The black cloud of gloom returned with a vengeance as I made my way back to the Street of the Assassins. Even the prospect of a pre-dinner Negroni didn't cheer me as much as it once would have. I gave Eduardo a wave but walked past the Magical Brazilian and straight upstairs to the flat.

It was still a surprise to me to see how well stocked the fridge was these days. Fede really had sorted me out. Aubergines, peppers, tomatoes, zucchini. All sorts of nice things that I could do. But nothing was really coming to mind. I never really enjoyed cooking for one. Pizza? No. Something healthier, something that would allow me to tell Federica that I'd got some vegetables into me. Baked aubergines topped with tomato and mozzarella. So simple it scarcely seemed like cooking at all. But at least it was cooking. I made myself a spritz and got to work.

The oven had only just warmend up when the telephone rang. Federica.

'*Ciao, cara*. Changed your mind about coming over?'

'Afraid not, *caro*. Way too much work on tonight and *Mamma* is back from Chioggia as well.'

I took another quick look inside the fridge. I could just about triple the quantities. 'Look, I haven't had dinner yet. You could all come over. You could just work away and I'll entertain your mum.'

'I'd love to but, really, there's a lot I need to get done.'

'I'll sparkle. I promise I'll sparkle.'

She laughed. 'Oh I know you will. People always tell me how lucky I am to have such a sparkly boyfriend. But I really can't.' Her voice changed, became more serious. 'Are you okay?'

I took a deep breath. 'Mm. Not really.'

'What's the matter? Have you been to see Nicolodi again?'

'Yes.'

'And?'

'I think this has all been a waste of time. Trying to help Paul. It turns out he's done bad stuff in the past. Really bad stuff.'

'What are you going to do? Talk to Vanni?'

'I don't know. There's absolutely no proof at all. I think I might just give it a few days. Just try and clear my head a bit.' I changed the subject. 'Anyway, tomorrow will cheer me up. We're entertaining Dario, remember?'

'Ah, I'd forgotten. With Valentina and his little girl?'

'Emily. No, they're off visiting grandparents. A shame, she's a sweetheart.'

'If you say so. Okay then, *a domani*.'

'*A domani*. Love you.'

'Love you too.'

I hung up, and smiled to myself. Maybe it hadn't been such a bad day after all. To hell with mysteries and art-obsessed serial killers. I had aubergines to bake.

Chapter 27

There was no surgery and precious little to do the following morning, apart from my early morning shout from Mr Blake-Hoyt; a routine that, by now, I was settling into quite nicely. I held the phone a comfortable few inches from my ear, said 'Yes' a lot, assured him I was still doing my best and that, yes, of course he should contact the ambassador if he so wished. Occasionally, I found it relaxing to make rude gestures at the handset. Mr Blake-Hoyt, I hoped, would never insist on Skyping me. Then I hung up, gently massaged my ear and made a second cup of coffee.

I needed to go and buy some fish for dinner. When I first arrived in Venice, I had chanced upon a stall in Campo Santa Margherita, and I'd used the same one for years. Less hectic than the Rialto market, and there was no shortage of bars in which to sit and watch the world go by. And then, one day, the stallholders – a father and son – weren't there any more. Dad, I learned, was getting on a bit and so his son had decided to sell up. In two years of shopping there I'd never even asked their names.

I never again went back to Campo Santa Margherita for fish. The two remaining stalls were run by perfectly nice people.

But two stalls didn't really seem to approximate a market, in the same way as three had. It seemed to be a sign to move on elsewhere. The Rialto market was closer, even allowing for the battle to get over the bridge. And despite the crowds, despite the occasional frustration of getting stuck behind tourists taking photographs of tomatoes, there was still something a little bit thrilling about the explosions of colours and smells, and the shouting in *Veneziano*.

It had taken a while to build up a relationship with Marco and Luciano. Marco was short and wiry with thinning grey hair and a few missing teeth. Luciano was younger and hipper; tattooed like a sailor, which clashed with his immaculately brilliantined hair. Crucially, they spoke a form of *Veneziano* that I could almost understand. I thought they might also knock a euro or two off the price of my shopping, but I could never be quite sure. What I did know is that whenever I asked for a piece of fish suitable for two people, they would sell me a piece suitable for three. Things would always, they assured me, shrink during cooking. They never did, but at least it meant I always had a well-stocked freezer compartment.

I had come to realise that I would never, ever be able to buy fish anywhere else again. Peter Parker's Spider-Sense was as nothing compared to their ability to detect me when I was wandering around the market. If I so much as glanced at another stall whilst cruising a lap, they would catch my eye and wave me over.

I quickly cast my eyes over the nearest stalls as I entered the market. Spider crabs. Spider crab with pasta would be nice. There were a couple left on the nearest stall to my left. I quickly checked Marco and Luciano's. No spider crabs. Okay, maybe this would be the first time I'd get away with it. Gently, ever so gently, I started to turn to my left . . .

'*Ciao, Nathan, come stai?*'

'*Abbastanza bene, Marco.*' We would not, then, be having spider crab that evening. I made my way over. Luciano was flirting with two American girls with the aid of a raw scallop. He cut the flesh into three, popped one piece into his mouth and made an exaggerated yummy sound. He passed the shell with the remaining pieces to the girls. 'Try one!'

One of them clapped her hands to her face. 'But it's not cooked!'

'Even better this way. Very healthy. See my dad over there.' He nodded his head towards Marco. 'He's eighty-three. You wouldn't think so, eh? It's because he eats raw fish every day.' Marco, who was neither eighty-three nor, for that matter, Luciano's dad did his best to enter into the spirit of things by giving them a broken-toothed grin. Then he turned to me and shook his head.

'*Incorreggibile.*'

'He's impressive though. I'd never have thought it possible to flirt whilst holding a mollusc. What's good today, Marco?' I had, by now, learned that it was never any good asking for what I wanted. Marco and Luciano would sell me what they wanted to sell me, and that was the end of the matter. So 'what's good today' was just shorthand for 'tell me what I'm going to be leaving with'.

'Ah, have the monkfish. Very good, very fresh today. You could eat it raw.'

I suppressed a sigh as I looked at a mountain of sardines, perfect for grilling. But if Marco said monkfish, monkfish it would be. 'That'd be lovely,' I smiled.

'How much?'

'Enough for three,' I said without thinking. He gave me the two biggest tails. Enough for four. 'Isn't that rather a lot?' I said.

He grinned. 'No no. It'll reduce when you cook it . . .'

Monkfish, then. I was pretty sure I had some stock in the freezer, and a couple of carrots in the salad drawer. A place that, until the arrival of Federica, might as well have had 'Here Be Dragons' affixed to it. It was a bit late in the season now, but not too late to pick up some asparagus, broad beans and fresh peas. I also bought some flowers for Fede to go with the second-hand ones I'd passed on to her. Bonus points, I thought. There were, I knew, better places to go for flowers in the city, places where the most gorgeous and exotic blooms would be trimmed and tethered, and beautifully presented. Knowing nothing about flowers, those places frightened me. The ones from the market might not be quite so artistically presented and might only last a few days, but they looked the part. I felt quite the model boyfriend as I fought my way back over the Rialto Bridge. Boyfriend? Was I too old to be a boyfriend? Probably. I didn't care.

I was still whistling a happy tune by the time I arrived home. I never whistled. I felt like glad-handing total strangers and ruffling the hair of street urchins. The weekly newsletter containing the latest offers from the nearest supermarket had been slid under the door, together with the electricity bill. A couple of flyers. And then, something else. An envelope. No address, neither handwritten nor printed. Advertising then. I stuck them all in the bag of vegetables and carried everything upstairs.

I had a small amount of translation work to crack on with that afternoon, and dinner to prepare. Nothing too complicated, just monkfish with spring vegetables, but it would take a little bit of work if it was going to look suitably cheffy and pretty.

I reckoned I had a little bit of time left to check out Francesco's story about Paul Considine. I stuck some early Jethro Tull on the stereo, and logged on.

It took a bit of searching. There were pages and pages about his art, about his being long-listed for the 2009 Turner Prize, and no shortage of comment, of course, about the unfortunate incident of a few days back. But no references to his arrest. I searched deeper. 'Paul Considine glass' just brought up pages of reviews and images. I changed it to 'Paul Considine glass arrest'. And there it was. A single article from the Standard, in 2005. He hadn't been famous at the time, just another struggling artist, and a fight in a London pub wouldn't have been enough to make the national papers. But from what I could gather, he'd been arrested after hitting somebody with a bottle in a pub. The other guy, it seemed, had had a knife on his person and hadn't pressed charges. Still. After one double whisky too many, Paul Considine, it seemed, had thought it a great idea to attack somebody with a glass bottle.

There were no other accounts of the incident. Strange. Surely it would have come back to haunt him when he became famous? Then I remembered what Gwen had told me about Lewis Fitzgerald, and his fondness for litigation and super-injunctions. For all his faults, then, it seemed as if he was very good at protecting his assets.

Francesco had been right. I didn't know much about art. Or, more precisely, I only knew about art by dead people. And maybe I didn't really know as much as I thought about people in general either.

I felt vaguely depressed. Considine had a violent streak. Lewis seemed like a spiv. Francesco . . . Francesco, I was starting to think was probably just a cheap crook. I started to worry if the Nice Welsh Lady really had actually murdered her husband. Everything just seemed a bit grubby and sordid. If that's what the contemporary art world was like, well they could keep it. I flicked through my diary. I had a few more openings to go to in the next few days, and more abstracts to translate, but my heart wasn't in it any more.

Cooking. Cooking would sort me out. The monkfish wouldn't take much time to cook, but a little bit of preparation would speed things up. And I'd need a starter as well. I replaced Jethro Tull with more Jethro Tull, and headed for the kitchen.

I prepared a dozen discs of polenta, and caramelised some red onions with a splash of balsamic vinegar. I put the onions on top of the polenta discs, and crumbled some cubes of mozzarella on top. I'd stick them in the oven when people arrived until the cheese melted, and they'd be just perfect as snacks whilst I cracked on with the fish. I set to preparing the vegetables.

Fede arrived at about six o'clock, paused only to remove the Tull from the hi-fi – she'd got it down to such a fine art by now that she scarcely needed to break her stride – and walked into the kitchen where she found me working on vegetables. She slipped her arms around me and kissed the back of my neck.

'What are you doing, *tesoro?*'

'Skinning the beans.'

'Why?'

'They just look prettier. Greener.'

'But do they really taste that different? Is it really worth it?'

'I'm not sure they taste any better. But they do look very pretty.'

'This is dinner for three, *caro*. Not *Masterchef.*'

I grinned. 'I know. But it's been a bit of a rubbish couple of days. This kind of cheered me up. Along with Jethro Tull of course.' I gave her my best hangdog expression.

She sighed. 'Okay, if it's been that bad I'll put it back on for you as a special treat. So, tell me all about it.'

I told her more about my meeting with Francesco Nicolodi and what I'd found out about Paul Considine. She wrinkled her nose. 'Okay, so Considine was an asshole ten years ago. Doesn't mean he is now. And it's a big stretch from "has fight in bar" to "serially murders critics with broken glass". Anyway, I still think there's no way he could have murdered someone like that. Far too many things to go wrong.'

'I know. It's just that I kind of went the extra mile to try and help him out. And now, well, everyone involved in this just seems a little bit seedy. I'm not sure I want to do any more. For that matter, I don't think there's anything else I can do.'

'Then don't. I mean, it's a shame we haven't got a real, proper mystery again. But it sounds as if you've done all you can. Let Vanni sort it out.' She gave me a peck on the cheek. 'The beans look lovely. Very green. And I'll put some nice Jethro Tull on for you.' She'd never used the words 'nice' and 'Jethro Tull' in the same sentence before. I thought to myself again what a lucky man I was . . .

Dario arrived about thirty minutes later, and we munched through polenta discs together as he showed us his latest batch of photos of little Emily. Federica smiled politely throughout.

'Aww, just look at her, Fede.'

'I'm looking, Nathan.'

'Isn't she lovely, though?'

Fede took my face in her hands. 'Okay, I don't know what you've done with him, but I want my old Nathan back, and I want him back right now.' Then Dario looked hurt, and she relented. 'She is lovely,' she smiled.

'Okay,' I said, 'I'm going back to the kitchen. You two can fight over control of the stereo in the meantime. If it's any help, Gramsci is going through a bit of an Alan Parsons Project phase.'

I poured some vegetable stock into a pan, and chucked in the asparagus. Just a minute or two, nothing more. Then the peas, then the beans. Just a couple of minutes more. Then the monkfish. Cover and cook, just five minutes. Then I poured the resulting stew into three bowls and served it up. Get this wrong, even by a few minutes, and you'd end up with a chewy piece of fish on a bed of stewed and overcooked vegetables. Get it right, and your friends would say lovely things about you.

Dario grinned, and took a sip of wine. 'He's very good, isn't he?'

Fede smiled at me. 'He is. That was very good, *caro*. Especially the very green bits.'

I had to agree. 'The green bits, I think, really made it.' I took the plates out to the kitchen and washed up. Then I cleared away the debris of the shopping. The morning's mail was still in the empty bag of vegetables. I put the electricity bill to one side and dropped the supermarket newsletter straight into recycling. I scrunched up the flyers and was about to drop them in as well, when something caught my eye. I unscrunched them. One of them was for a pawn shop in Mestre which may or may not have been a front for money-laundering. The other was for the exhibition on Lazzaretto Vecchio.

I smoothed it out. An image of the lazzaretto against the background of the lagoon, together with a list of participating artists and their works. Considine's name was at the top. His piece in the British pavilion, I remembered, was called *Seven by Seven by Seven*. This was simpler, *Seven by Seven*. The opening date and time had been scribbled out, and underneath someone had written *Friday 20 May 2015. Midnight.*

My own, personal *vernissage*.

I shook my head. Whoever you are, I don't think so. I turned it over. The reverse was blank, except for the words *Help me, Nathan.*

Oh hell.

I checked my watch. Nearly nine o'clock. How the hell was I going to manage this? Dario and Fede, I knew, would try and talk me out of it. Or, worse, they would insist on coming with me. Moreover, Fede was supposed to be staying over with me tonight. Somehow, I needed a way of steering us back to the Lido.

I tore open the blank envelope. It was a postcard. I saw the image on the card, and nearly cried out. Then the thought struck me that it might just be a solution. I folded the flyer away, and ran back into the living room. 'Fede, Dario. I think I've got a problem.'

'You've forgotten your quarterly tax return?' said Dario.

'Again,' whispered Federica, but not quite *sotto voce* enough.

I shook my head. 'No, this is different. This is *weird* different. Take a look at this.' I waved the postcard at them. 'It arrived in the post this morning. Or, more to the point, it was slipped under the door this morning.' I passed it around. A gaunt, cloaked figure, bearing a scythe, astride a horse, flying through the clouds; leading a host of demonic, bat-winged creatures.

'Gustav Doré,' said Federica.

'I thought it might be. The Angel of Death?'

'Almost certainly.'

'Where's it from? The *Inferno*?'

She shook her head. 'No. Not the *Inferno*. Not the *Rime of the Ancient Mariner*. I'm really not sure. Perhaps his series on Edgar Allan Poe?'

'It's from his illustrated Bible. Round about 1870, I think,' said Dario. There was silence around the table.

'You what?' I said.

'He illustrated a French edition of the Bible. This is called "The Vision of Death". From *Revelation*, the opening of the fourth seal. "And I looked, and beheld a pale horse: and his name that sat on him was Death, and Hell followed with him".'

'Yes yes yes but . . . how?' I asked.

'It's the cover of Hawkwind's "Angels of Death".' He looked puzzled. 'You should know that, Nathan.'

'I know the track. There's an album called *Angels of Death*?'

'Sure. It's a compilation of their three RCA albums.'

'*Sonic Attack. Church of Hawkwind. Choose Your Masques.* That explains it. I had the three of them already.'

'Ah, you see there was a distribution problem in Italy. *Church of Hawkwind* didn't come out over here until the 1990s. But there are four tracks from it on the compilation.'

'I didn't think you were a fan?'

'Not really, but there's usually a track or two on each album worth listening to.'

'Any bonus tracks on there?'

He shook his head. 'No. Nothing at all. If you've got the originals you don't need it. But the cover's really good.'

We stopped talking. We became aware that Federica was staring at us. Not in a good way.

She closed her eyes and held her hands in front of her face, palms outwards. 'Can we just stop talking about this? Please?'

'Sorry,' we both said.

'Good. So what is this? A warning? A threat?'

'Someone's stuck a picture of a man with a scythe under my door. It might not be a threat, but it'll do until something better comes along.'

'I don't think so,' said Dario.

'It's a man with a scythe, Dario. A man with a scythe.'

'Sure.' He poured himself some more wine then patted my arm. 'If you ask me, it's this guy Nicolodi. You've had two big fights with him in the last few days, right? And he knows all about that guy losing his head and the picture found in his pocket. He knows where you live because you gave him your card. So he walks by one afternoon, sticks this through your door in the hope that it'll scare you.'

I drew a deep breath, and nodded. 'You're probably right. It does make sense.'

'Almost,' said Federica. 'With one problem. Where did he get the card?'

Dario shrugged. 'Does it matter?'

'Yes it does.' She reached over for the card, and turned it over so that the reverse side was facing us. 'Where's it from? There's no way to tell?'

'It could have come from anywhere,' I said. 'Any church or gallery shop in the city.'

'Maybe. Maybe not. Because I'm absolutely certain this image isn't in any church or gallery in Venice. Which means whoever bought it must have done so before they came here. Before they ever met you. Now why would someone do that?'

Dario shook his head. 'The Accademia. The Cini foundation. The Correr museum. There must be others. Any of them might be selling copies of this.'

'They might. But I'm not so sure about that.'

'You know,' I said, 'I like Dario's theory. It's kind of reassuring.'

'It is,' said Federica, 'but there's something not quite right about it. I don't think that postcard was bought in this city. Now who travels around with a copy of "The Vision of Death" with them, just on the offchance?'

'People who listen to too much Black Sabbath?' suggested Dario. I smiled, but he continued, 'Or, I don't know, weirdos . . . murderers . . . serial killers . . .'

'That's not helping, Dario.' I stopped him before he could go any further. We sat in silence for a few moments.

'So what are we going to do?' said Federica.

'I'll call Vanni in the morning. I know it's not much to go on, but it's all I can think of.'

She nodded. 'Okay, do that. But why not call him now?'

'He won't be there now. It'll just be some cop that I don't know. And I'll have to tell him that someone's sent me a picture of a man with a scythe. And I'll seem like a mad person. I mean, in the morning it'll probably all seem like nonsense. And Dario's probably right.'

'Mr Blake-Hoyt was found beheaded with a picture of Judith beheading Holofernes in his pocket. And all that could have been a coincidence. You get attacked with a glass arrow, and a picture of Saint Sebastian is stuck in your pocket. Stretching the definition of coincidence. Now you get a picture of the Angel of Death slid under your door. And now that doesn't seem like a coincidence any more.'

I nodded. I opened my mouth to speak, and closed it again. They'd both given me an opportunity here, but I was going to have to lie to them.

'You all right, buddy?' asked Dario.

I shook my head. 'No. No, I'm really not.' I paused, 'Fed, is your mum still with you?'

'She went home yesterday, why?'

'I'm just thinking – you know the idea was for you to stay over tonight?'

'Yes. Ah, I know what you're thinking. You'd like us to go back to the Lido?'

I breathed a sigh of relief, but not for the reason they were thinking. 'It's stupid, I know, but—'

'No, it's not. I don't really think we're going to be horribly murdered in our beds tonight, but it's not stupid at all. So would you feel better if we headed off back to my place?'

'Thanks,' I breathed. 'What about Dario?'

'Only if I get to choose the music.'

We all laughed. 'I'll head back to Mestre, *vecio*.'

'You sure?'

'Sure I'm sure. I haven't met any of these people. If there is a psycho stalking the streets I'm pretty sure he's not looking for me.'

'Thanks. That makes me feel better. A very little better.'

'Thanks for dinner.' He leant over and kissed Federica. 'Look after him, okay?'

'I'll call you tomorrow, Dario,' I said.

He grinned. 'I hope so.'

I finished the washing-up after he left. Fede fetched our coats. 'I think there's everything you need over there, isn't there?' I nodded. 'And you've got no surgery tomorrow, or any openings to go to?'

I shook my head. 'Just some translating. I can do that on your PC. I'll just drop back to feed the cat.'

'Good.' She hugged me. 'This is all silly, I'm sure. But why give this Francesco guy the satisfaction? In a day or two he'll be out of town, and this will all be done with.'

I hugged her back. 'Yep.' We moved to the stairs, only to be interrupted by a little *meep* from behind us. I turned. Gramsci stared up at us. 'I don't suppose we could bring—'

'Don't push it.'

I sighed. I grabbed the card again and held it up in front of his face. 'Okay buddy, if you see someone like this,' I pointed to the cloaked figure with the scythe, 'you make your own call okay? Take him down if you think you can, but it's okay to go and hide if you want.'

I locked up, and ten minutes later we were on the boat to the Lido. My personal opening view lay ahead of me.

Chapter 28

'Are you coming to bed?' said Federica.

I flopped down on to the sofa. 'Not yet. I think I'll stay up for a bit. I just need to clear my head.'

'Okay. Shall I stay up with you?'

I was prepared for this. 'That'd be great. I brought *Theatre of Blood* with me. I thought we might watch it again.'

'Are you mad? How is that going to make you feel better?'

'Trust me, it just will.'

She shook her head. 'You really are mad. Would it surprise you if I said I don't need to see it a second time?' I made a sad little face. 'Just keep all the doors closed, okay? I don't want all that screaming waking me up.'

'Thanks. I don't suppose you've got any cigarettes?'

She sighed, and reached into her handbag. 'Here you go. But not indoors.'

'I promise. You're a star.'

'I know.' Then she smiled, and bent over to kiss the top of my head. 'Are you all right?'

'I will be. Promise. I'll be through in a bit.'

I gave her thirty minutes, before I padded over to the bedroom door. I could hear gentle snoring from inside. Then

I crept over to the front door, pulled on my shoes, and let myself out as gently as I could. If she heard anything, she'd just assume I was going for a smoke and go back to sleep. Hopefully. Lazzaretto Vecchio was perhaps five minutes' walk from Fede's apartment on the Riva di Corinto. With a bit of luck she'd never know I'd been gone.

I made my way downstairs and through the garden of the *condominio*. As soon as I left the main gate, I could see the shadow of the island in the lagoon. A clear night, a moonlit night. I made my way along the street, empty of traffic at this hour. The shape of the island became clearer as my eyes adjusted. Then, out of the silence, from behind, came a great roar and two voices shrieking hysterically.

I jumped, and spun around. Two kids flashed past on a *motorino*, laughing and shouting. I bent over, placing my hands on my knees for support, and breathed deeply. Then I smiled. Daft kids, coming back from a late-night party. And riding way too fast. I hoped they'd make it home safely. I also hoped that the noise hadn't woken Federica.

I walked along the *riva*, staring out at the island more in hope than expectation of actually seeing something. Beyond the Lazzaretto, I could see the silhouette of Venice in the moonlight, a city of domes and spires. Silence now, occasionally broken by the sound of far-off traffic. Out on the lagoon, I could see tiny dots of light marking late-night water traffic.

I stood and stared out at Lazzaretto Vecchio. Directly beneath me, a temporary bridge – installed for the duration of the Biennale – led from the shores of the Lido to the island. I walked along the *riva* until I found a set of steps leading down to the shore.

My feet crunched on the shingle, breaking the stillness of the night as I made my way across the rocky beach. The bridge was closed with a low gate. I tested it with my hand. Locked, but it was a simple matter to clamber over.

I stopped halfway across, and looked back. Federica would be worried if she woke up to find me gone. And there'd be merry hell to pay if she ever found out I'd been telling her a pack of lies. So this was, almost certainly, an incredibly stupid thing to do. The postcard, I was convinced, was just Francesco playing head games with me. In fact, I'd probably given him the idea during our conversation the previous day. The invite was another matter. I'd given Paul 150 euros, following which he'd disappeared. What if he really had gone and done something stupid? Didn't I have some responsibility for that? There was, I thought, no choice but to go on.

The bridge led to a small landing stage, where visitors' boats could moor in the daytime. I made my way across some scrubby grassland, until I came to a rickety wooden bridge that led through a gap in the great brick walls and into the Lazzaretto itself. It seemed darker and quieter once I had crossed the bridge, an effect of the surrounding walls.

I had never been here before, and struggled to remember what I knew about it. It was the oldest of the quarantine stations in Venice, where incoming crews would remain for the statutory forty days before being allowed to proceed into the city proper. And then, during the era of the great plagues, it served as a house for the dying. Over fifteen hundred skeletons had been unearthed here during the restoration project and hundreds, perhaps thousands more, lay beneath my feet.

I found myself within a courtyard. A *vera da pozzo* sat in the middle whilst, to my left, stairs led up to a loggia. Straight ahead of me lay the monumental main entrance. San Rocco and San Sebastiano stood either side of San Marco, above a doorway leading into darkness. If you had been brought here during the period of the great plagues, this would be the last you would ever see of the outside world. *Abbandonate ogni speranza, voi ch'entrate.*

I had no idea where to go or what, if anything, I was looking for. Perhaps if I was higher up, I could get a better idea of the layout of the place. I took the stairs upwards, my shoes crunching on the crumbling stone. The entrance to the loggia itself was blocked by a padlocked iron grille. I gave it a shake, but it wouldn't shift. Probably just as well, given the chances were it was closed for safety reasons.

I turned around, and gave a start. Down below, I could see a shadow in the courtyard. Someone standing just by the entrance. Watching me.

My throat was dry, but I managed to cry out. 'Paul?'

The figure took a step towards me. I instinctively stepped back, and my feet slipped on the crumbling stone, sending me sliding towards the edge of the staircase. I scrabbled for purchase, desperately trying to stop myself from falling over the edge. Then my hand closed around the iron grille and I was able to pull myself upright. I fought to control my breathing, and then forced myself to look down into the courtyard once more. The figure, if it had ever been there, was gone.

I made my way down the stairs, keeping myself as close to the wall as I could. The entrance to the main gallery lay open. I could see nothing inside. I cursed myself for not bringing a torch. Did I even own a torch? The one on my phone would have to do. I made my way towards the entrance and then, for a moment, my foot slipped on a smooth surface beneath me and, as I tried to regain my balance, my feet scrunched against gravel, the noise ringing out against the silence. I looked down to see what I had slipped on. A black, polished surface reflecting the feeble light from my phone. I bent to take a closer look. The surface was semi-obscured with dirt and gravel, but I could still see some writing etched into it. I wiped away the debris and bent closer to read.

Death was here.

I stumbled back. *Calm, Nathan.* Presumably it was part of this year's Biennale installation, or the remnants of one from a previous year. I moved forward again, and stopped on the threshold. The door was open, with a sign affixed with the usual list of prohibitions for a tourist site. No eating and drinking, no smoking, no dogs. Okay, that was a good sign. If visitors were allowed in then the basic structure must be safe, and I wouldn't have to worry about the floor giving way beneath me.

I stepped inside. High windows in the walls let in the moonlight, which was of slightly more use than the dim light from my phone. I switched it off to save the battery, and paused to let my eyes become accustomed to the small amount of natural light. And then, in the moonlight, I saw seven motionless figures facing me. I stepped back, shaken. The figures repeated my motion. I stepped forward again. The seven figures did the same. My eyes sharpened, and I laughed. Seven figures to my left, seven figures to my right. The entire space was a hall of mirrors, presumably part of Considine's exhibition. *Seven by Seven*, of course.

I made my way through the gallery. On the other side lay another doorway, this time leading into pitch-blackness. I stepped through, switched my phone back on, and, again, gave my eyes time to adjust.

The light helped only a modest amount and I paused every few metres just to scan the floor ahead of me for obstacles. I turned around. I could still see the entrance back to the main gallery illuminated by the moonlight. Good. As long as I could see that, I'd be able to find my way out again. I moved further into the darkness; perhaps ten or twenty metres.

There was no sound at all now. 'Paul,' I called. The sound echoed back at me and made me start. I counted to ten, and then called again. 'Paul. It's Nathan.'

Silence. Absolute silence. I screwed my eyes shut, praying that when I opened them again I'd find myself back in bed. I opened them again. Almost complete darkness. I directed my phone at the floor, and moved forward a few metres, then swung the light to my right, and then to my left. Something on the wall. Some marks in red. I moved a little closer. Writing. Possibly in Arabic, but I couldn't be sure. I shone the light further along the wall. The image of a figure, scratched into the stone. An angel. Scrawled there centuries ago by one of the ill-fated inhabitants.

I moved forward again. More fragments of writing, some of it intelligible. Just names, of people and ships and cities, the work of bored seamen in quarantine, wanting to leave a little record that they'd passed this way. They must have been older than the angel, from the time when the island was merely a place of quarantine, and not a house for the dying.

And then something more abstract. In red, like the other markings, but this time a long red Jackson Pollock-style spray of colour. I followed the curve with my torch until it ended in a larger, deeper patch of red. Rothko, this time, not Pollock. And then, as I moved the beam of light down, I saw a dark shape on the floor. I moved closer, holding my makeshift torch out in front of me. And then the beam illuminated the bloodied face of Francesco Nicolodi, his eyes wide open and face contorted in a terrible grin.

I screamed, and dropped my phone. There was a brief clatter of plastic upon stone, and then absolute silence. And absolute darkness.

Chapter 29

'Francesco. It's Nathan. Can you hear me?'

Silence.

'Francesco, are you all right? Can you speak?'

Silence.

I felt the fear rising within me but strove to keep my voice calm. 'Francesco, I don't know if this is a joke. I don't know if you're just trying to scare me. But if you are, then well done, yes, I'm scared. Okay. But just say something. Please.' And then it struck me. The silence was absolute. I was, perhaps, less than a metre away from him and yet there was no sound of his breathing.

I turned around. Slowly, ever so slowly. There was, I knew, a source of light at the end of the corridor. Find that, and I could find my way out again, get home and ring the police. And in the midst of the blackness I could indeed see a pale square of blue light to guide me out. Then, nightmarishly, I saw the square grow smaller and smaller and then disappear altogether. From far off, there came the faint thud of a door closing.

Absolute silence. And absolute darkness.

Calm. Keep calm. What's the worst that can happen? Someone will be here in the morning. Just keep calm and wait. And then I was aware that the silence was not absolute. There was a scratching and a scrabbling from the walls.

Pantagane. Rats.

Perhaps it was the thud of the door closing that had disturbed them. I didn't know. Carefully, oh so carefully, I dropped to my knees and pressed my hands to my ears to block out the sound. Rats don't attack people, I repeated to myself. Rats don't attack people. They'd only been stirred up by the sound of the door closing. But who had closed the door?

I removed my hands from my ears, trying to ignore the sound of the rats in the walls and listen for footsteps instead. Slowly, the scrabbling and scratching fell silent and, again, I was alone in the darkness and silence.

I fought down the panic. Keep thinking, Nathan. Francesco isn't going to hurt you now. The rats won't hurt you. Probably, the rats won't hurt you. There are no footsteps, therefore no one is coming. All you need is a source of light and you can get out again. A cigarette lighter? I ran through my pockets, and swore. An image came to mind of it lying on my bedside table. The thought brought Federica to mind again, and, again, I fought down the panic and guilt.

Light. Get the lights on.

I placed my hands on the ground. I swept my right hand slowly along the surface of the floor. Not slowly enough. My fingertips sliced across something, and I snatched my fingers back. I placed them to my lips. Blood. I screwed my eyes shut, and tried not to let the tears flow. It would be easy, so easy just to start screaming. But that wouldn't get me home.

I tried again. Slower this time. Sweeping my hand across the floor hadn't worked. I tried moving my hand up and down and around, in a patting motion. My palm came to rest on something round, something smooth. I tightened my fingers. A handle of some kind, possibly wood. I moved my hand upwards, gently relaxing and tightening my grip all the while. The feeling of the surface changed. Not wood any longer, but smoother. Metal? I carefully moved my thumb from the centre of the surface to the left. Sharp. A blade.

I raised my hand again and continued the patting motion and then, to my blessed relief, it landed on something that felt like plastic. I brought it to me and ran my fingers over it. The spongy feel of a cheap plastic keypad. But too light. I ran my fingers over the back. Hollow. The phone had come apart when I'd dropped it.

Okay. It was a start. I dropped my hands to the floor again, and continued the sweeping, patting motions. Somewhere in this area would be the battery. It was entirely possible, of course, that it had bounced metres away. In which case I could be here all night. I tried not to think about that.

My fingers came to rest on something soft and damp. Cloth. A jacket, a shirt? Something was clinging to my fingers. My blood? Francesco's blood? And then my fingers encountered something solid. Rectangular, indentations at one end. The battery.

I had never, ever felt so grateful for not having a smart-phone. If I'd dropped one of those on to a stone floor, I'd be spending the rest of the night in darkness. But I'd dropped my cheap thirty-euro mobile time and time again. I knew that it would break apart every time. I also knew that it could be put back together every time.

I snapped the battery in. Nothing happened. I gently prised it out again, and ran my finger around it searching for the contacts. I tried again, and was rewarded with the most beautiful sound in the world as it plinged into life and the screen briefly illuminated. Long enough for me to activate the torch.

I held my breath and shone it around me. The beam was too faint for me to see down the end of the corridor, but I at least had an idea as to where the door might be. At the limits of the beam, squat black shapes skittered away into the darkness. I swung it back into my immediate vicinity, and on to my left hand. The fingertips were bleeding, sliced as if by a razor blade. I shone the beam in the direction of Francesco, and braced myself.

The face was as I remembered. The eyes open, the lips clenched in a terrible rictus grin. His hands were raised above his head, tied to each other and lashed around a spike driven into the wall perhaps just one metre off the floor. A blade protruded from his neck. Metal? No, not metal. A great curved blade had been driven through him, from one side of his neck to the other. The force of the blow had caused the blade to shear in two, and half of it lay on the ground where I had opened my fingertips on it. I forced myself to look closer. Not metal, no. Glass. A glass blade. A glass scythe.

I gagged, and turned away to vomit. And then I crawled away, my telephone shaking in my hand, all the way to the door. It still opened, thank God. Blown shut by the wind? And then I ran through the door, through the gallery, out of the Lazzaretto and into the clean air and shining moonlight.

I ran over the bridge, vaulted the gate, and tore along the riva and back through the condominial gardens. My keys shook and rattled in my hands as I raced up the stairs, back into the apartment and back into the bedroom where I collapsed sobbing in front of an uncomprehending Federica.

Chapter 30

'How are your fingers?'

I looked down at them, as if to check they were still there. The cuts had been clean, but I'd thought it best to swab them with surgical spirit and plaster them up. 'They're okay. Not painful. Going to make typing a bit difficult for a few days though.'

Vanni nodded. 'Nathan,' he said, 'why the hell didn't you call me before going over there?'

'It just seemed,' I fumbled for the words, 'so pointless. What was I going to say? As far as I knew, it was just Considine wanting to talk. Wanting some help.'

'You think he wrote those words on the flyer?'

'I don't know. I thought so. I gave him some money, and then he disappeared. I was starting to worry he'd fallen into his old bad habits . . . drugs, booze, whatever. And that would be my fault.'

'And what about that card you received? The man with the scythe.'

'I was going to call you about that in the morning. But last night it just seemed too difficult to explain.'

'You mean you think we wouldn't have taken it seriously?'

'Not really, no.'

He nodded. 'Well, to be honest, we probably wouldn't. Okay, let's just run through a few things. The man in the courtyard. Can you describe him at all?'

'Not at all. I can't even be sure that it was a man. He was about my height. Maybe wearing a long coat, I don't know. He was just a shadow. The only other thing was – the way he moved. He took a step towards me. Just to see what I'd do. Then I slipped. I took my eyes off him for a second, and then he was gone. It's as if it was some kind of challenge to me.'

'That's it?'

'That's it.'

'Mmm. Doesn't help much. Tell me about Francesco Nicolodi.'

'I don't know that much. There was something not right about him though. He said he was a journalist, but I couldn't find anything published by him prior to that article in *The Times*. He was staying in some flophouse over in Dorsoduro for a few days, and then checked into one of the most expensive hotels in town.'

Vanni nodded. 'So you'd been following him for a couple of days? Checking him out?'

I paused. 'Yes. Yes, I suppose so.'

'Any reason why?'

'*Boh*. I guess I was just trying to help Considine. Francesco was one of the first witnesses on the scene . . . at the pavilion, you know? I just thought I'd talk to him again. Just to see if there was anything else he might remember. And then, well, I kind of got sucked in, I suppose.'

'So you followed him around the city?'

'I didn't follow him. I went to the two hotels he was staying in.'

'And on the last two occasions you met him, you had a fight.'

'Not a fight. We exchanged a few strong words, that's all.'

'Then you went to meet him in the early hours of the morning, alone, on the island of Lazzaretto Vecchio.'

'I didn't go to meet him. I found him.' We sat in silence for a few seconds. 'What are you trying to say, Vanni?'

'Nat,' he never called me Nat, 'we know you followed Nicolodi around the city for two days. We know you argued on the last two occasions that you met. We know you were the first to find him, late last night, at a location that you knew would be deserted.' He paused. 'And we have a murder weapon with your fingerprints on it.'

I went cold. 'Wait a minute. Now wait a minute, Vanni. I told you, I cut my fingers when I was reaching around in the dark. And then I grabbed the handle and the blade of the scythe. You don't really think I had anything to do with this? Come on, we've known each other for years. You can't think I had anything to do with this.'

'I don't, Nat. Really, I don't. But there are other people who would very much like to think that you did.'

'What do you mean?'

'Look, we've had two deaths in the last ten days. Both linked with the Biennale. There are two hypotheses. One is that the first death was an accident, and the second death was down to you. The other is that we have a serial killer. Now tell me, which is the easiest solution for everyone?'

'So what are you saying? Am I under arrest? Do I need a lawyer?'

He shook his head. 'No. I'll do what I can to help. I promise. But in the meantime, you step right back from this. Right back. You go home, you do your translations, you help people with lost passports. That's it. You understand?'

I nodded.

'You understand?' he repeated.

'I do, Vanni. I do. What about—' I paused.

'What about Paul Considine?' I nodded. 'Let me worry about him.'

'Do you know where he is?' Vanni said nothing. 'Okay, I understand. I'll just stay out of things.' I half rose from my chair but he motioned me back down again.

'There's one other thing, Nathan. Vincenzo Scarpa came to see us yesterday.'

I gave a watery smile. 'Let me guess. He wants to know my address so he can send his business associates around for a chat?'

'A bit more serious than that. He says you followed him a few days ago, locked him inside the *ovovia* on the Calatrava Bridge and then came up with some threatening story about a serial killer using methods found in famous works of art.'

'I wouldn't put it quite like that.'

Vanni reached into his desk drawer, and drew out an envelope. 'Then yesterday, he found this in his mailbox.' He opened the envelope, and took out a postcard. He pushed it across the desk to me.

A man, slumped in a bathtub. His head bound in a towel, his eyelids drooping as if in sleep. His right hand, clutching a quill pen, trails along the floor. The smile upon his face is almost beatific, yet his chest is stained with blood, and a bloodied knife lies upon the floor.

Jacques-Louis David, *The Death of Marat*.

'My God. Oh my God.' Vanni said nothing. 'What do you want me to do?'

'I want you to do exactly what you promised, Nathan. Go home. And do nothing.'

'But what about,' I gestured at the postcard, 'this?'

'Leave that to us. In the meantime, go home. Do nothing.'

I nodded my head.

He reached across the desk and patted me on the shoulder. 'Thanks, Nathan. Try not to worry about it.'

Federica was waiting outside for me. She looked tired and drawn. 'Are you okay?' I said.

She nodded. 'Tired. I don't think I'll be going up any scaffolding today. How about you?'

'Fine.' I said.

Silence hung in the air between us. 'Are you sure?'

'Yes, it's fine. I just told Vanni exactly what happened.'

'And so everything's okay now?'

'Yes. Well, there are still a few things that might need to be checked out.'

'So it's not "fine" then?'

'Well it is, basically.'

She sighed, and looked around the reception area of the *Questura*. 'I'm tired. Feels like I've been here for hours. Let's go and get a coffee.' We walked to the same bar on the corner of Piazzale Roma where I'd shared a coffee and a cigarette with Anna a week previously. The city was starting to come to life now, as commuters from Mestre crammed themselves on to *vaporetti*.

Fede tipped two sachets of sugar into her coffee. She stirred it clockwise. And then anticlockwise. Then she sipped at it. 'So, tell me all about it.'

I shrugged. 'There really isn't very much to say. Vanni just told me to step back a bit. Concentrate on the day job.'

She paused. 'Nothing more?'

I hesitated. 'Nothing more. Nothing important, anyway.'

She slammed two euros down on the counter. 'Nothing important. Okay, let's go.' And she left without a backward glance.

I hurried after her as she made her way across Piazzale Roma. 'We're not getting the boat then?'

'I'm going to work, remember. You can do what you like. And I don't want to be stuck on a *vaporetto* having a row in front of other people.'

'Oh. Are we having a row then?' I was finding it hard to keep up with her. I reached out for her arm, but she shook it off. 'Come on,' I said, 'what's the matter?'

She stopped and turned on me. 'Okay, Nathan, I'll tell you what the matter is. Something is wrong, something's worrying you. But you won't tell me what it is. Just that "it's all fine".'

'It is all fine.'

'Shut up. Please, just shut up.' Her voice was cracking. 'You went off on your little adventure last night without even waking me up. Vanni has obviously said something to you, something serious, and you won't tell me what it is. Stop cutting me out of everything. Why can't you be honest with me? And why didn't you at least tell me where you were going last night?'

'I didn't want to worry you.'

'Right. So when I woke up and found you weren't there, what was I supposed to think?'

'I don't know. I didn't think.'

'You didn't think. Exactly. At first I thought you'd gone outside for a smoke. Then when you didn't come back, I didn't know what to do. Were you in trouble? Should I call the police? Or do you just have another woman?'

'Good God, no, of course I don't.' Our voices were raised now, and it was evident that people were listening to us. A full-blown row in the middle of the street. Well done, Nathan.

'No. No, I don't think you do. But why will you not let me in?'

'As I said, I didn't want to worry you.'

'Well, that's not working, because I am worried. You know what the problem is, Nathan? It's that you won't grow up.'

'What?' I was genuinely losing the thread of the conversation now.

'You won't grow up. It's all just a lovely game for you now, isn't it? You've got your job, you've got your cat, you've got beers and rock music with Dario. And now you've got another little adventure. The one thing that you won't do is let me in on any of this. Just jokey little asides and "don't worry about it". Well, I am worried about it. I'm worried you're going to get hurt.'

'Well, thanks for that.'

'Quiet. Just quiet. I'm worried that you're going to get hurt, or at the least end up in trouble, but I can cope with that. What I can't cope with is you not being honest with me. You lied to me last night, again and again and again.'

I stopped walking. I closed my eyes, and nodded. 'You're right. I know you're right. I'm just—' Again the words would not come. 'Look, all I can say is that I don't want to worry you. I'm sorting all this out.'

'Fine. Well give me a call when you've sorted your life out.'

'Look,' I pleaded, 'can't we just talk about this later? If you come round about seven, I'll cook and—'

'I don't think so. I've got a lot of work on at the moment, I'll need to do some tonight.'

'No worries. Shall I just come round to yours then, I can cook dinner and you can work.'

'It's not a good idea. I'm busy. As I said, you sort out your little mystery. Sort things out with Vanni. And if you can do all that, then give me a call and we'll see if we can sort out our relationship. If we think we can.'

'Whoah. Wait a minute, wait a minute. What do you mean "if we think we can"?'

She stopped walking. 'It means what it means, Nathan. It may be working for you at the moment, but it's not working for me. You need to decide if you want to have a proper, grown-up relationship. And that means being honest with me. Maybe it means being honest with yourself as well. So when you've decided what you want, call me.'

'You're, what, leaving me?'

She shook her head. 'I don't know. I'm saying come back when you've decided what you want.'

'But I love you.'

'And I love you too, *tesoro*. But right now I don't like you very much. And I have to go to work.'

And with that, she was gone, leaving me standing alone in the midst of the hordes of tourists in the Campo dei Frari.

Chapter 31

'You've done *what!*' said Dario, his beer halfway to his mouth.

'Pretty much as I said. Implicated myself in a murder case. Very probably going to lose my job as consul. Oh, and Federica's left me.' I lit up a cigarette. 'Still, you've got to laugh, haven't you?'

Dario flapped away at the smoke. 'I thought you were giving those things up?'

'I was. Doesn't seem much point now.'

'Ah, Nathan . . .'

'I mean, if it wasn't for the self-medication I'm sure I'd be feeling a lot worse.'

'So what have you been doing all day?'

'Sulking, mainly. Went back to bed for a bit. Smoked too much. Listened to some Leonard Cohen to cheer myself up.'

'So what are you going to do now?'

I took out my diary and flicked through it. 'Let me see. After you go home, I've got a couple of hours of drinking too much scheduled. Then there's a late-night horror on RAI to watch. Following which, I think falling asleep on the sofa and waking up in my clothes seems like a good idea.'

'Nat. Stop this. This isn't helping.'

'I'm fine Dario, really. Things could be worse. It could be raining.'

Dario breathed deeply and put his head in his hands. I lit up another cigarette. He stretched across the table, yanked it from my fingers and ground it underfoot. I reached for the packet but he was too fast for me and snatched it from my grasp. Then slowly and deliberately he crushed it in his hand, and dropped it back on the table.

'Dario?'

He said nothing, but just rubbed his face. And then stared directly at me. I tried to hold his gaze but failed. Finally, he spoke. 'Have you thought that she might be right?'

'What do you mean?'

'Look at you. Just look at you. She was the best thing that ever happened to you, and you've broken it. And instead of working out just how you can put things back together again, you're behaving like a self-pitying little shit.'

'That's a bit unfair. You've forgotten the desperate attempts at gallows humour.'

'See what I mean? She was right. You need to grow up. Come on, what are you going to do? Sort things out, or just smoke, drink and sulk for the rest of your life?'

'Well, now you mention—'

'And if you say that sounds like a pretty good idea I really will hit you. Do I look like I'm joking?' And again, he stared directly into my eyes. We sat in silence for a few seconds.

'Dario. You're my friend. You're my best friend.'

'I know. And what does that mean?'

'I don't understand.'

'It means that sometimes it's all Pink Floyd and one too many beers, and me knowing that you'll probably buy cigarettes on the way home because you know I don't like you smoking but I don't really care because my buddy is happy and he's going home to snuggle up to lovely Federica. And other times, it means being honest and telling you that your haircut doesn't suit you or you really need to buy a new jacket. And other times it means telling you that you're being a selfish, self-indulgent asshole and you need to snap out of it before you really screw your life up.'

'Wow. You're pretty sure of yourself.'

'Yes I am.' He got to his feet. 'I'll get these.' He walked inside, and returned a few seconds later. 'Okay, this is what you're going to do. You're going to go straight upstairs to bed. You're going to sleep on it. And then in the morning you're going to have a serious think about how to sort this all out. Federica, and the case.'

'The case? Dario, there is no case. Vanni told me to step back.'

'The police won't be stepping back on this, *vecio*. Trust me, if they can pin this on you they will. Vanni might not want to but others will.' He patted me on the shoulder. 'Okay, I'm off. Speak tomorrow, eh?'

'What about you?'

'I'm going home and I'm going to think about how to sort your life out. That's what friends are for, right?' And he walked off, down the Street of the Assassins, and into the night.

I went inside, and up to the bar. 'I'll have a Negroni for the road, please, Ed.'

He shook his head. 'Sorry Nathan, I can't do that.'

'What? What do you mean you can't do that?'

'Your pal Dario. He said he'd kick my arse if I sold you anything else tonight.'

'What is this, an intervention?'

'Maybe. But he said he was just being a pal. Got me thinking that maybe I should be one too. Just go home, Nathan. And I'll see you for breakfast tomorrow, on the house. Okay?'

I nodded. 'Tomorrow.' I turned to go, and then looked back. 'Thanks.' My voice cracked, and I hurried out of the door before he could see my face, and made my way upstairs to the flat.

My phone started ringing as I turned the keys in the lock. I fished it out of my pocket as I made my way inside, gently prodding Gramsci back up the stairs with my foot. Federica? Please let it be Federica. Or Dario. Or even Eduardo, telling me I'd left something down at the bar and giving me an excuse to go back. Then I looked at the number and my heart sank.

'Sutherland?'

'Mr Ambassador. How are you?'

'Good, good. Well, actually not. You seem to be in the news again.'

'Ah. You've heard then?'

'We've heard. Look, Sutherland, this is a bit embarrassing for everyone . . . in fact it's very embarrassing for me . . . but we're wondering if you need to step back from things for the moment.'

'What?'

'It's nothing personal, please do believe me on that but – well, this is twice in ten days now that you've been in the newspapers. And perhaps it doesn't make us look all that good.'

'Ambassador Maxwell, please, you were in the pavilion at the same time as me. You can't believe I'm involved in any of this.'

'Oh, of course not, of course not. But until it's sorted, we think it might be best if you just stepped back a bit. Just direct any queries to the consul in Mestre . . . It is Mestre, isn't it?'

'Yes,' I answered, automatically.

'Good. And then just let the police do their thing.'

'So what are you doing? Are you sacking me? Sacking me from my voluntary job?'

'Nothing like that, Sutherland. Just let our chap in Mestre take over for now, and then, hopefully, when it's all cleared up, well, we can all have another think, eh?'

'Sure. Of course.'

'Good man. Good man.' I said nothing. 'Well, I won't keep you any longer. I'm sure you've got plans for the evening. Who knows, this might even be rather a nice little break for you.' He hung up.

I slipped the phone into my pocket, closed my eyes and breathed deeply. There came a little *miaow* from around my ankles. I bent down and scratched Gramsci behind the ears. 'We'll be all right, eh, buddy? We've still got each other, haven't we?' He yowled, and slunk from the room.

I went through to the office and looked at the papers strewn on the desk. The front pages from last week's newspapers. Scribbled notes on Nicolodi, Fitzgerald and Considine. The postcard of 'The Vision of Death'. The invitation to Lazaretto Vecchio.

Somewhere, in the midst of it, was the answer. But I was tired now, dog-tired. I'd sort it out in the morning. Sort the case out, then sort my life out. And then everything would be fine. Everything would, probably, be fine.

Chapter 32

The phone rang at about 6.30. I rubbed the sleep from my eyes, and stared at the screen, waiting for my vision to clear so I could make out the number.

'Dario?'

'*Ciao, vecio*. How are you doing? Did you take my advice?'

'Yes I did. Still, it's a bit early.'

'Well, we've got a lot to do.'

'I know, I know. But beyond making coffee and feeding the cat, I don't know where to start.'

'You'll think of something, Nat. I know you will.'

'And what about you?'

'Working from home.'

'On a Sunday?'

'Yeah, we've got a project going live next week. I've got test plans and all sorts of crap to review and sign off. I'll sort out your love life and save you from prison in my lunchbreak. I'll see you later, okay?' He hung up.

It was tempting to turn over and go straight back to sleep but Dario, I knew, had called specifically to make sure I was up and about. Besides, I had to admit, I actually felt pretty good after taking his advice of the previous night.

I showered and shaved, wincing a little as the water hit the wounds in my fingertips and shoulder. And the little shock of pain seemed to spark an idea. Glass arrows. A glass scythe. Like the ones in Considine's exhibition. Were they actually the same ones? I had no idea if it would lead to anything, but it might be worth investigating.

The only problem was, how to get access to the exhibition space. The police, I was pretty sure, would have finished with it, but it was technically a crime scene and so would remain under lock and key for months. How was I going to get in there?

There was one way. I didn't like the idea, but I couldn't think of a better one. I pulled my jacket on, and gave Gramsci a little scratch under the chin as I headed for the door. He snatched at my hand. The one certain thing in an uncertain universe. It made me feel a lot better.

I hopped on the next boat to Giardini. There were seats outside, but I preferred to sit alone on the inside, and think. I had a plan, but it wasn't much of one. And it could jeopardise a friendship.

I still had time to kill before the pavilions officially opened, so I took a quick coffee at Paradiso and ran through my plan one more time. Then I made my way through the gardens to the French pavilion. It struck me that I had no idea if Gheorghe would even be working that morning. Still, he was smart and he was local, so the odds were he'd have tried to bag the cooler early-morning shifts for himself.

There were a few early-morning visitors milling around the space between the German, British and French pavilions. The police tape, I noticed, had been removed from outside the

British exhibition. I ran up the steps just in case, against all my expectations, the doors were unlocked. No such luck. They were securely padlocked. I made my way back down again, and tagged on to a tour group as they made their way into the French pavilion.

Four men, in white tie, stood in the four corners of the room. Four women, in evening dresses, stood facing the centre of each of the four walls. We appeared to be the first visitors of the day. Then, from somewhere, a band struck up the strains of Chet Baker's 'Let's Get Lost' and the four men and four women turned to face us, smiling. A statuesque blonde lady walked towards me, arms outstretched but, before she could reach me, Gheorghe had grabbed my hands and whirled me into the centre of the room. He had a broad smile on his face.

'Nathan! Thanks for coming.'

'A pleasure. You might have let me dance with the blonde lady, though.'

'Oh, her. She's nice, but she's not much of a dancer. Trust me, you're better off with me. Social foxtrot okay for you?'

'Oh yes. I just about remember how to do it. Listen, Gheorghe, I need to speak to you.'

'You mean you're not just here for the art?'

'Not exactly. Can you take a break for a few minutes? I mean, right now?'

We reached a corner, rock turned, and promenaded across the central space. 'It's a little tricky. But we always have a few spare dancers just in case. Let me go and ask. I'll just pass you over to Analiese.' Almost without breaking stride, he handed me over to the statuesque blonde.

'Analiese.'

'Nathan.'

'It's a pleasure.' She twirled me around. 'Do you come here often?'

'Well, to be honest, only every two years.'

'A shame. You dance quite well. You should come more often.'

'I think perhaps I should.' And then Gheorghe had seamlessly interposed himself between us, and danced us off towards the door. 'Oh. I was enjoying that.'

'Too much, Nathan. Your girlfriend will be jealous.' I felt a stab of guilt. It must have shown on my face. 'Have I said something wrong?'

'No. Not at all. Come on, let me buy you a coffee.' We walked back to Paradiso. I grabbed a table outside, overlooking the *bacino*, making sure we were a proper distance from other customers. 'What are you having?'

'*Marocchino*, please.'

'*Marocchino*?'

'Sure. If you're buying.'

'You know what, I'd like a *marocchino* too.' Bar staff, I'd noticed, were not always thrilled at having to make *marocchini*. Painstakingly building layers of coffee, chocolate and foam took time, and ordering one always made me feel like the man at the bar who waits until the very end of his order to ask for a Guinness. Still, it wasn't busy yet, and hopefully the *barista* wouldn't be too put out.

'You look happy, Gheorghe. I mean, properly happy.'

He grinned. 'Yeah. It's going well, Nat. I'm bringing some proper money in from this job. Then I'm picking up work from elsewhere. There's always people needing help with translation work. If it carries on like this I won't need to worry about carrying dogs over bridges any more.'

'That's brilliant.'

'It's taken a long time. I've been here, what, nearly three years now. But things are coming together.'

'I'm pleased for you. Really,' I said, and felt like a shit. Our overly complex coffees arrived. We stared at them for a moment, admiring the sheer precision and beauty of the stratigraphy, and then, as one, stirred in our sugar, turning them into a nondescript brown.

'So what's this about?' asked Gheorghe.

'I need a favour, Gheorghe. And I'm sorry, but I don't know who else I can ask.'

He sipped his coffee. 'Ask away, Nathan.'

'Okay. It's like this. And I know it sounds stupid. But in the British pavilion there are three walls with different weapons made of glass. Seven daggers. Seven arrows. Seven scythes. That's what there should be. I need someone to get in there and check for me.'

He put his coffee down. 'Seriously?'

'Seriously. I'm not crazy. It's important.'

'Okay.' He fell silent. Something was troubling him. I knew what it was. 'Nathan, why are you asking me?'

'Gheorghe, you work next door to the British pavilion. You're the obvious person to ask.'

He nodded. 'Is that all?'

'Of course.'

'Right. But just one thing. Why can't you do this yourself?'

'Gheorghe, if I get caught doing something like this I'll be in trouble. Big, big trouble.'

'And I won't be?'

'Yes, but . . .' My voice trailed off.

'So ask the East European guy to break the law, he's probably used to it. Is that what you were thinking?'

'No.' I could hear the edge of desperation in my voice. Because I knew he was right. 'I'm in trouble, okay. Maybe big trouble. But there have been two murders in the city in the past ten days, and maybe one attempted murder. All using glass as a weapon. It's long and difficult to explain, and I will tell you, I promise. When it's all over. But believe me, I really need to know what's in that building. And I don't know who else to ask.'

He swirled the dregs of his coffee. 'Okay. I'll do it.'

'You will?'

'Sure. You're a friend, after all.' Gheorghe Miricioiu had been in Italy for three years. He had done an endless series of crappy jobs trying to make ends meet and send money home. And now, when things were looking up for him, I was asking him to break the law.

'Thank you. Thank you.' I reached over and grabbed his hand. 'I'll make it worth your while, I promise.'

He snatched his hand back, as if burnt. 'You won't.'

'Sorry?'

He got to his feet, shaking his head. 'I'll do this for you, Nathan. But not for the money. I'll do this because you're a friend. You understand?' He walked off, without looking back.

I waved to the *barista*, and fumbled in my pocket for some change. 'I understand,' I whispered.

Chapter 33

There was little more to be done until Gheorghe got back to me and I had no idea how long that might be. I walked through the gardens, as far away from the British pavilion as I could find. Perhaps some mad art would clear my head. Austerity art from the Greeks, physical theatre from the Romanians, something scary with razor blades from the Serbs and something unintelligible from the Austrians. The Poles, at least, had a sixty-minute film and comfortable seats. It was getting hotter now, and I took my jacket off. The temptation was to grab a little snooze but that would be wasting the day and I knew I'd have to explain it to Dario.

I went to the café and treated myself to a small beer and a sad little sandwich. Fitzgerald – Nicolodi – Considine. The answer was to be found there somewhere.

Nicolodi was an alleged journalist, albeit one who never seemed to have published anything and who probably didn't even have an Italian journalist's card. I had no idea how easy it was to get accreditation as a journalist for the Biennale, but I was pretty sure you needed more than an empty website.

It was a place to start. There was, I knew, a press centre in the Padiglione Centrale. I made my way back through the gardens. The sun was high in the sky now, but the choice was to walk along the dusty gravel paths in direct sunlight, or to stick to the shadows where the mosquitoes lay in wait. The temporary discomfort seemed like the better option. The skies had been clear for days and Gwenant Pryce's grisly image of Lewis Fitzgerald would soon be materialising in its full gory glory.

The temperature dropped slightly inside the pavilion, and the air-conditioned interior of the press office was positively blissful. A young woman was seated behind a desk. Gothic-looking, with slightly too much eye-liner and black-painted fingernails, she reminded me of Lucia Popp's Queen of the Night. She inclined her head to one side. 'Can I help you?'

'Yes. I hope so. Well maybe?'

She gave me a closer look. 'I'm sorry. Have we met? I can't remember your name.'

'We might have. During *vernissage*. I'm Nathan Sutherland, the British honorary consul.' Or at least I am for the moment.

She nodded. 'Perhaps we did. How can I help?'

'Well I'd like to know how someone might get press accreditation for the Biennale.'

'I see. Is this for yourself?'

'It's, er, for a friend. In the UK.'

'For the film festival, next year's architecture Biennale or the art Biennale in two years?' She riffled through a sheaf of papers, and looked at me expectantly.

'No. For this one.'

She put the papers down, and looked at me as if I were simple-minded. 'It's too late for this one. Your friend should have submitted three months ago.'

'Oh. Oh dear.'

'Anyway, why does your friend need to come now? The openings have almost finished. He should have been here a week ago.'

'Well, he's just starting out. I think he thought it would be good experience. Or something.' I forced out a laugh. 'I'm just trying to help him out. As a friend. Is there no chance?'

She sighed, and passed over an application form. 'You need the name and address of the publication. A covering letter from the editor. You – your friend – needs to attach three published articles for review. And you also need to attach a copy of your press card.'

'Wow. That's quite difficult.'

'It needs to be. Otherwise every dilettante would be swarming over the gardens for months. For free.'

'Must be easier for online journalists, though.'

'No. It's the same thing.' She ticked them off on her fingers. 'Covering letter from the editor. Three articles. Press card.'

'Oh.' I paused. 'That's strange.' I shook my head, then folded the application form away within my jacket and stood up. 'Thank you for your time, Ms . . . ?'

'Wait a moment. What do you mean "that's strange"?'

'It's just that I met a guy on the opening day. At the British pavilion. He said something about, well . . .' I trailed off and did my best to look embarrassed.

'No, go on, please. What exactly did he say?'

'Well, it's probably nonsense. I think he might have had a glass or two of prosecco. But he told me how easy it was to blag a press pass for the whole Biennale. Just pretend to be from an online publication, he said, nobody ever checks. And bingo, you get into all the parties, all the events for fr—'

She waved her hands at me. 'Yes, yes. Sit down, please. Just a moment. Do you remember this man's name?'

'Erm, it'll come to me in a minute. Is it important?'

She tapped away furiously at a keyboard. 'Yes it is. If somebody's issued a press pass without properly checking, I'll make sure they're fired for it. Security implications, if nothing else.' She looked up at me. 'Well?'

'Let me think.' I was milking it now, but for the first time in days I was actually enjoying myself. 'Nicolini . . . Nicolucci . . . Nicoletto . . . Nicolodi. Yes, that's it. Nicolodi.'

She hammered away at the keyboard. 'First name?'

'Let me see. Filippo . . . Fiorenzo . . . Fortunato.'

She flapped her hands at me again. 'Never mind. I've found him. Francesco Nicolodi, is that right?'

'Ah yes, that's it.'

'The name's familiar.' I fervently hoped the stresses of her day job didn't leave her time to read the newspapers. She clicked away with her mouse, and then leaned back in her chair, looking visibly relieved. 'It seems *signor* Nicolodi was, as you might say in English, pulling your leg, Mr Sutherland.'

'He was?'

'He was. He didn't have a press pass. Simply an invitation to the opening of the British pavilion as a guest of the artist.'

'Oh, right. So he was just trying to look important.'

She shrugged. 'It happens. There are a lot of famous people around. Some people like a little bit of reflected glory.'

'Well, I do feel silly.'

'Yes.'

I smiled, and got to my feet. 'Well, I'm very grateful for your help. On behalf of my friend. Thank you so much for your time.'

I walked back through the pavilion and stopped at the central arena to sit down and collect my thoughts. A pile of suitcases was arranged on stage, whilst atonal electronic music blared out. Stockhausen. I quite liked Stockhausen. In small doses. I looked at the title projected behind the stage. Ten minutes in length. That was small enough.

I'd proven Nicolodi was a chancer, but I'd known that anyway. But what did 'guest of the artist' actually mean? A guest of Considine, or a guest of Fitzgerald? What was the connection between them?

I had the arena to myself by the time Stockhausen's mini-epic had weebled its way to its conclusion. Then a few visitors came in and took their seats as two people appeared on stage, positioned two hefty scripts on music stands, and started to read. The first reader was a pretty young woman who read with a light South Welsh accent. I looked at the title card again. A live reading of Friedrich Engel's *The Condition of the Working Class in England*. She handed over to her companion, an older, more bohemian-looking figure with curly hair and a moustache. American, this time. I felt a twinge of annoyance. It was beginning to look as if every foreign resident in Venice was working at the Biennale, with the exception of myself.

It was tempting to stay and watch the whole performance, but time was getting on. I'd head back home and try and get all my thoughts in order before meeting up with Dario. I made my way outside, into the afternoon sun, and made my way back to the exits.

'Nathan!' It was Gheorghe. 'Over here.' He waved me over.

'What is it?'

'That thing you asked me about. This morning.'

'Yes.'

'Now's a good time. Come on.' He grabbed my arm and steered me away from the exit, and back up towards the British pavilion. 'Have you got a cigarette?'

'I didn't know you smoked?'

'I don't. But you do. Come on, straight round the back, we'll make it look as if we're on a crafty cigarette break.'

'Why would we be doing that?'

'Management don't like us smoking in front of the pavilions. Think it looks a bit rough. So all the smokers go round the back of the British pavilion. The public don't come round here because it's all closed off.'

'Brilliant.'

He gave a half-smile but still appeared tense, and looked around. 'There's a fire door at the back. Doesn't fit properly. Remember, this whole space was remodelled after the last Biennale. It isn't difficult to open, come on.'

He gave it a firm thump with his shoulder, there was the faintest of clicks, and we made our way inside.

'Quite something, isn't it?' The space was much as I remembered it, although in semi-darkness now. The only light shone in from the door of the fire exit, itself shielded by trees. Still, it was enough to see by. The area around the shard of glass that had separated Gordon Blake-Hoyt from his head was stained a deep, rusty brown.

I put my foot on the stairs leading up to the gallery and then stopped. At least one panel, I knew, had been loosened. How many more might have been tampered with? I turned away from the steps, and moved around the outside of the field of glass, craning my head upwards. It wasn't easy to see in the half-light, but it was good enough.

I grabbed Gheorghe by the arm. 'Okay, let's be quick.' I pointed upwards. 'One, two, three, four, five, six, seven. Seven daggers. You agree?' He nodded. 'Good. Now over here.' I walked him over to the entrance, in front of the locked and bolted main doors. I pointed upwards. 'How many arrows?'

'Seven.'

'Exactly. Now the last one.' We made our way to the opposite wall, and looked up at the gantry. 'How many scythes? Seven?'

'Yes.'

'There we are then. Seven by seven by seven. Nothing missing.'

'I don't understand. What does it mean?'

'Francesco Nicolodi was killed with a glass scythe. Exactly like the ones up there. Lewis and I were attacked with glass arrows. Exactly like the ones up there. Now if none have been removed from here, it figures that the murderer has had duplicates made.'

'But where?'

'Where would you go to get something as specialist as a scythe made out of glass? Murano. It says so on the abstract.'

'So all you have to do is find the right workshop on Murano . . .'

'. . . and I've found the murderer.'

Gheorghe grinned. 'Brilliant!'

'You know, I can't find it in my heart to disagree with you. But I couldn't have done it without you. I'm sorry I put you in an awkward spot.'

'It's all right, Nathan. Really.'

'Anyway, let's get out of here before . . . Oh bloody hell.'

We heard footsteps from outside and, before we could move, a shadow fell across the fire exit.

Chapter 34

'Oh bloody hell,' I repeated under my breath. Gheorghe looked at me in despair. I could tell what he was thinking. He was going to lose his job over this. Unless . . .

'Punch me in the face!' I hissed.

'What?'

'Punch me in the face! Do it. Now— Owwww . . .' I'd been expecting it, but Gheorghe's blow still managed to catch me unawares. It was also rather harder than I'd been hoping for. I sank to my knees, and clutched at my nose, already feeling the blood starting to flow.

'*Che cazzo è?*' I looked up. The figure was dressed in a heavy beige uniform with reflective strips. A fireman. Of course, there was always a team from the fire department in attendance at the Giardini. 'What the hell's going on?' Neither of us spoke. 'English? Italian?'

I got to my feet, a little unsteadily. 'I can explain.'

'I'll bet you can. And who's he?' He pointed at Gheorghe, resplendent in full evening dress.

'I'm one of the Dancing Frenchmen.'

'Oh, right. Yes, I suppose so.' He turned back to me. 'This place is closed off for a reason. It's too dangerous to walk around. You want to try explaining?'

I nodded. 'I'm sorry, there's been a terrible misunderstanding. I was here on the opening day. When the accident happened. I realised this morning that I'd lost my *carta d'identità* and wondered if I'd dropped it here.'

'Why didn't you just go to lost property?'

'Thought I'd see if it was open. The fire door wasn't locked.'

'It was when I checked earlier.'

'Well, check harder next time. Next time might be important.' He stiffened, but he couldn't be completely sure that I wasn't telling the truth. 'Anyway, I must have made some noise. This gentleman,' I gestured at Gheorghe, 'must have heard me and thought I was breaking in.'

Gheorghe nodded. 'Sorry.'

I shook my head. 'S'okay. Shouldn't just have walked in. Stupid of me.'

'Did you find it?' asked the fireman.

'Find what, sorry?'

'Your *carta d'identità.*'

'Oh that. No. I'll try lost property.'

'Should have done that in the first place. Damn stupid just wandering around here with no proper lighting. One step out of place and you could kill yourself.'

'You're right. Sorry.'

'I need to be getting back to work,' said Gheorghe.

The fireman nodded. 'No worries. At least you were here. And I'd better get this door fixed up.'

'I guess so,' said Gheorghe. 'Oh, erm, could you not say anything about me? Hitting the visitors, that sort of thing – it doesn't go down well.' He turned to me. 'No hard feelings, I hope?'

'No hard feelings,' I said. We shook hands.

'Thanks,' he whispered.

We made our way outside. Gheorghe headed off towards the French pavilion, where Louis Armstrong was striking up with 'All of me'. I dabbed the blood from my nose, threw the handkerchief in the nearest bin, and headed off to lost property under the watchful eye of the fireman, where I proceeded to fill out an entirely fictitious claim. Then I made my way to the *vaporetto* stop, crammed myself on to a sweaty and over-crowded boat, and fretted all the way home. I hopped off at San Samuele and scurried along the *calli* until I reached the Brazilians.

I could, should, I told myself, just head straight upstairs and get to work on the computer. On the other hand, I'd done a good day's work and, more to the point, been punched in the face for my pains. I deserved a drink.

'Evening, Ed. Negroni and smartphone, please.'

'Negroni coming up. What's a smartphone?'

'An advanced type of mobile phone offering features more typically associated with a personal computer. In other words, something way too advanced for me. But I'm sure you've got one, so can you look something up for me?'

'Pre or post fixing the Negroni?'

'Post. It's only my personal reputation and liberty at stake.'

'Sure. Do you want it flaming?'

'Like never before.'

He quickly peeled a strip of peel from an orange, and folded it in two. Then he struck a match on the bar, waited a few seconds for the sulphur to burn off, and then set fire to the citrus oils. My drink flared, briefly, in the evening light, attracting the attention of a couple of tourists who looked in my direction with the expression 'I want one of those' in their eyes.

'You're an artist, Ed.'

'And you're a different sort of artist, Nat. Now. What do you want me to check out?'

'I need the abstract for the British pavilion at the Biennale.'

'Sure.' He tapped away. 'You could do this yourself, though, right? I mean, you do have a computer upstairs?'

'Yes. But that would involve me having to mix and set light to my own drinks. That might put the entire city at risk and I'm not prepared to do that.'

He tapped away at his phone, and then slid it across the bar to me. I scanned through it. The glass weapons. Who had made them?

I reached the end of the text, where Considine thanked his gallery, his agent and the British Council for their support. And then, '*All glass objects were fabricated according to traditional methods on the island of Murano.*'

Oh hell. I hadn't expected that. I'd thought that, at the very least, the glassmakers would have wanted a credit. Ed saw the expression on my face. 'Something wrong, Nat?' he said.

I ran my fingers through my hair. 'Nah, it's okay. Something just became a little more complicated than I needed, that's all.' How many glass foundries were there on Murano? 'But this, Ed,' I said, 'is a two-Negroni problem.'

He smiled sympathetically, and slid another across the bar. I looked around. There were a few familiar faces, faces I'd known for perhaps five years. And how often had I spoken to them. I mean, really spoken to them?

I looked to my left. A football trophy sat in a case in front of a fading certificate. A team of accountants who'd beaten a team of lawyers in an amateur tournament how many years ago? And yet, it was something that had been worth recording. It must be difficult to beat a team of lawyers at football, I thought. Doubly so in Italy.

This was getting me nowhere. Go home, call Dario, get as early a night as possible. It would be a bit of a pain trogging around every foundry in Murano, but so be it. I pushed my money across the bar, said goodnight to Ed, and left.

I made my way upstairs. 'Fed?' I called. There was no answer. 'Fede?' I called again. 'I'm sorry. You know that. I'm—'

She wasn't there. Of course, she wasn't there. I sighed, hung my jacket on the back of the door and made my way into the flat, which seemed very, very empty.

Chapter 35

Seven knives. Seven arrows. Seven scythes. Seven by seven by seven. Nicolodi had said something at our last meeting. Something about looking out for Considine running at him with a glass scythe. Why had he chosen to use that particular word?

I printed off the address of every *fornace* and glass showroom on Murano. It was going to be a hell of a lot of work. But it was something to go on.

I took my mobile from my pocket, placed it on the table and stared at it. Then I shook my head, closed my eyes and tried to concentrate on the problem in hand. Lewis and Paul. They must have been in Venice over the past few days. As Nicolodi had said, it wouldn't have made sense for them to return to the UK only to fly back for Paul's second opening a few days later. They had to be in the city. And had Paul really been off on his own personal lost weekend – with my money – as Lewis had suggested?

Fitzgerald. Nicolodi. Considine. What was the connection between them? If only there was some way of getting hold of Paul, of speaking to him again.

There was, of course, something else I needed to do first.

It had to be faced. And it had to be done now. I sighed, and ran my hands through my hair. I opened my eyes. The phone, as expected, was still there. Then, thankfully, the doorbell rang. I picked up the intercom.

'*Chi è?*'

'*Ciao, vecio.*'

'Dario! Come on up.'

He was carrying a small rucksack. 'Any chance I can stay tonight, Nat?'

'Sure. Any reason why?' Then a thought hit me. 'Oh no, don't tell me you've had a row as well?'

'No no. Nothing like that. But I'm working in Venice tomorrow. If I get in early I might be able to finish early afternoon, and then I can help you with the case.'

'And Valentina and Emily?'

'Still in Trieste with Val's parents.'

'Great. Just like the old times, then. Pizza, beer and Pink Floyd?'

He shook his head. 'Maybe later. We've got some work to do first. So what's happened today?'

'Let's go through to the office.' I cleared some papers away to make space, and dragged the visitor's chair round to my side of the table. 'Sit down here, eh? Now, the first thing is, we need to find a way of getting hold of Considine. So we can talk to him. Really talk to him. The other thing is this.' I reached for the list of glass furnaces on Murano, and tapped it with a pen. 'Somewhere on Murano is the furnace that made a set of glass weapons for him. And if we can find that, just maybe we can get a name, a description or—' I broke off. Dario was shaking his head.

'Not that. I meant the important stuff.'

'I don't know what you mean?'

He reached across the desk to my mobile phone and set it spinning with a flick of his fingers. We sat there and, in silence, watched it rotating ever more slowly until it came to a stop. Then Dario turned to me.

'I think you do, *vecio*.'

I nodded.

He got to his feet. 'I'm going down to Ed's, okay? Come down when you're ready. Take all the time you want. But you know what you have to do, don't you?'

'Yeah. You know I do.'

He smiled, and then left without saying another word.

I picked up the phone, and turned it over in my hands. Then placed it back on the desk, and spun it around again as I drummed my fingers. Then I took a deep breath, grabbed it and dialled.

'*Pronto?*'

'Fede. It's me.' There was silence on the other end of the line. Good. It made things just that bit easier. 'Just listen, please. Hang up after if you want, I'll understand. But please just listen. There are things I have to say.'

My legs were still shaky as I made my way downstairs, and through the door of the Magical Brazilian. The bar fell silent as I entered. Dario, a half-empty glass of beer in his hand, stared at me, trying to read my expression. Ed, frozen in the act of polishing glasses. The same half-dozen regulars who I hardly knew turned to face me.

I made my way to the bar, conscious of everyone's eyes on me. 'What would you like, Nat?' said Ed, trying to keep his voice neutral.

'First of all, I'd like everyone to start talking again and behaving normally.' Then I looked over at Dario. And then I could no longer keep the smile off my face.

Dario leapt from his chair, picked me up and spun me round. 'You bastard! You had me scared for a minute! So everything is—?'

'Fine. Really fine. Really, properly fine.' He threw his arms wide. 'But please, don't hug me again. I think you might have opened the wound up.'

He grinned, and turned to Eduardo. 'Get this man a Negroni.'

Ed shook his head. 'He had two earlier.'

'Okay then, get him a beer. A large one. And give him a cigarette as well, he's earned one. But only one.' Ed reached under the counter, took a packet of MS out and passed one to me.

'Thanks. Just give me five minutes, eh?' I made my way outside, and sat down at the one empty table. My hands shook as I lit up. Then I closed my eyes and leaned my head back, taking in the smell of cigarette smoke, the chatter of excited passers-by and the warmth of an early summer's evening. I could feel the stress draining from me, the muscles in my shoulders unclenching.

'Excuse me?' I opened my eyes. The accent was American, the speaker a big, grey-bearded man on the adjacent table, which he was sharing with a woman of similar age, and two young girls. 'We were just wondering if we should say Happy Birthday?'

'I'm sorry?'

He pointed towards the inside of the bar. 'There seemed to be some sort of celebration going on. We wondered if it was your birthday.'

I smiled, and shook my head. 'You see the big guy at the bar?' He nodded. 'That's my best friend. And he's just saved my life.'

Dario joined me at the table, and set two beers down. 'Okay then, let's get to work. Tell me about today.' Then he broke off, and leaned closer in, staring at me. 'Have you been in a fight? What have you done to your nose?'

'I asked a friend to punch me in the face.' I ran through the events of the afternoon with him.

'I don't get it.' He looked confused.

'I thought I'd try and make it look as if I was an intruder and Gheorghe had come to investigate.'

'Yeah, that I understand. But why didn't you just pretend to be hurt?'

'You know, I never thought of that.'

He shook his head. Then he grinned again. 'Okay, let's finish these and go.'

'Go? Go where?'

'Pizza and beer, *vecio*. And then we've got a crime to solve.'

Chapter 36

'Bacon and eggs?'

'Strictly speaking it's pancetta and eggs. It's not quite the same, but it's a guilty pleasure. Fede never understood.' I smiled, 'Doesn't understand – the need to fry things first thing in the morning.'

Dario laughed. 'Make the most of it then. She'll be back over tonight and you'll have to get used to proper food again.'

'Or, I could, you know, be in prison?'

'You worry too much. As we were saying last night. You go to Murano. You find the right *fornace*. You get the name of whoever ordered the weapons. And then you go straight to the police. Game over.'

I sighed. 'I don't want to go to bloody Murano. Can't you come with me, at least?'

'Sorry, buddy. I've got to work this morning. I'll take the afternoon off though, okay? Give me a call when you get back.' He got to his feet and wiped his lips. 'Terrible breakfast, Nat. See you later, eh?'

Bacon and eggs was one of the few things that Gramsci would never attempt to scavenge. It at least made breakfast a little less stressful than it was wont to be. I finished Dario's as well, then chucked the plates in the sink and then I looked through my pile of newspaper clippings. I needed a good clear shot of Considine, Fitzgerald and Nicolodi. I tore the front page from *La Nuova* and folded it away inside my jacket.

It was a pain to get to Murano from this part of town. There was no direct *vaporetto* service via the Grand Canal. I could get a boat up to Ferrovia or Piazzale Roma, but the boats from there would inevitably be choked with tourists setting out on a day trip to buy glass souvenirs. It would take forever, or at least feel like it.

I walked up to the Rialto, and struck out north, skirting the church of San Canziano, and then made my way up one of the long, straight *calli* that led towards Fondamente Nove. I always felt there was a mournful air hanging over this part of the city. The narrowness of the *calli* and the absence of light felt oppressive. Then, at a certain point, you started to become aware of the unusual number of flower shops. Then of the number of stonemasons that specialised in headstone work. Then of the number of businesses offering funerary services.

The reason became obvious when you emerged from the *calle* and looked out upon the cemetery island of San Michele. But there was something about the view that never failed to lift the spirits. On a cold, clear winter's day, the snow-capped Dolomites would be visible on the horizon. The weather was already too warm for that, but the view across the northern lagoon cheered me up. Dario, I knew, was right. The job of finding the right *fornace* might be a little tedious, but the process would be a mechanical one and, who knows, there was always the chance of striking lucky first time. I grabbed the next boat for the island.

My good mood evaporated in the fifteen minutes it took to arrive, as the amount of work that might be required started to sink in. I looked at the printout I'd brought with me, of the names and addresses of every glass furnace and factory on the island. There were more than twenty of them. Still, it had to be done, and the island wasn't all that big. I got off at the Faro *vaporetto* stop, next to Murano's lighthouse. It was the obvious place to start. I could make my way down as far as Murano's very own Grand Canal, then cross over and walk back on the other side. And, if need be, I was going to stop at every damn shop, factory and furnace along the way.

I stopped for a cigarette about an hour later, less than halfway to the halfway point. I'd forgotten what I didn't like about Murano. Or rather, I'd forgotten just what I disliked most about it: namely, shopping for glass.

Tourist guides tended to suggest steering clear of Murano, unless actually going there with the specific purpose of buying souvenirs or visiting a glassblowing demonstration. I'd always thought that was a mistake. The buildings were smaller than in the *centro storico* proper, which gave it a lighter, airier feel than Venice itself. The Grand Canal was pretty enough, there were a few churches worth visiting and some decent bars and restaurants. I could never imagine living there, as the place seemed to shut down after dark, but, as a place to visit, I'd always found it quite pleasant.

As long as, that is, I was not engaged in the business of buying glass.

I remembered trying to buy my first-ever Christmas present for Federica. I circumnavigated the entire island, twice; got lost in the thick, freezing fog that had settled over the city like a blanket; discovered that the warming winter drink enticingly described as a 'hot spritz' actually tasted of a distillation of evils; and I had found nothing, nothing at all that seemed quite right. I walked past shops displaying chandeliers of exquisite workmanship that would have looked absolutely stunning if one happened to have the entire *piano nobile* of a baroque palace in which to hang them. Shops with vases of extraordinary complexity and beauty that would have been ideal for people with pockets of infinite depth and non-destructive pets. Jewellery of every imaginable kind, none of which I could imagine on Federica, which made me swear I would never, ever again go shopping without her.

And that was just the good stuff. I walked past seemingly endless window displays of stuff that was simply godawful, including an entire nativity scene displaying a Holy Family so terrifyingly ugly that it made me momentarily wonder if Herod had not, perhaps, been on to something. 'Everything for a euro' shops where the works bore no official stamps of authenticity beyond the teasingly ambiguous 'genuine Italian glass'.

I finally ended up buying a Father Christmas bottle stopper from the very first place I'd visited. Fede pretended to like it, said it was the thought that counted, and I had never loved her more.

In short, Murano was a great place to walk around. Except for the glass.

And so I walked the length of the Grand Canal and stopped at every shop, outlet and *fornace* along the way. *Signore, you want to buy a knife? A glass knife? A scythe? From us?* I got used to every shop assistant stepping back from me. Christmas presents from Murano, I figured, were not going to be a problem. Or even an option. Because nobody gave the impression they'd be desperate for my custom in future.

I dropped into a side street for another cigarette. Come on, Nathan, just stick with it. Doesn't matter if it's the last place you look. Face it, it probably is going to be the last bloody place you look. Stick with it.

I walked along the *fondamenta*, in the midst of hordes of excited tourists; kept a fixed smile on my face as I queued behind a French couple swithering between a set of glasses retailing at €13.50 and another at €18.50 and fought down the impulse to scream that both sets were made by small children in the Far East and worth a couple of euros at most; and cursed myself for getting grumpy whilst waiting in line behind people who were, after all, on holiday and trying to have a good time.

I reached the bridge that crossed over the Grand Canal, and saw a sign outside an unprepossessing shop window. Fornace Vianello. Despite my mood, I couldn't help but smile. Vianello, the most Venetian of surnames. Back in Aberystwyth, this place would have been called Jones the Glass. I took a closer look in the window. At first glance, it looked like the usual crap – gondolas, harlequins, generic masked figures. It also looked too small to house an actual *fornace*, but perhaps there was space for a workshop at the back. But then something caught my eye. An arrow. A glass arrow! I couldn't be absolutely sure that it was exactly the same type that had put a hole in my jacket and three stitches in my shoulder, but, by

God, it was a glass arrow! I gave a little jump and an excited little *meep* sound that raised a sad shake of the head from a passing Venetian, evidently disappointed at how little it took to impress a tourist.

Inside, a middle-aged moustachioed man was working on a thin *millefiòri* cane with a micro torch. There was no one else inside, and he gave no sign of acknowledging me. I gave him a couple of minutes and then wondered if I should clear my throat, or possibly just try coming in again, when he switched off the torch, pushed back his protective glasses and smiled. 'Good morning. Can I help you?'

'I'm sorry. It seems like I'm disturbing you.'

'No, no, please. I'm sorry too. You need to concentrate a lot with this type of work. Sometimes I concentrate a little too much. Someone comes into the shop, I don't notice them and suddenly – *bum* – I look up, somebody is leaving the shop and I've lost a sale. But what can I do? Or more importantly, what can I do for you?'

'There's something in the window that caught my eye. Something a bit unusual. A glass arrow?'

He nodded. 'Oh that. Well, it was a commission. That was my first attempt. To be honest, it's not very good, I could let you have that one at a special price.'

'A first attempt? I would never have guessed, it looks beautiful.' We both smiled and nodded at each other, both aware that these were the first steps in the dance of negotiation. 'A slightly unusual thing to commission, though.'

'Oh yes. It was a strange order. The gentleman was an artist, I believe.' I must have started, because he noticed my reaction. 'Yes, yes. It's not unusual at this time of year. We always get a few, shall we say, idiosyncratic commissions during the Biennale.'

'Glass arrows. Perhaps he was just buying early for Valentine's Day?'

He laughed. 'Oh, I hope not. You ought to have seen the other things he wanted. A glass knife, for one. And a glass scythe. Can you imagine that? A glass scythe!'

'Wow! Okay, hopefully not for Valentine's Day then.' We both laughed, and then he looked at me expectantly. 'Can you tell me his name? The man who commissioned them?'

He stopped smiling. 'Are you police?' I shook my head. 'Then why should I tell you?'

'I'm trying to help someone. I'm the UK's honorary consul in Venice. I believe a British national is in trouble, and I'm trying to help him.' That person being me.

He shook his head. 'I can't do that. You have a problem like that, you need to go to the police.' He brushed past me, made his way to the door and held it open. 'I'm sorry. I think you'd better go.'

I didn't move. 'I don't need his address. I don't need a phone number. All I need is a name. And I wouldn't ask if it weren't vitally important. Please?' He continued to hold the door open, staring at me.

Last throw of the dice. The shop was a little bit off the beaten path. There was a cheapo shop selling Chinese glass next door. I was the only customer on a sunny morning during one of the peaks of the tourist season. I reached for my wallet. I took out a fifty and placed it on the counter. He didn't move. I took out another. He let the door slam shut. I put a third note down. 'It is important,' I repeated. He said nothing, but stared at the counter. I took out a fourth note, the last I had, and placed it on top of the pile. 'Vitally important.'

He turned the sign on the door so it read 'Closed' in three different languages, and went behind the counter. 'Okay. If it's important.' He quickly swooshed the notes off the counter and into the till, in one fluid motion. 'Let me see.' He ran his hand down a ledger. 'Now, I don't normally keep a record of this sort of thing, but commissions are a bit different. Here we are.' He paused.

'The name?' I asked.

'Considine. Paul Considine.'

Chapter 37

There are times when only the words, 'You what?' will do.

'You what?' I said.

'Considine. Paul Considine.'

I shook my head. 'I don't think so.'

'I don't understand.'

I ran my hands through my hair. 'It can't be. It just can't be.' I was thinking out loud now. 'Do you remember what he looked like?'

'Not so much. A little, maybe.'

'Was he about my height? Longish hair, possibly unshaven. Probably wearing lots of black. Looked just a bit rock 'n' roll?'

Vianello smiled. 'Oh no, *signore*. Not at all. He was a bit more like you, you know?'

'Meaning not very rock 'n' roll. Okay, no time for hurt feelings.' I pulled out the clipping from *La Nuova* and spread it on the counter. 'Do you recognise anyone in this photograph?' He looked at the photo for a few seconds, and then up at me. 'Not me. Apart from me!' He bent over the photo again, and then moved his finger to Francesco Nicolodi.

'It was him.'

'Are you sure?'

He shook his head. I tried to keep the frustration out of my voice. 'But it could have been?' He nodded. 'You're sure it wasn't him.' I pointed first to Considine and then to Fitzgerald. 'Or him?'

'No *signore*. Not them. I am sure. But I don't understand . . . ?'

'I think I'm beginning to.'

'Have I done anything wrong?'

I shook my head. 'No. You've done me a very big favour. Thank you.' I made for the door.

He gave a gentle cough. 'As I said, I can do you a good deal on the arrow.'

I stopped dead in my tracks. Something had just occurred to me. 'A glass arrow. Could you actually shoot a glass arrow?'

He looked confused for a moment and then laughed. 'Shoot one? From a bow? Oh no, *signore*, these are just for decoration. They're not balanced like an arrow. They would probably break as soon as you tried.'

'You could never shoot one. But you could stab someone.' He took a step backwards. 'Of course, you could stab someone! Someone close to you,' I laughed.

Vianello took another step backwards. There were small beads of sweat on his forehead. '*Signore?*'

I smiled at him. 'You've been very helpful. Thank you so much.' I took a quick look around the shop. 'You know, you have some lovely pieces here. I must come back for Christmas presents.'

He nodded, his eyes wide, never moving his gaze from me.

I smiled at him one final time, then turned and left the shop. As soon as the door closed behind me, I heard him scurrying across the room to lock and bolt it.

*   *   *

Francesco Nicolodi. Nicolodi, who had told me that Paul Considine was a fragile, damaged man with a history of violence. Nicolodi, who had been right next to me when I picked up a wallet with an incriminating piece of evidence inside. Nicolodi, who had commissioned a glass arrow, a glass knife and a glass scythe using Considine's name.

Nicolodi, who was now dead.

There was another problem. I'd not seen him at the Arsenale, and now – with the CCTV records having been deleted – there was no way of proving he'd ever been there. Yet, there had to be a connection. For some reason, Nicolodi had been trying to frame Considine for murder. It was an almost perfect solution. Were it not for the not inconsiderable problem of his death.

I rubbed my face and felt a twinge of pain from my nose. Dario's words came back to me: *Why didn't you just pretend to have been punched?*

Why didn't you just pretend . . . ?

I'd intended to head directly for the *Questura* at Piazzale Roma and tell Vanni everything. The case against Nicolodi made sense, but it was imperfect, incomplete. Vanni, I knew, would scribble copious notes and then give me a very stern warning about not interfering. No, there was still more that I could do for myself.

I jumped off the boat at San Samuele and made my way home. Gramsci gave a happy little yowl as I stepped through the door, and started scrabbling away at the sofa. Time for a feed. Or time to play ball. Or both.

I picked him up, tucked him under my arm and then plonked him unceremoniously on the desk next to my laptop.

Then I brought my face down level with his and stared directly into his sulphurous eyes. 'Okay, it's like this. We're going to solve this case and then, and only then, do you get fed. Then, and only then, do I agree to start throwing balls for you. And if you start walking back and forth over the keyboard, or chewing on cables, or pulling plugs out of sockets, then you're going to be a very hungry and bored cat. Do we have a deal?'

I logged on. How far back did online newspaper archives go? Maybe twenty years at most? That would have to do. That would probably be enough. I had a quick search on the name 'Francesco Nicolodi'. It returned a few names but a quick check was enough to assure me that we weren't talking about the same person. 'Lewis Fitzgerald' then. More hits, this time, mainly in the context of being Paul Considine's agent. 'Lewis Fitzgerald Francesco Nicolodi' returned nothing. I typed 'Lewis Fitzgerald Italian' and crossed my fingers.

And there it was. An image of Lewis at a party in the mid-1990s. I didn't recognise the others at first sight, until I looked at the caption. Gwenant Pryce, her red hair clipped short; and Adam Grant, then a mere beardless youth. Paul stood between them, with an arm around Gwenant's waist. He could only have been in his early twenties, but already had something of the rock star about him. They all looked so happy. Lewis, almost glamorous and with a full head of hair, stood next to a young man who, the caption informed me, was named Riccardo Pelosi. Fitzgerald's assistant.

There was another image, this time from a *Guardian* article of 2008. Two men arriving at court. Lewis, his hair thinning by now, looking tired and drawn as he tried to smile for the cameras. The other was a man, the caption said, who had been convicted of threatening behaviour and arson. I took a closer look. A man who bore an uncanny resemblance to Francesco Nicolodi: Pelosi.

The two of them, it seemed, had spent several days in court. Fitzgerald had pleaded not guilty to all charges. And Pelosi had accepted complete responsibility, and said he was acting alone. In the end, Fitzgerald had been acquitted and Pelosi ended up with a seven-year prison sentence. In 2008. With good behaviour he could have been out a year or two ago.

I printed off the article and photograph, went through to the kitchen, and poured out Gramsci's kitty biscuits. He jabbed at a cheesy one, and then looked up at me in disbelief. I stared down at him. 'You'll have to weed out the ones you don't like yourself.' He glared back at me, but I felt sufficiently brave to turn my back on him. I practically skipped down the stairs. For the first time in a very long time, I actually felt in control of events.

Five minutes later, I was back upstairs. 'Sorry Grams, I've just realised I forgot something.' I took the top copy of *Il Gazzettino* from the pile of unread newspapers. I was on my way out when he gave a pathetic little *n'yeep* sound. He hadn't moved from his bowl, and was staring down at the contents.

'Oh for God's sake.' I put the newspaper down, picked up his bowl, removed the cheesy biscuits and set it back down again. Without so much as a single *meow* of thanks, he settled down to eating. I watched him for a few moments, then shook my head, picked up the newspaper and headed back downstairs. I was in complete control of events. More or less.

The door to Santa Maria Ausiliatrice was closed. I knocked, and it swung open at my touch. 'Gwen,' I called. 'Gwen?'

'Nathan. Come in.' Her voice was ragged. I stepped inside. Gwen was righting an upturned chair. 'Can you give me a hand with this, *cariad*, it's a bit heavy for me?' She indicated a wooden easel lying on the floor, and a large canvas. I grabbed one side of it and together we shuffled it into the corner. Then we moved the canvas into position. What had once been the macabre portrait of Lewis Fitzgerald had been slashed to pieces. Gwen stood back. 'Not quite what I had in mind perhaps, but I think it's still got something.' She smiled at me but her eyes were red.

'What the hell happened here, Gwen?'

She shrugged. 'An overenthusiastic critic, perhaps? Take a look around.'

I walked into the blue room. The mirror had been smashed, and the painting cut to pieces. Blue, purple, green, orange, white, violet, black. In every one, a slashed painting and a broken mirror. Forty-nine years of bad luck.

'Gwen. Oh Gwen, I'm so sorry.'

She dabbed at her eyes, and patted my arm. 'It's all right, my love. It's only art. Not people. Only art.'

I put my arms around her and hugged her. 'It was him, wasn't it? Fitzgerald.' She nodded. 'Were you here? Did he hurt you? I'll bloody kill him.'

She moved away from me, and patted my chest. 'Sit down, *cariad*. I'll make us a cup of tea.' She filled the kettle, and switched it on. 'At least this still works. No, I wasn't here when it happened. But I know it was him.'

'How?'

'Because he telephoned me this morning. Said he'd enjoyed my exhibition, and hoped I didn't mind the little interventions he'd made. Then he told me to leave Paul Considine the hell alone if I knew what was good for me. And if I received anything – anything at all – in the mail in the next few days, I was to give it to him straightaway without opening it.'

'What?'

'He said he was "collecting an insurance policy for a friend". I don't know what he meant by that, do you?' I shook my head. The kettle finished boiling, and she filled two mugs. 'Earl Grey all right?' I nodded. 'Biscuit?'

'Oh Gwen, to hell with the bloody tea and biscuits. What are you going to do about Fitzgerald?'

'I think, *cariad*, that I'm going to do as he says.'

'Call the police. He's caused thousands of pounds' worth of damage here. More than that, he's actually threatening you.'

'Oh, he's very, very good at that. Remember what I told you last time. He knows some nasty people.'

I took out my phone. 'Well, if you won't call them, I will.'

She touched my arm. 'No you won't, Nathan.'

'I think I will.'

'No, you won't. If you do, he'll hurt Paul. Seriously.'

I stared at her for a few seconds, then nodded and put my phone away. 'Okay. Then we need to find another way. Where is Paul, anyway?

'He stayed with me for a couple of days. Then went back to Lewis last night. He said his head was in the right place now. He was going to break with him. Take control of his own affairs again.'

'He stayed with you?' I smiled at her. 'Did you enjoy lunch the other day, Gwen?'

'I'm sorry?'

'A shame Ai Mercanti was closed. Paul wanted to take an old friend out to lunch, and was very keen that Lewis didn't find out about it. I hope you found somewhere nice?'

She laughed her tinkly little laugh, and, for a moment, the lines seemed to drop away from her face. 'We found some terrible old tourist trap on the way to Piazza San Marco. Frozen pizzas, and cost us a fortune.' She smiled. 'But it was still lovely.'

'You and Paul. You were more than just friends, weren't you?'

'Clever, Mr Consul. Yes, we were more than just friends. For a while at least. A long time ago now.' She smiled. 'You've been taking Adam's advice then? Asking all the right questions?'

'And the wrong ones, it seems. But this next one's important. Take a look at this.' I took out the article from the *Guardian*. 'Do you recognise anyone here?'

'That's Adam, of course. And Paul there. Handsome boy, wasn't he? And me. Looking all lovely and glammed-up. I can't really be sure where that was taken. Some opening at Lewis's gallery, I expect. Before he started representing Paul. Before we started wondering where all our money was going.'

'And who's this?' I pointed at the figure of Riccardo Pelosi.

'I remember him. Lewis's assistant. Not a nice man. I think he went to prison.'

'He did. He set fire to an artist's studio, "as a friendly warning". A warning to people like you and Adam, I imagine. Not to push Lewis Fitzgerald too far. The thing about artist's studios though, is that they're liable to be full of inflammable materials. And the whole building went up like a torch. Bloody lucky that no one was killed.' Gwenant didn't speak. I put the photograph from the clipping directly next to the one from the front of the *Gazzettino*. 'They're the same person, aren't they? Riccardo Pelosi is Francesco Nicolodi. Lewis Fitzgerald's fixer. A man who went to prison for seven years. A man, we might say, who knows where the bodies are buried. He was murdered on Lazzaretto Vecchio two days ago.'

She looked over at me and nodded. I continued. 'A man who arrived in town for the Venice Biennale, staying in a flophouse in Dorsoduro. And who later moved into one of the most exclusive hotels on the Grand Canal.'

'I don't understand.'

'I'm not sure I do, not completely. Come on, let's game it through. Francesco Nicolodi – let's call him that for now – spent the last week and a half dripping poison into the ears of anyone who'd listen. About Paul Considine. A man with drink and drugs problems. An artist who might be a plagiarist. A man with a violent past who depends on medication to control his bipolar disorder and who could potentially become aggressive if he forgets to take it.' I paused. 'Now, I've known him for just over ten days, Gwen. That doesn't sound like the man I've met. But you properly know him. Was he ever that sort of person?'

She shook her head. 'The problem with Paul is that he became too famous, too quickly. Too many people queuing up to tell him how brilliant he was. That sort of thing's never good for you. So yes, he drank too much. Smoked too much. Spent way, way too much. Self-destructive, oh yes. Broke my heart. But never violent.'

'Nicolodi told me he'd glassed someone in a fight. Did you ever hear about that?'

'There was a fight. A fight in a pub. Somebody pulled a knife and a glass was broken. And he got hurt. But that was it. That was years ago when he was young and stupid. And it scared him, scared him to death. That's when he got the idea of working with glass. Trying to work everything out in his head, trying to exorcise things.'

I nodded. 'There we go, you see. Nicolodi trying to plant the idea of the psycho artist with a thing about broken glass. Now then, when did you find out he was bipolar?'

'I think I heard about it shortly after we broke up. It explained a few things. The mood swings. That self-destructive streak.'

'And what if he forgot to take his medication?'

'I don't know, Nathan. I'm no expert on this sort of thing.' She sounded tired now.

'Neither am I. But what's likely to happen? That he becomes depressed and anti-social? Self-destructive? Maybe so. But I'm pretty sure it wouldn't turn him into a psychopathic master criminal trying to kill everyone who'd ever wronged him in ever more convoluted ways.'

'And he was always taking his medication.' She sipped at her tea. 'At least, I know he has been the last couple of days. But how does this tie in with Lewis?'

'Think back to 2008. Nicolodi takes the fall for Lewis. He serves however many years in prison and keeps his mouth tight shut the whole time. And then he gets out. He knows Lewis has been embezzling money from Paul for years. Lewis is getting edgy as Paul is showing signs of wanting to take back control of his affairs. He also owes Nicolodi more than a few favours. He needs to keep him on his side. So he cuts him in to a deal.

'They plan to set Paul up as this crazy, violent near-psychopath. A man who should in no way, shape or form be left to look after himself. Make him out to be crazy, maybe even a killer. People would just shake their heads at poor, mad old Paul Considine and think that at least his manager had tried to look after him.

'Nicolodi lifts Paul's wallet, and plants some incriminating evidence in it. And he drops it right at the feet of the honorary consul in Venice, a man, he's sure, who will make certain it ends up in the hands of the police. Only he's been lazy, hasn't done his research properly. He doesn't know that the Priadol tablets he's managed to score are the wrong dose for Paul Considine.' I smiled. 'And that's when Mr Honorary Consul starts to take an interest.

'Then Francesco Nicolodi becomes very greedy, very quickly. He wants a bigger share. He's got an article in *The Times* in which he takes a shot at Considine's management. Now Lewis has the problem of getting rid of him as well. So he lures him out to Lazzaretto Vecchio and puts a glass blade in his neck.'

'Lures him out there. How would he do that?'

'I'm not sure yet. But I think he tells him that this Sutherland guy is nosing around. That he's found out a bit too much. More than that, he's screwed up their plans by sending Paul off with some spending money when he was supposed to be attacking people with glass arrows in the Arsenale. So they've got to get rid of him and make it look like Considine was responsible. And then Nicolodi turns up to find that I'm not there, and the only other person there is Lewis. Waiting for him with a scythe.'

She nodded. 'It's complicated. But it could be.'

'The two of them were working together. Nicolodi got greedy. Lewis killed him. That's it. That's got to be it.' I paused. 'And now I need you to tell me where Lewis and Paul are staying. Because I don't think they've left Venice at all. I think Lewis has unfinished business.'

'Unfinished business? With who?'

'This "insurance policy". Something Nicolodi was holding over him. Whatever it is, it wasn't enough and Lewis called his bluff. But whatever it is, I don't think Lewis will feel safe leaving Venice until he's got it.' I smiled. 'So come on, Gwen. Do you know where they're staying?' She said nothing. 'Gwen, I know you think you're protecting him but—'

'He said he'd hurt him!' she snapped back.

'He has already. He's probably stealing all his money. He's tried to frame him for murder. He might even be switching his medication. How long before we read about tragic Paul Considine accidentally overdosing?'

She dabbed at her eyes again. 'They're at the Palazzo Papadopoli. Or at least they were.'

'Figures. I can see how it would have appealed to Nicolodi. Another little way to torment Lewis. To see him sitting there, drinking expensive drinks on his money.' I got to my feet. 'Okay, I need to go.'

She grabbed my hand. 'Do you actually know what you're doing, Mr Consul?'

'In all honesty, not really.' I made my way to the door. 'But I'm going to sort it out. I promise. And for what it's worth, Gwenant, I still think you're a lovely Welsh woman.'

Chapter 38

Dario and I leaned on a table outside the Birraria La Corte in Campo San Polo.

'This isn't going to work, is it?' I said.

He took a drink of beer and wiped away a foam moustache. 'Erm, possibly not. Maybe not. In fact, probably not.'

'That's not making me feel any better.'

'Sorry, buddy. Can't think of anything better. Can you?'

'Nope. All I can think of is that we somehow need to separate Considine from Fitzgerald. And if we can do that, maybe we can get him to talk.' I caught Dario's expression. 'No, not like *that*. Well, there is an alternative. We just stake the place out until he leaves.'

Dario shook his head. 'Won't work. What if he leaves by water taxi? There's no way we can watch the front entrance unless we're on the other side of the Grand Canal. Anyway, that'll take time and that's something you're running out of.'

'What do you mean?'

'How long before the cops have the same idea you did and go knocking on the door of every *fornace* on Murano? "Yes, officer, we did have a man making enquiries about fashioning deadly glass weapons. A foreign gentleman he was."'

'Yes, but they'll soon twig that it wasn't me.'

'Oh sure. Depends on their definition of "soon", though, and how long you're prepared to spend *in gattabuia* waiting to find out.'

'You're right.' I'd made a few prison visits. I had no desire to learn any more about them from the inside. 'Okay, let's do it.' I drained my glass and left a few euros on the table.

Dario laughed. 'What are you doing?'

'Just leaving the money for the drinks.'

'We're not in Mestre now, *vecio* and this is not Toni's. This is,' he checked the menu again, 'eight euros a bottle.'

'Eight euros!'

'Yep.' He picked up the bottle. 'But it's no ordinary beer. This has a delicate aroma of lemon, pink grapefruit and orange, offset with delicate hoppy notes.'

'Eight euros, though!'

'Sure, I know it's a lot. But I thought it might be nice to come somewhere really good for your last beer as a free man.'

I fished a tenner out of my wallet. 'Brilliant. All of a sudden an enforced vacation as a guest of the president doesn't seem so bad. Come on, let's go.'

We made our way across the campo, down through San Polo and towards the Palazzo Papadopoli, where we tailgated a couple of guests through the front gate.

'Who's going to do this?' I whispered.

'Gotta be you, buddy. I can't do an English accent.' It seemed unfair, but he was absolutely right. We walked separately into reception. Dario nodded and smiled at the receptionist, sat down in an armchair and opened a newspaper, as if waiting for someone.

I walked up to the desk. There wasn't much chance this was going to work, but – given that Considine didn't seem to be the most extrovert of people – there was always the slight chance that he'd never made much of an impression, ideally visual, on the hotel staff.

'Hi there,' I said. 'I'm sorry, this is really awkward, but I've lost my room card.' I kept my head down and stared at my shoes.

'No problems sir, I'll get you one immediately. Your name . . . ?'

'Considine. Paul Considine.'

'Mr Considine. In room 313?'

'That's it.'

'Okay, I'm just doing that for you now, sir.' She reached into a drawer, took out a stack of blank cards, and placed one into a card writer. 'Oh, there's some mail for you as well.' She reached behind her, took an envelope from a pigeon hole, and passed it to me. Then her expression changed, became panicky, as if she'd realised she'd done something wrong. 'Oh, I'm sorry, I do need you to sign this first.' She slid a form across the desk to me.

'Of course.'

She looked a little embarrassed. 'And I do need to see your passport. Or driving licence. Anything like that.'

'Ah. Oh yes, of course you do.' I tucked the envelope away in my jacket before she could say anything, and made great play of checking my pockets. 'I'm so sorry, I must have left them in my room.'

'Okay. It's probably best to make sure you've always got it with you, though. You are supposed to have some form of identification with you. Just in case.'

'Of course. Silly of me to forget. It's just that we don't have ID cards in Britain. Imagine that, eh?' I laughed, a little too loud and a little too long. 'Well, I'll just fetch it from upstairs and bring it down.' I reached out my hand for the card.

She put her hands to her face, flushed with embarrassment. She'd got the protocol just a little bit wrong, and that had now put her in a difficult position. I smiled, but didn't move my hand. 'I'll just be two minutes,' I said.

'Is anything wrong, Sasha?' I recognised the voice at once. The manager. I was unable to prevent myself from stiffening up, and snatching my hand back. Out of the corner of my eye, I could see Dario discreetly folding his newspaper away.

'Nothing wrong, ma'am.' The relief in the young woman's voice was tangible. Someone more senior was going to have to deal with it. 'It's just Mr Considine's lost his room card.'

'Oh dear. Well, not to worry, Mr Considine, Sasha will soon . . .' She stopped, and her face clouded as she stared at me. 'You're not Mr Considine.' Her eyes narrowed. 'I know you. We've met before. You were here just a few days . . .' Her voice trailed off.

I gave her the best smile I could manage. 'I can explain.' Dario, I noticed from the corner of my eye, had got to his feet.

'Can you?'

I shook my head. 'No. Not really.'

'Sutherland. What the hell do you want?' There was no mistaking the voice. I turned to see the familiar figure of Lewis Fitzgerald, side by side with Paul Considine.

'Sasha, call the police please,' said the manager.

'Yes, Sasha, please do that.' I pulled the envelope from my jacket. I had no idea what was in it, but that didn't necessarily matter. It only mattered that Lewis believed that I did. I held it out towards him, like Peter Cushing brandishing a crucifix. 'It's over, Lewis. Everything's in here. Pelosi's insurance policy. It's all over.'

Paul took a step towards me, and smiled. For a moment he looked ten years younger. Then Lewis grabbed his arm and yanked him back. He spun him round to face him, grabbed his face with both hands and hissed at him. 'Remember what I said, Paul?'

Paul looked back at me and shook his head. 'I'm sorry, Nathan.' Then the two of them turned and broke for the entrance, haring back the way they had come, with Dario and I in pursuit.

'You know, that went better than I expected.'

'They're calling the police, Dario. And when they find me they're going to throw away the key.'

'You worry too much, *vecio*!'

Neither Lewis nor Paul looked in great shape, but they had a surprising turn of speed. I had no idea if they knew where the hell they were going. After a few twists and turns down narrow *calli*, I was convinced that I didn't. Surely, I thought, just one more turn and they'll find themselves in a dead end, or the only exit directly on to the canal, and then we'll have them. They hurdled a pair of small dogs, as a couple of *abusivi* selling bags flattened themselves against the wall, and turned right towards the Grand Canal.

San Silvestro. Somehow they'd ended up at San Silvestro. Ahead of us I could see the *vaporetto* stop, and the next boat pulling in. They still had a good fifty metres on us and leapt aboard. Dario and I ran like hell, and hollered for the *marinaio* to wait for us. He looked at us, sizing up the distance and shrugged apologetically before casting off.

We stood, panting, at the side of the canal. 'The number,' said Dario, 'did you see the number?'

'San Silvestro. It's a 1,' I said, trying to catch my breath. Got to be a 1.'

'So next stop is—'

'Sant'Angelo.'

'Okay, we can cut him off there. Come on.'

'Dario, there's no way.' I looked up the Grand Canal. 'We'd have to double back on ourselves and cross the Rialto Bridge. 'There's no way we can get there in time.'

'Yes there is.' He grabbed my elbow and half-dragged me along the *fondamenta* and over the wall of the adjacent hotel. He sprinted through the garden, scattering waiters and tourists to the left and to the right, as I followed shouting apologies as best I could. Then we were up and over the wall on the other side, and at the San Silvestro gondola station. Before I could stop him, Dario had pushed his way to the front, and gently but firmly dragged two elderly tourists back from the pontoon where they were about to embark. 'It's okay,' he said, pointing at me, 'he's a cop.'

'You are?' the husband looked unconvinced.

I shook my head. 'No. But I'm an honorary consul, if that helps.'

He shook his head.

'Get in!' shouted Dario.

'Dario this is insane. This is a gondola. It's not built for a high speed chase.'

'Get in the goddamn boat, Nathan. And don't tell a Venetian about what a gondola can and can't do.'

I jumped in. Dario yammered away in a *Veneziano* that was far too quick for me to attempt to understand, and made frantic gestures in the direction of Sant'Angelo. The gondolier looked confused, but nodded and kicked back at the jetty in order to push off. He waved his hand at us, 'Can you sit down please?' We looked at each other for a moment, and then the two of us plumped ourselves down into a red plush heart-shaped chair. 'Thanks, that's better. You want me to sing?'

'No. No, we don't want you to sing, thanks. Just get us to Sant'Angelo as fast as you can.'

'Sure, I can do that. But it's a busy time of day. If you like, I can go off into some of the side canals. Much quieter, more beautiful.'

'Please. Just get us to Sant'Angelo. As fast as you can. Row. Row like the wind.'

He shrugged, and fell silent. I turned to Dario. 'This is never going to work.'

'It is going to work, *vecio*. Somebody once piloted a gondola to Croatia, you know?'

'And how long did that take them?'

'About a week. Now just watch.'

The *vaporetto* was well ahead of us and – despite the best efforts of our gondolier – extending its lead. And then, as we were watching, an Alilaguna boat for the airport slid into the Sant'Angelo pontoon, collecting a group of tourists with heavy luggage. Behind it, two taxis jostled for space; whilst ahead of it, the *traghetto* service started out across the canal. Dario grinned at me. 'Busy time of the day, Nathan, on the busiest stretch of the canal. It was an easy bet that something would hold it up.' And, indeed, we sat and watched as the *vaporetto* waited for the passage to clear and, slowly but surely, we made up ground.

We were almost level by the time the pontoon was clear. As soon as the *marinaio* had moored, and opened the gate, Lewis and Paul were away across the bridge and across the *campo*. As soon as the gondola was within distance, Dario leapt ashore, setting the boat rocking alarmingly. I let the gondolier pull up to the jetty and then set off in pursuit, before I felt an arm pulling me back.

'Eighty euros please, sir.'

'Eighty euros! We've only had a five-minute trip.'

'It's the standard charge sir. Please, if you want to check . . .' He indicated a laminated page fixed to the side of the gondola.

'I know it's the standard charge. We didn't want the whole experience. We just wanted to cross the canal.'

'I'm sorry, sir. For crossing the canal, there are the *traghetti*. If I don't charge you eighty, well, there are customers back there that I have lost.'

I sighed, and reached for my wallet. Seventy-five euros. I smiled at him. 'Enough?'

He shook his head.

I reached into my pocket and took out a handful of change. 'One . . . two . . . three,' I counted. 'Four euros. Four-fifty. Four-seventy. Four-ninety. Ninety-five. Ninety-seven. Ninety-eight. Ninety-nine.'

'I'm sorry sir, but that's not a *centesimo.*'

I looked again. 'Ah, you're right. It's a one-penny piece. Wonder how that got there?' I turned again to my handful of small change. 'And two *centesimi*. There we go.'

'Thank you, sir.' He smiled at me, and held my gaze in expectation of a tip that was never going to come. Then he handed me a card. 'Please leave a review on TripAdvisor.' He smiled once more, and kicked off from the jetty, back in the direction from which we had come.

I tucked the card inside my pocket, and looked around the square. Dario, of course, was long since gone.

Chapter 39

I went back to the flat. There didn't seem to be much else to do. It was getting dark outside now. Dario would call in a few minutes. He knew the Venetian maze of streets better than most, but it wouldn't have surprised me if Lewis and Considine had managed to lose him, even if more by accident than design. He'd be back, sooner rather than later. Fede was supposed to be coming around tonight and we'd all have a big old laugh about what a great pal Dario was.

In the meantime, there was the package to examine. I tore it open. It contained a sealed envelope, a sheaf of newspaper clippings and what appeared to be bank statements. There was also a USB stick. I opened the envelope within. Cheap note-paper, printed with a 'Hotel Zichy' logo, a budget attempt at looking upmarket. The message 'For attention of Paul Considine, Nathan Sutherland, Gwenant Pryce'. There were two signatures. Francesco Nicolodi and Riccardo Pelosi.

I checked the postmark on the package. Saturday 21 May. The day after he was murdered. There was no mail on Sunday. Why those three names?

I scanned through the financial statements as quickly as I could, but found it difficult to get my head around them. Too much for me. My *commercialista* might be able to explain it properly but I could understand little more than that large sums of money were being moved around – how many accounts? Four? Five? I shook my head, and moved on to the clippings.

They consisted of photocopies of old newspaper articles detailing various legal actions against Fitzgerald, all of which had finished with cases being settled out of court or dropped. Insubstantial stuff on the face of it that did nothing except demonstrate that Lewis Fitzgerald had never broken the law. The final photocopy was the same one that I had seen in the *Guardian*, where Lewis Fitzgerald had walked free and Riccardo Pelosi had been sent to prison for seven years.

I sighed. I'd been expecting a smoking gun, and this didn't seem quite enough. I plugged in the USB stick. There was just a single document. Confiteor.pdf. *Confiteor. I confess.* I clicked it open.

It was a scanned document. There were pages and pages of it. Each page made reference to one of the enclosed news clippings, in which Riccardo Pelosi detailed how he had hired thugs to intimidate Gwenant Pryce and Adam Grant, how he had bribed and intimidated jurors, colluded in false account-ing and committed arson 'just to send out a very clear signal'. And how he had done all this with the full knowledge and collaboration of Lewis Fitzgerald. Each page was signed and dated. The final page held a scan of a passport in the name of Riccardo Pelosi, and an Italian ID card in the name of Francesco Nicolodi.

I closed the document, ejected the USB stick and dropped it in my pocket. Then I shuffled the news clippings and bank statements together, and replaced them in the envelope.

Nicolodi's insurance policy. Just to keep Fitzgerald in line in case he decided to have second thoughts about their deal. And then Nicolodi had become just a bit too greedy, and his bluff had been called.

It was probably enough. This time I wasn't going to mess around playing private detective, this time I was going to do what I should have done in the first place. Go to the police. Tell Vanni everything.

The telephone rang. Dario's. His landline, in Mestre.

'Dario! What are you doing at home?'

There was a brief pause. 'Nathan. It's Valentina.'

Dario's wife. We'd always had a bit of a spiky relationship. I couldn't remember her ever having rung me before. And that could only mean she was worried.

'Is Dario with you? We've just got back from Emily's grand-parents. We thought he'd be at home.'

Oh shit.

'Valentina. *Ciao, cara.* He'll probably be home soon. He was working in Venice today. I know he said he'd be in a meeting for hours so he'd have his mobile switched off.'

'Oh good. Good. Thank you, Nathan. Silly, I know, but I worry if I can't get hold of him.'

'He's probably on his way back, Valentina, and just forgotten to switch his phone back on.' Why was I even saying this? I knew it almost certainly wasn't true.

'Thanks, Nathan.' There was a brief pause. 'You've always been a good friend to Dario. And I am grateful for that, you know?'

'Thanks, *cara*. I'll give you a call if he calls me first, okay.'

She hung up.

Oh God. Dario, please call. Please call now. I've just lied to your wife who doesn't like me very much anyway, but has been trying to be nice because she's just starting to get scared. Please call. I sat there and drummed my fingers on the desk. Gramsci hauled himself up on to the windowsill and mewled for food, but I ignored him. It was dark outside. The tourists would be making their way back to their cruise ships, or back to the mainland. Another hour and restaurants would start putting chairs on tables. I could, should, call the police straight away. But if I did that, there was every chance they'd telephone Valentina and that would frighten her. And there was still a chance that Dario would call, and everything would be okay.

The phone rang again. Fede's number.

'*Ciao, caro.*'

'*Ciao, tesora!*'

'I've just got off the phone with *Mamma*. She's safely arrived back home. I think you made a big impression on her. She says you must come around and cook for us next time. Anyway, I know it's a bit late, but I'm free at last. So are you coming over here, or am I coming to you?'

Hell.

'Er, I don't really know, sweetheart. Things are kind of busy now. Just a few things to put to bed and then I'll be free tomorrow. Maybe we can do lunch?'

A pause. 'You're lying.'

'What do you mean?'

'You never call me "sweetheart". Not in English. You know I'd kick your arse if you called me anything as insufferably twee as that. What's going on?'

'Nothing. Everything's . . .'

'Fine?' The question hung in the air like a challenge, and I suddenly realised that there were two paths to follow. One would lead to us irrevocably breaking up. And so the other, painful as it might be, was the only one to follow.

'No. It's not fine.' I tried to keep my voice level, and failed.

There was the briefest of pauses. '*Caro*, what can I do? What's going on?'

'Dario. He's not answering his phone. I know that doesn't sound like anything, but we were trying to solve this bloody mystery. He was trying to sort my life out.'

She laughed. 'I thought he would be. Bless him.'

'Valentina called me only five minutes ago. She's starting to get worried. I can tell. And I don't know what to do. Fede, he's my best friend and . . .'

'Shhhh. Shhhh *caro*. I'm coming over, okay?'

'You don't have to.'

'Yes I do. I can help. I can be with you.'

Again, I tried to control my breathing. 'Thank you. I love you.'

'I love you too. I'll be there within forty-five minutes, okay?'

We hung up. The phone rang again within thirty seconds. I saw the number and my heart leapt.

'Dario! You silly bastard, I was getting properly scared.'

There was a pause. 'Dario can't come to the phone at the moment, Sutherland.'

'Lewis! Well, this is an unexpected pleasure. What can I do for you?'

'Oh, I thought you might like to come over, Sutherland. Have a little chat, that sort of thing.'

'At the Palazzo Papadopoli? I'd be delighted. I trust you'll be buying the drinks, though?'

'Not at the hotel. I'm sorry, I'm afraid I've checked out. I think you know where to go. But just in case you don't, I've gone to the trouble of arranging a guide for you. Take a look out of your window.'

I shooed Gramsci off the windowsill and peered out. A figure was standing in the shadows, just outside the pool of light cast by the Brazilians'.

'Lean out. Give him a wave.'

The figured turned to me and looked up. I couldn't read the expression on his face, but I recognised him immediately. 'Hello, Paul,' I said. He nodded.

'Well done, Sutherland. Now just keep speaking to me. I want you to go and buzz Paul up to your flat.'

'What's he going to do? Kill me? I'm not in great shape, Lewis, but I think I'd have a pretty good chance against a man who looks like he hasn't slept in days.'

Lewis chuckled. 'If I were a gambling man I think I'd go evens. No, he's not going to kill you. I just want him to accompany you over here. I don't want you getting any ideas about phoning the police. Are you still there, Sutherland?'

'Yes, I am. *Stai tranquillo!*' I pressed the entrance buzzer and heard the door click downstairs. 'Did you hear that?'

'I did. Keep talking to me.'

I heard Considine's footsteps coming up the stairs. I had, perhaps, twenty seconds at most. Leave a message. How? Where?

Gramsci yowled and nudged at his empty bowl.

Of course.

'What would you like me to talk about, Lewis? The weather?' I shook some biscuits into Gramsci's bowl. Not too many.

'What was that?' said Lewis.

'My cat. He's getting in a state. I'm just putting some food down for him.' I grabbed the front page of *Il Gazzetino* from my pocket, scrunched it into a ball and stuffed it into the box of biscuits.

'Do you have to?'

'Up to you. If I don't, he'll start howling until the guy from the bar downstairs comes up to see if I'm still alive.'

A pause. 'Okay.' Then he chuckled. 'You might want to put a lot of food down, Sutherland.'

I stuck the box on top of the fridge, and then went to open the door. 'Hi Paul, thanks for coming round,' I said.

'Okay, Sutherland, give your telephone to Mr Considine, please.' I passed it over.

'I've got it, Lewis,' said Paul.

'Mr Fitzgerald, if you please. I'm hanging up now. I'll see you both soon. Or, just to remind you, Sutherland, *signor* Dario and I will both see you soon.'

Paul and I made our way downstairs and I locked the door. We looked at each other. 'So,' I said, 'Lewis is going to kill me then?'

He couldn't meet my gaze, but his eyes were red, and he looked drawn and gaunt. 'I don't know. Nathan, I'm sorry. I'm so sorry.'

'It's all right, buddy.' I paused. 'We could always just phone the police, you know?'

He shook his head. 'I can't let you do that. I'm sorry.'

'It's okay. I understand. Just tell me, what did he say to you?'

'That he'd hurt Gwen. Really hurt her.'

I nodded. 'He said the same to her, you know. Blimey, you're a couple, eh? But how's he going to do that from the inside of a cell?'

He shook his head again. 'I can't risk it, Nathan. And he's got your friend as well.'

'Okay. Don't worry. We'll find a way. So where are we off to, then?'

'The Giardini.'

I nodded. 'I thought so.' I checked my watch. 'Okay, there's a boat in five minutes.'

'Isn't it quicker to walk?'

Of course it's quicker to walk, I thought. But I need to eat some time up. 'We could walk, but there's *acqua alta* tonight. It'll be a pain, and neither of us have got boots.'

We were well beyond the season for *acqua alta* but Considine, I reckoned, wouldn't know that. Sure enough, he nodded. 'Where's the nearest stop?'

'Rialto. Come on. It's only a couple of minutes.' A couple of minutes' walk, but a couple of minutes in the wrong direction, that could add ten precious minutes to the boat journey. We made our way down through Campo Manin, to Campo San Luca and then through one of the narrow *calli* that linked with the Grand Canal. A *vaporetto* was pulling in just as we arrived. Busy, but not too busy. The weather warm, but not that warm. Good. We'd be able to get seats outside.

'Shall we sit at the back, Paul? Have a bit more privacy?' He nodded. We made our way through the cabin to the seats at the back. I sat down next to him, and looked around us. 'Wonderful isn't it? It's the best time of day, to be honest. And the best time of year. One more month, and it'll be starting to get too hot, but now . . . you can just sit here and watch the whole of the city unroll before your eyes.'

We both smiled. It was impossible not to. However low you felt, there was something about the city at night that worked magic on you. 'I've never been to Venice before,' he said.

'No? Has it been all you expected?'

He gave a dry laugh. 'Not exactly.'

'I'm sorry, Paul. Really.' I leaned back in my seat, closing my eyes. I felt the bump of the *vaporetto* against the pontoon. Where were we now? San Tomà, probably. Federica's boat would be at least thirty minutes away. If I was lucky. I opened my eyes again. 'Okay, Paul,' I said, 'I need you to trust me on this.'

'What do you mean, Nathan?'

'Just what I say. When we get there. Just trust me on this. I think I can get us all out of this.'

'You think?' I nodded. 'But you can't promise?'

I shook my head. 'No. Wish I could. But there's a chance we can get this bastard off your back for ever. So, are you going to trust me?'

He was about to speak when the doors opened and a family of four joined us. Mum and Dad struggled to manoeuvre two big rucksacks through the swing doors, whilst the kids ran to the rearmost seats and knelt on them, waving excitedly at a group of tourists in a water taxi heading in the opposite direction. I smiled at them.

Paul and I sat in silence, the only noise now being the chattering of our new companions as they watched the city slide by. Under the Accademia Bridge, and past the church of the

Salute, glowing in the moonlight. The kids, pointing at every new wonder along the canal. Mum, with her hands on their shoulders, gently but firmly preventing them from leaning out just a little too far. Dad, trying to find out exactly what they were looking at from his guidebook. I looked at the cover. *Venedig*. German or Austrian, then. It seemed like it was their first visit. How lovely for them.

We'd passed the Salute now and were moving into the more open water of the *bacino* of San Marco. To our right lay the Basilica of San Marco and the Ducal Palace, clear, now, of the swarming hordes of visitors, and resplendent in the moonlight. I smiled over at Considine.

'Not bad, is it?'

He smiled back at me. 'Not bad at all. You're lucky, you know?'

'I know I am. Maybe not so much at this precise moment.' He started, and looked guilty, but I just chuckled and gave him a pat on the back.

The *vaporetto* pulled in to the San Zaccaria stop, and I held the swing doors open for Dad as best I could, as Mum set off in pursuit of the two kids haring their way through the cabin. '*Schoenes urlaub,*' I said. He smiled and nodded.

We had, perhaps, ten minutes. I reached into my pocket, and brought out the envelope I'd taken – stolen – from his hotel. I passed it over to him. 'It's all in there, Paul. Everything he's done. All those people he threatened. Those careers he ruined. And buried deep inside are the details of all the money he's ripped off from you.'

He nodded. 'We don't really have a choice, do we?'

'Not really.'

'And I just have to trust you on this?'

'That's pretty much it.'

'Can you tell me what you're going to do?'

'No.'

'Why not?'

'Too dangerous.' But mainly because I hadn't actually thought of anything.

He closed his eyes for a few seconds, and then smiled. 'Okay, Nathan. Let's do it.'

'Good man.' I heard the engines of the boat spinning into reverse as we slowed down and approached the Arsenale. We paused only for a few seconds to allow some passengers to get off, and then the *marinaio* had cast off again. Another few minutes, and we drew near to the trees and green spaces of the Giardini.

'Let's go.' We made our way through the cabin of the *vaporetto*, and were the only ones to alight. Indeed, there were precious few reasons to get off at Giardini at this time of night. 'Lovely when it's like this, isn't it? No one else around. And it's Monday night. Which means the gardens have been closed all day. Which means the lightest of security details, and probably not even worth activating the CCTV.' Yes, Lewis had thought it through pretty well. 'Would a cigarette be good?' He nodded. My phone, in his pocket, started to ring. He began to reach for it, but I waved my hand. 'Ignore it. It's probably not important. Let's just enjoy the moment, eh?' He smiled again, and we stood there and smoked in silence, looking out across the *bacino* to the city under the moonlight.

I ground my cigarette underfoot. 'Guess we'd better go, then?' He followed me into the gardens, and along the path to the fenced and gated area that separated the public gardens from the Giardini della Biennale proper. 'I take it we're going inside?' He nodded. 'Okay. If we try to get in here we'll probably set off all sorts of alarms. Follow me round here.'

I took him into a thickly wooded area, perhaps a hundred yards to the right, where the metal fence was thickly concealed. 'Hope you've not got your best jacket on,' I joked, as we hauled ourselves over. I could see the main path leading up to the British pavilion shining in the moonlight. 'I think we'd best stay off the beaten track, don't you? We'll go around the back way. Just be careful where you put your feet, the ground is a little bit treacherous.'

We crept through the undergrowth until we reached the fire door at the back of the pavilion, now open again with a faint light glowing from inside.

'Okay, Paul, I think we're here. Let's go in. Good luck, eh?'

I checked my watch. Nearly eleven. I'd burned up as much time as I possibly could. Still, Federica would only just be turning the key in the lock.

I was depending on her, now. More worryingly, I was also depending on Gramsci.

Chapter 40

'Where the hell have you been?'

I looked around, but couldn't quite identify where Lewis Fitzgerald's voice was coming from. 'Had to be careful, Lewis. I didn't think you'd want anybody spotting us on the way in.'

'Fair point, Sutherland. And I'm up here.' I looked up to the gantry where Fitzgerald was leaning – more than somewhat theatrically, I thought – upon the glass barrier, his body silhouetted by the emergency lighting shining from behind him.

'Good pose, Lewis. I'm not sure I'd trust those barriers, though.'

'Trust me, this one is absolutely fine. I'd stake my life on it.'

'I'll bet. Where's Dario?'

There was no answer.

'Where's Dario?' I repeated, trying to keep my voice steady.

'He's up here, Sutherland. And still in one piece. Tell Considine to come up here, would you?'

'Tell him yourself, Lewis. Better still, ask him. He's your friend after all. Isn't he?'

'You're right. Paul, come up here a minute would you? There's a good lad.'

Considine looked at me. 'It's all right, Paul,' I said. 'You go on up. It's all going to be fine, I promise.' He looked scared, but nodded, and then made his way up the stairs, and along the walkway, his boots clanking on the metal.

'Now you, Mr Honorary Consul.'

I shrugged. 'Sure.' I followed Paul up the stairs, and was halfway along the walkway when Fitzgerald's voice rang out. 'That's enough.'

I stopped.

'You know why you're here, Sutherland?'

'Well, it's one of two things, I guess. I'm hoping this is an exclusive private view and this is all just part of the experience. Or . . .'

'Or?'

'Or you're going to horribly murder the three of us and make off with Considine's money.'

He smiled. At the mention of his name, Paul looked over at him. 'Lewis, I don't care about the money. Take it all. Just go, and leave us alone.'

Fitzgerald smiled, and patted him on the cheek. 'Oh Paul, but I've looked after you so well. *Signor* Nicolodi wrote some horrible things about you and got his just deserts. Nasty old Vincenzo Scarpa gets the shock of his life.' He chuckled. 'Silly old fool's probably at home right now wondering if it'll ever be safe to take a bath again. And that spiteful old queen Gordon Blake-Hoyt meets a nasty, brutish and short ending as well. Everyone who's been horrible to you. I've done so much to help you, haven't I?'

'Except, of course, it isn't quite like that, is it Lewis?' He looked over at me, an expression of mild irritation in his eyes.

'Nicolodi's article wasn't aimed at Paul, was it? It was aimed at you. "Look at me, I'm in print now in a big, proper national newspaper and perhaps I'm starting to think I'm not getting enough from this deal of ours. Because I know about every last skeleton in your closet, and where every last body is buried and, you know what, this hotel is just a little bit small for my tastes, can you do anything about that?"'

'Balderdash, claptrap and bunkum, Sutherland. In no particular order.'

I ignored him. 'And grumpy old Vincenzo Scarpa? He was just a great big red flapping fish, wasn't he? Somebody to send a scary postcard to. Somebody who you knew would create a big scene and throw us off the scent.'

'Shut up, Sutherland. You're boring me.'

'It's all true though. Isn't it? Paul and I had a nice little chat about it on the boat. He's seen all the documentation. Nicolodi confessed to everything. Intimidation, arson, false accounting. Even murder. And your name is linked to everything.'

Paul's hand trembled as he pulled the envelope from his jacket. 'He's right, Lewis. He's telling the truth. I've seen it all in here. You frightened me. Told me I'd be blamed for GBH dying and that only you could help me. And then, when that didn't work any more, you told me you'd hurt Gwen.'

Lewis just smiled his shark's smile.

'I trusted you for years. I thought you were trying to help me. And now, all that money? All that money I'm supposed to have made. Where is it, Lewis? What have you done with it?'

Lewis continued to smile. 'Paul, it's all safe. It's all where it should be.' He reached out to him, as if to pat him on the shoulder, and then his fist lashed out and he punched him in the face. Paul's head jerked back and banged against the wall. He slumped to the floor and didn't move. Lewis kicked him in the face anyway, whether to be absolutely sure or just out of sheer spite I couldn't be certain. He wiped his hands, just for effect, with a handkerchief. 'The money is all safe. In my account. And that's where it's going to stay. Oh, and I'm sorry if I said terrible things about your Welsh glamorous granny.'

'That hand seems to be healing up well,' I said. He nodded, finished wiping his hands, and tucked the handkerchief inside his jacket. 'Of course, it was never really badly hurt to begin with, was it? There was never anyone else there at the Arsenale. You just took a swipe at the nearest person – didn't matter if it was me or Scarpa – and then just cut your palm enough to make it bleed. And then you grizzled all the way to the hospital about how it had gone through your hand. And I believed you. I really started to believe you were the manager of some drug-crazed psycho artist who was going on a killing spree.' I touched my nose. 'Dario gave me the idea. "Why didn't you just pretend to be hurt?" he said. And, of course, that's exactly what you did.'

At the mention of his name, Dario groaned. I couldn't quite make him out, half concealed as he was by Considine's unconscious body.

'Dario, are you okay?'

He raised himself, ever so slightly, and nodded. 'I'm okay, buddy.' His forehead, I noticed, was bleeding. His hands, I could see, were tied behind his back but he made an effort to get to his knees.

'The gorilla is fine, Mr Sutherland. The trouble is, he didn't have one of these.' He brandished a revolver at me, twirled it in his fingers and then, almost casually, smacked Dario across the face with it.

'Bastard!' Dario slumped backwards.

'Language, please,' drawled Fitzgerald, and drew back his hand to hit him again.

I held up my hands. 'Stop it. Please, Lewis, just stop it. Don't hit him again. It's nothing to do with him.'

Lewis shrugged. 'I'm sorry, Nathan, but it seems to me it's very much to do with him.' He hit him once more, and this time blood sprayed from Dario's nose.

'For God's sake, he's got a wife and kid.'

'Tragic, isn't it?'

'Please. It's me you want. Just let him go.'

'Well that's very noble of you, Nathan, but you're just going to have to wait your turn.'

'But why, for God's sake?'

'Well, it has to look convincing. I mean, look at poor old Considine down there. He doesn't really look like he's capable of fighting the two of you to the death, does he now? Still, we'll do our best to make it look good.'

'Lewis, please think. This is insane. You can't kill all three of us.'

He scratched his head. 'I rather think I can, you know.'

'So what's the idea? Dario and I were trying to clear my name, only to be killed in a showdown with the crazy serial-killer artist?'

'Pretty much. Something like that. Well done, Sutherland, well thought out.'

'Oh look, just think. People will find out. It's a stupid idea, too many people already know about it.' He hesitated. 'People know about you and Francesco Nicolodi. How many people do you think he had his insurance policy sent to? They'll join all the dots up.'

Lewis scratched his chin. 'It's possible. Trouble is, I don't really see an alternative now.' He gave a little jump, and the gantry shuddered, ever so slightly. I clenched my eyes shut, and grabbed the guardrail. He smiled. 'Not very good with heights, are you, Nathan? What if I do it again?' He stamped down, properly hard this time, and again the gantry shook.

'You stupid bastard, you'll kill us all.'

'Not all of us. Only you. My bit is perfectly secure.'

I grabbed for a railing but, before I could put my weight on it, I felt it wobble underneath my hand. I leapt back from it, my movement making the gantry shudder terribly, and then watched as the section of glass crashed to the floor below.

Lewis reached inside his jacket, and took out a hex key. 'Sorry, Nathan. Truth is this whole thing is a bit of a lash-up. It can be put together in a few hours. And dismantled in round about the same time.' He stamped again, and I dropped to my knees and gripped the floor beneath me.

'I don't think that'll help, you know. Remember poor old Gordon Blake-Hoyt, Nathan?' I said nothing. He stamped again. 'I said, do you remember poor old Gordon, Nathan?'

It took all my strength of will to keep my eyes open. 'How could I forget?' I said.

'Do you ever wonder what it must have felt like? When he realised he was falling? Do you?'

I nodded.

'This, I imagine, must be worse?'

Again, I nodded.

'The difference is, you now have time to think about it. Gordon would have had, what, a fraction of a second as he fell? But you, every time I do this,' he stamped again, 'you have so much time, so much time to wonder, will this be the last time, will this be the time the structure collapses, what will I hit, is there any chance I'll survive? It must be terrifying. Mustn't it?'

I screwed my eyes shut, took a deep breath and raised my head. Then I slowly, ever so slowly, got to my feet and forced myself to keep my eyes open. It was difficult to keep my voice steady. 'Yes, I'm scared,' I said.

I reached my hand out to the wall on my right. Solid, reassuring. Yet nothing to hold on to. Nothing that would help me if the gantry, which swayed beneath me, collapsed. 'I'm scared,' I repeated, 'but I'm going to give you one last chance.'

I could hardly see his face in the semi-darkness, but I could imagine his expression. 'You what?'

'One last chance, Lewis. You leave us now. You run like hell out of here. You leave me, Dario and Considine unhurt. You get on the next flight to China, or Belarus or Iran or somewhere else that doesn't extradite. And you have my word – my absolute word of honour – that I will say nothing about you, nothing about the past, nothing about what's happening now. I'll let you get away with murder if you let us go. Do you understand?'

There was a brief pause, and then he laughed. 'You must be absolutely mad.' He stamped again, I clung to the wall, and something metallic dropped from the gantry and pinged off the floor. It wasn't going to last much longer.

'I'm not mad. I'm giving you a chance. There's a stack of evidence against you in that envelope.'

'Oh yes. Thanks for reminding me.' He reached down, and picked it up. 'I'll make sure to take great care of it.'

I nodded. 'Okay. But I did try.' I reached into my jacket, and drew out the USB stick. 'You know what this is?'

Lewis had his foot in mid-air, ready to bring it down again. He paused.

'Ah, you do, don't you?' I tossed it in the air, and caught it in my left hand. The right, for what it was worth, still clinging to the wall. 'You want this?'

Lewis stepped forward. The gantry shook, just a little, and so he stepped back. He ran his hands through his hair, and forced a smile upon his face. 'Oh, poor Mr Sutherland. I don't know what you think you've got there, but – and I am most terribly sorry – it really isn't going to help you.'

'Isn't it?' I said. 'Okay. Stamp on the gantry again.'

He raised his foot. And then he paused.

'Come on. Do it. Once, twice more and I'll fall. The only thing is, this,' and I brandished the USB stick, 'is going to fall with me. Because everything is on here. Nicolodi's complete, signed testament. And you'll have to find a way of getting it back from the midst of a forest of broken glass.'

And then I heard it. A long way off, but unmistakable. A siren.

Federica. Gramsci.

They'd done it.

I put my hand to my ear. 'Listen. You hear that? That's a police boat coming across the lagoon.'

'Liar!' he shouted.

'Of course I'm not a bloody liar, Lewis. You did everything you possibly could to stop me contacting the police. But you're holding my best friend captive, so of course I'm going to find a way. What do you think this is, some shit movie? And in the end it wasn't that difficult. You know why? Because my brilliant girlfriend is smarter than you. More than that, my cat – my cat, Lewis – is smarter than you.'

'Bastard!'

'Now you're not even using sentences any more, Lewis. Come on. Step out of here. Step back. The deal still holds if you want to.'

'Bastard. Lying bastard.'

'Yes, you've said that before. Both of those I know. Come on, be original.' Again, I raised my hand to my ear. 'Closer now. Must be at San Zaccaria. Maybe another two or three minutes to get here, perhaps another few minutes to find us. We are making rather a lot of noise.'

'Give me it, you bastard. Or I'll kill them. I'll kill both of them.' He spun around and trained his gun on Considine, who was trying to get to his feet.

'Not much of a threat, Lewis. I don't really know him. So I don't really care. Sirens are getting closer, aren't they? Try again.'

He raised the gun and smacked it against Considine's forehead. Then he moved on to Dario. Dario, still dazed from the beating, tried to raise himself. Lewis, slowly, deliberately, put his boot on his chest and forced him back to the floor. Then he pushed the barrel of the gun against Dario's forehead. He turned and looked at me.

'Lewis. Please.'

He continued to stare.

'Lewis. He's my best friend. Maybe my only friend. Please don't do this. He's got a wife. His daughter isn't even a year old. Please.'

He smiled.

'It's your last chance, Lewis.'

His expression changed. 'What do you mean?'

'Well, give up now. Obviously. What did you think I meant?' By now, under the blare of the sirens, I could hear the crunch of boots on gravel.

'Son of a bitch,' Lewis swore, pushed his gun against Dario's forehead and forced him to the ground. Did I see his finger tighten on the trigger? To this day, I can't be sure. All I knew was that Valentina and Emily were waiting at home for him. *Make him angry, Nathan. Make him so angry he'll stop thinking.* I gripped the USB stick in my fist. 'Okay, Lewis. Here we go. Come and take if off me, eh? Come on boy. Fetch!' And I tossed it over the side. There was a gentle plink from below, and I gestured with my left hand. Twenty feet below, the stick lay in a maze of jagged glass.

There was silence for a moment except for the sound of hammering at the door. Lewis' shoulders dropped for a moment, and then he raised his head to look at me, and grinned. And then he launched himself at me.

I had the advantage in that I thought he might. I raised my knee to fend off his attack, but his forehead cracked into my jaw. Lights flared within my skull, yet I still remembered. Hold on. Just hold on, Nathan. I grabbed on to the floor of the gantry as, with a tearing metallic sound, the side nearest Lewis collapsed. We swung towards the floor, and banged into a supporting pillar, the impact of which was enough to dislodge him.

There wasn't even time for him to scream. He fell silently on to a forest of broken glass. And then there was silence, about the space of thirty seconds, interspersed by the sounds of the police hammering outside. Then I was aware only of a creaking sound from above, a metallic pling as the last supporting bracket fell to earth, and I was aware – if only for a few seconds – of my own voice, screaming, and of a blinding flash of pain.

Chapter 41

'So you're telling me your cat saved your life, Nathan?' Vanni smiled across at me as he scribbled away in a notebook.

'I wouldn't put it quite like that. I certainly wouldn't tell him, just in case he understood. Might give him airs and graces. But I knew I had perhaps thirty seconds at most before I had to let Paul in through the door. I also knew Fitzgerald would have warned him to check I hadn't tried writing a message on the back of the door or anything like that. So I just tipped a few kitty biscuits into his bowl.'

Vanni shook his head. 'I don't understand.'

'He won't eat the cheese-flavoured ones. And if they're in his bowl he will just sit there and yowl and yowl and yowl until somebody comes along and takes them out. Federica, I knew would be along within about forty-five minutes. She arrives, I'm not there. She settles down to wait. She gives me a call, but I'm not answering. Then she notices that Gramsci is whinging. Now, you might be able to bear that for a couple of minutes. Maybe even five. But nobody could stand it for any longer. So she goes to his bowl, starts picking out the cheesy kitty biscuits. He starts crying for more food so she takes down the box, and there right at the top is a scrunched-up page from *Il Gazzettino* with a "Death at Giardini" headline. She worked the rest out.'

'You trusted your life to your cat?'

'No, I trusted it to Federica. Although it did rather depend on Gramsci's fundamentally bad nature as well. Anyway, I couldn't think of a better idea.'

'You're crazy, Nathan.' I shrugged, and then winced as the pain in my shoulder shot through me. 'How is it?' he asked.

'Hurts when I move it. But that's to be expected. I was lucky. Bloody great glass spike went straight through, missed all the major arteries. Going to need some physio when the wound heals, but the doc says I should be okay. I'll probably have some sort of manly scar, but I'm hoping Federica will like that.'

Vanni laughed. 'When do you get out of here?'

'Tomorrow morning with a bit of luck.'

'Good. Good. Anything I can do in the meantime?'

'There's something I still don't understand.' He raised an eyebrow. 'Pelosi's insurance policy. How was that supposed to work?'

'We spoke to a young Romanian guy at the Zichy. Pelosi gave him three packages. Told him that he was to send them off if ever he failed to telephone him at four pm. Paid him a hundred euros a day. So, there was no mail on Sunday. Considine's arrived first on Monday. Your copy and Ms Pryce's are probably waiting for you at home. Three people he trusted to do the most damage.'

'But not the police?'

Vanni laughed. 'My goodness me, no. He was a career criminal. Old habits die very hard.'

'I thought he hated me.'

'Quite possibly. He still trusted you, though.'

'I'm flattered.' I shifted painfully in my bed. 'Is there any chance you could lend me a cigarette?'

'In a hospital room? I'm afraid not. There are limits even to my powers.'

'Are there? Oh dear.'

He took out a packet of MS, and slipped a couple into the pocket of my dressing gown. 'At least open a window,' he said.

I smiled. 'Thanks, Vanni. Your powers are great indeed.'

'No problems. Oh, and try and drop by the *Questura* as soon as you can. There are some forms that need signing. There's a body – actually, make that two bodies – that need repatriating.'

The painkillers were making me drowsy, and I must have dozed off for a while. Then I became aware of someone else's presence in the room. Someone holding my hand.

'Fede?' I said, sleepily, and opened my eyes. Then I smiled. 'Gwenant!'

'How are you, *cariad*?'

'Not too bad. The doctors tell me that one day I might be able to play the piano again.'

'There's an old joke coming up there, isn't there?' We smiled. 'I just wanted to say thanks, Nathan. Thanks for what you've done for Paul. And for me.'

I shook my head. 'I don't understand it, Gwen. I don't understand you. What was all the big mystery, all the "you have to be the one that asks the difficult questions" business?'

'Easy for you, my dear. Lewis knows me from way back. I couldn't go around sleuthing. And besides, as I said, he played me and Paul off against each other. He knew how to scare us. He didn't know how to scare you.'

'Oh, I think you'll find he did. So what now, then?'

'What now?'

I raised an eyebrow, but even that seemed painful. 'What now? You and Paul?'

She laughed her tinkly little laugh. 'Oh, well he's going to need help getting back on his feet again. While they try and track down just how much of his money Lewis never got around to spending. I know a couple of decent agents, I'll get him set up with one of them.'

'That's not what I mean, and you know it.'

'Oh, *cariad*, I'm far too old for all that sort of nonsense now.'

I shook my head. 'I don't think you are. *Cariad.*'

She said nothing, but smiled and stroked my hair, her own face only a few inches from mine. Then she kissed my forehead, whispered 'Thank you' once more, and then Gwenant Pryce, lovely Welsh woman, was gone.

Chapter 42

'You're doing very well, *cara*!'

Federica stopped pitching the ball for Gramsci. 'Don't push it, *tesoro*.'

Dario grinned. I shrugged, and then winced with pain. 'Look, I'd do it myself, you know. But the doctor says it could be another six weeks until my throwing arm is back to fighting strength. And if Gramsci's not entertained in the meantime he could unleash a wave of destruction.'

'So what about cooking?'

'Oh, I'm a master at one-handed cooking. But tonight Federica's in charge.'

'Indeed I am.' She moved behind me, put her arms around my neck and hugged me. Perhaps just a little too strongly, as it drew an 'ouch' out of me. 'We have beer in the fridge, and Rosa Rossa on speed dial. That's my equivalent of one-handed cooking.'

'You're a lucky man, Nathan.'

'I know.'

Federica went back to the kitchen and returned with three bottles. 'Beer to be going on with?' We nodded. 'So what happens now? To Considine, I mean.'

'Hopefully, he'll get some proper help now. There's a lot of people there wishing him well, especially after what's happened. I don't know if he'll ever get all his money back – it's going to take a long time to untangle Fitzgerald's affairs – but there's a chance of a new start for him at least. And there'll be Gwenant there as well.'

'Do you think they might? Get back together that is.'

'Oh, they're both adamant that they won't. But they better had. I'd feel cheated otherwise.'

'And what about you?' said Dario.

I sighed. 'Busy few days coming up. Two bodies now to be released back to the UK, but Vanni thinks the authorities will be amenable. Then they can just wash their hands of it all. The Italians can deal with *signor* Nicolodi, or Pelosi, or whatever name he'd like to be buried under. And I'll never have to be shouted at by Mr Blake-Hoyt's brother again.'

'And your job?'

'Oh, that's different. Various other people will want to shout at me for certain. The ambassador was on the phone earlier. Yes, I can have my unpaid, voluntary job back but I certainly mustn't get involved in this sort of nonsense in the future. Not the sort of thing Her Majesty expects, apparently. *Signor* Scarpa and his three lovely boys might still like to have a word with me, but I get the impression he's got a short attention span when it comes to this sort of thing. There are probably far more important people in the art world in need of bullying by him, and he's a very busy man.'

Gramsci mewled again. Federica sighed, and reached for his ball. 'You know, is there actually anything preventing you from throwing with your left arm?'

'My technique's rubbish. Trust me, he'd notice.'

'Six weeks, the doctor said?'

'Six weeks.'

'Okay. I can manage that. But then I really am leaving you.'

'You can't do that. He's got used to you now. He'd miss you.'

'He'd miss me? What about you?'

'Me? Oh yes. Me too. Well, I suppose so. Definitely a bit.'

She threw the ball for Gramsci and he swatted it with great force in my direction, bouncing it off my nose. The two of them looked at each other with satisfaction. 'Okay, cat,' said Federica, 'maybe we can get used to each other.'

Dario smiled, and grabbed me around the shoulders. A little harder than I'd have liked. 'Thanks, *vecio*.'

'What for?'

'You saved my life.'

'Nah. You saved mine. Really.' We all clinked bottles. 'So Valentina and Emily are coming into town with you tomorrow?'

'Tomorrow afternoon, yep.'

'Great. There's an event at the Thai pavilion. I did some work for them. I can get you all tickets if you want to come along?'

He looked dubious. 'I'm not sure it's their sort of thing, *vecio*.'

I smiled. 'Of course it is, Dario. After all, the best part of the Biennale is always the *vernissage*.'

Acknowledgements

The inspiration for this novel came in the summer of 2015, which I spent as part of a group performing a live reading of Marx's *Das Kapital* in the central pavilion of the Venice Biennale. I would like to thank the artist Isaac Julien and the filmmaker Mark Nash for the opportunity, as well as my brilliant co-performers and friends Steven Varni, Francesco Bianchi, Jenni Lea-Jones, Jacopo Giacomoni and Ivan Matijasic.

With the exception of the non-existent Hotel Zichy all locations in this book are as described, although I have occasionally changed names. I have also taken some liberties with the location of Federica's apartment and the San Silvestro *vaporetto* stop.

I would also like to thank my friend, and occasional cat-sitter, the artist Duncan Robertson, who makes wonderful art from wedding dresses and many other things; and Sergio Gallinaro for many happy hours spent discussing progressive rock music under the guise of English lessons.

Thank you to my wonderful agent John Beaton, Gregory Dowling for his support, my editor Colin Murray; Krystyna Green, Clive Hebard, Rebecca Sheppard, Jess Gulliver, Kate Hibbert and Andy Hine at Little, Brown; and, of course, my wife Caroline for her love, support and inexhaustible patience.

The Venetian Game

PHILIP GWYNNE JONES

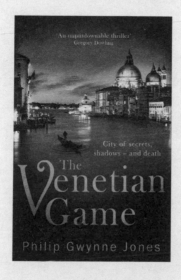

From his office on the Street of the Assassins, Nathan Sutherland, English Honorary Consul to Venice, assists unfortunate tourists as best he can. It is a steady but unexciting life that dramatically changes when he is offered a large sum of money to look after a small package containing a prayer book illustrated by the Venetian master Giovanni Bellini.

Unknown to Nathan, from a palazzo on the Grand Canal, twin brothers Domenico and Arcangelo Moro have been playing out a complex game of art theft for twenty years. And now Nathan finds himself unwittingly drawn into their deadly business . . .